MAKING IT WRITE

* available from Severn House

MAKING IT WRITE

Betty Hechtman

SEVERN
HOUSE

First world edition published in Great Britain and the USA in 2022
by Severn House, an imprint of Canongate Books Ltd,
14 High Street, Edinburgh EH1 1TE.

Trade paperback edition first published in Great Britain and the USA in 2022
by Severn House, an imprint of Canongate Books Ltd.

severnhouse.com

British Library Cataloguing-in-Publication Data
A CIP catalogue record for this title is available from the British Library.

ISBN-13: 978-0-7278-5093-5 (cased)
ISBN-13: 978-1-4483-0753-1 (trade paper)
ISBN-13: 978-1-4483-0752-4 (e-book)

All Severn House titles are printed on acid-free paper.

MIX
Paper from
responsible sources
FSC® C013056

Typeset by Palimpsest Book Production Ltd.,
Falkirk, Stirlingshire, Scotland.
Printed and bound in Great Britain by
TJ Books, Padstow, Cornwall.

ONE

I sat back from the computer and read over what I'd just written before I pressed save. Derek Streeter, my fictional detective, had just announced that he was ready to close in on the bad guy – or was it bad *gal* since in this case the killer was a woman? My business was words so I took a moment to think it over. 'Bad guy' seemed sort of unisex, but these days you had to be so careful about what might be considered offensive to somebody. I spent a bunch of time checking out the derivation of 'gal' and decided it sounded dated and was more likely to offend. I left it as guy and finally hit save.

It had been a long haul writing this book, but the end was finally in sight. There had been so much stopping and starting as I agonized over the words. The problem was the first book in the Derek Streeter series, *The Girl with the Golden Throat*, had been a nice success and I was worried the second one wouldn't measure up. I hated to admit that it had paralyzed me and my writing had become labored, like squeezing words out of a toothpaste tube or, said in a more colorful way, like having word constipation.

Not that mystery writing was likely to make me rich or even take care of that many of my bills. Only the superstars made the big bucks. That was why my real work was as a writer for hire. I wrote anything and everything as long as it was legal – that included love letters, promotional copy, food descriptions, wedding vows, celebrations of life for funerals, and more. I'd just finished a gig coming up with interesting names for paint colors where the names were more poetic than they were actually descriptive. It was about emotion rather than the shade. I came up with names like Twilight's Last Streaming for a soft pastel rose and Autumn Touch for a mellow yellow-gold. I did a lot of work with food places creating descriptions of menu items, ice-cream flavors and coffee blends. It was always an adventure since it got me into all kinds of interesting situations with all kinds of people. I also ran a writers' group out of my apartment. Every Tuesday night they gathered around my dining-room table and shared their pages along with bits of their lives.

The computer screen went dark and I pushed away from my desk. In a rush of inspiration, I'd taken my morning coffee and gone right to work on the mystery. I stopped writing as I had an appointment with a potential client and I was still in my sleepwear. It seemed like it was going to be a meet and greet to see if we hit it off. I wanted it to work out because it was a dream gig. It would mean that I'd have to put Derek Streeter on hold for a while since the client was looking for someone to assist her in writing her memoirs. I knew nothing about her besides her name, Maeve Winslow, and had no idea if she'd done anything noteworthy or if she was just longing to have someone create interesting word snapshots of her life.

I not only wanted the gig, but needed it, too. My only other writing job at the moment was creating love notes for a math professor. And who knew how long that would last? I usually required knowing about the obstacles and the people involved. But much as I'd tried to get information about who the notes were for, all he would tell me was that he and his wife had had a falling out and he was trying to get her back. I gathered that he was the one who did something wrong and whatever it was, it was pretty terrible – enough so she wouldn't even talk to him. Thanks to a previous client, I'd discovered that there was a responsibility to writing love letters. I certainly didn't want to help a stalker or someone out to deceive a person. Everything about Caleb's demeanor said he was neither, and I really needed the money.

He seemed too lost in his world of numbers to manage being a stalker and too awkward to pull off any sort of deception. His plan was to send the notes I created attached to gifts. It seemed like a good plan to me. Who isn't going to read a note attached to a box of really good chocolates or flowers or cookies? He was willing to try just about anything. But so far, the notes and gifts had no effect. It felt like throwing spaghetti against the wall and none of it had stuck. I paused in my thoughts, wondering if the spaghetti thing counted as a cliché. I scolded myself for ruminating about clichés. True, I thought the meaning could be said in a fresher way, but fussing about clichés made me seem set in my way, old maidish – which wasn't really accurate since I had been married briefly a long time ago – and, worst of all, no fun. I really needed to be more of a *whatever* sort of person.

The point was that it wasn't going to go on forever with Caleb. Either the notes and gifts would get through to her or he'd realize it was a hopeless cause and give up. I was hoping at the very least that he'd finally tell me what he'd done to make her so upset that she shut off all communication.

Another reason I wanted the memoir gig was that Maeve lived a short walk away. I figured there would be numerous meetings and having her close by made it so much easier. For the moment, I was car-less, depending on public transportation with the occasional Uber or Lyft. The idea of being able to walk a block or so was a lot more appealing than all the time it would take up if I had to depend on trains or buses. I didn't want to jinx the deal and had avoided trying to do any research on her in advance of our meeting, which meant I was going in cold.

I took my coffee mug into the living room to get a look at the day. The window in my office looked out on the brick wall of the next building and it was hard to get a take on the weather. The living room was my favorite room in the apartment. It and the kitchen were the only rooms with a view that didn't involve the brick wall of the building next door. The bayed windows looked out on the tree-lined street and across to the other side to several other brick three-story walk-ups like mine. Already the leaves were looking a little wilted now that it was late September, but they still clung to the branches, keeping them from being the bare brown skeletons they'd be soon. Fall was my favorite time of year in Chicago. The hot humid days were over and the icy-cold days were still off in the future. For today, the sky was a bright blue, and when I opened the door to the balcony to check the temperature, it felt comfortably warm.

My smart watch vibrated on my wrist, reminding me of my

upcoming appointment, and I hustled to get ready. I always tried to dress to suit the occasion. The point was for Maeve to feel at ease with me, which meant dressing too formally might put her off. But too casual might make me seem unprofessional. I went back to my bedroom and thumbed through my closet, choosing a paisley print tunic and black jeans outfit that seemed to hit a sweet spot in the middle. I'd add a silver necklace and some silver bracelets to finish it off.

I stuffed some samples of my work into my peacock blue messenger bag and slung it over my shoulder, wished myself luck and went out the door. I was on my way down the stairs when the second-floor apartment door opened and a toddler rushed out. I heard a voice from inside sounding a little panicky as she called for him to stop.

'Hey, Mikey, where are you headed?' I said laughing as I snagged the little boy just when his mother rushed through the door.

'Good timing,' Sara Wright said with relief, picking him up. 'His escaping has become my nightmare ever since Mikey learned how to open the door.' She looked at my messenger bag and picked up that I was wearing makeup. 'Where are you off to?'

Sara was my neighbor and my friend. We were about the same age, though at different places in our lives. I gave her the rundown of where I was headed and how much I wanted the job.

'I'm keeping my fingers crossed for you,' she said. 'Let me know how it goes.' She turned to go inside, muttering something about needing to get some other kind of lock on the door.

It felt warmish when I first stepped outside but as soon as I reached the corner and turned on 57th a gust of wind hit me in the face and blew my breath away. The wind was coming off Lake Michigan and had a sharpness that made me wonder if I needed a jacket. Ah, Chicago weather – you honestly never knew what was around the corner.

Since I didn't have far to go, I braved the wind and kept on going. It was late morning, so the coffee shop on the corner was in that quiet spot between breakfast and lunch. Someone walked out of the cleaner's with an armload of clothes in plastic. I glanced in the window of University Foods which was so convenient and so pricey. Four joggers passed me seeming unbothered by the wind. They were wearing maroon T-shirts with the UChicago logo.

As I reached the corner, the hairdresser in University Styles looked out at me as I passed and smiled. Was she imagining what she'd do with my rather plain brown hair?

The wind abruptly stopped when I turned onto the side street, thanks to the Metra tracks. They were on a raised embankment and acted as a barrier. I took a moment to recover my breath and push the hair out of my face. I really did want this job, I thought, looking down the street, thinking again about the convenience. I might have thought it was bad luck to find out about the woman I was meeting, but I knew all about this two-block stretch of houses. It was like its own little community within the Hyde Park neighborhood. The street had been developed as a planned community in the 1880s, before Hyde Park was even part of Chicago. The Queen Anne and shingle-style homes had a view of the lake, since at that time the Metra tracks were level with the ground. They were called the Rosalie Villas after Rosalie Buckingham, who had been involved with the development until she went off to marry Harry Selfridge. They moved to London where he started the hugely successful Selfridges department store.

The information had come courtesy of one of my writers' group people. Tizzy was writing a time-travel novel; she was into the history of the neighborhood and was generous in sharing what she found out. I was curious to see the interior of Maeve's house. Would it have the charm it had been built with, or would the inside have been gutted and altered to go with the current fashion of making the common area into one big space.

I kept checking addresses and stopped in front of a Victorian-style house painted lavender with fish-scale siding. The covered front porch had a wicker settee decorated with a pumpkin surrounded by gourds and Indian corn in anticipation of Halloween. I glanced at the stained-glass strip above the top of the door as I felt my nerves kick in. This was it. It was show time. I wished that I could be cool, calm and collected, but whenever I met a potential client I always got butterflies in my stomach. I gave the doorbell a push and looked in through the glass pane on the upper section of the outer door, putting on what I hoped was a friendly smile.

And then nothing. I was considering giving the bell another push, when a woman opened the inner door and eyed me with a blank expression.

'Maeve?' I called out, looking at her.

There was no friendly smile in return as she finally opened the outer door.

'Maeve?' I repeated, giving her a quick appraisal. She seemed in her late twenties and hadn't seemed to have lived enough yet to be writing a memoir.

'Hardly,' she said in a sharp tone. I waited, expecting her to say something more, but the woman continued to stare at me. Calling her a woman felt too old. But calling her a girl didn't seem right either. The *woman-girl* thing was a conundrum. Women in their seventies talked about the *girls* getting together. Maybe it was a frame of mind rather than an age thing. In the end, I gave up and went with considering her a woman. I stopped myself from my mental ramblings and focused on the moment. She made no pretense at being gracious.

'I have an appointment to see her,' I said. 'Do you suppose you could get her?'

'What exactly are you here to see Maeve about?' she demanded. There was an arrogance about her and I had the feeling she didn't care much for the woman I was there to meet. I considered how to answer. Some of what I was hired to write was secretive, like the love letters. A memoir might be the same. While we did our stare-off and I thought about what I wanted to say, I took in more of her appearance. It was like second nature to come up with a description that was more of an impression than based on things like height and eye color. In the few seconds I looked at her, I noted that she had a low center of gravity and that she managed to camouflage it with a burgundy knit dress that hung just loosely enough to skim her body. She had a long silk scarf hanging loose which directed your eye to her face. Her dark-blonde hair was pulled up on top of her head and, by the bundle, I assumed it was quite long. My impression of her personality from her appearance was that she was calculating.

'It's about some writing she wants help with,' I said finally.

'Writing?' the person repeated and her eyes seemed to narrow. 'You mean like invitations?'

Since Maeve hadn't made an appearance and she didn't seem to be getting her, I figured she was the gatekeeper and – unless I satisfied her – I wasn't going to get any further.

'No, it's something about her life,' I said. 'More like a biography.' I thought it sounded more impersonal than memoir.

She choked on a laugh. 'Isn't she the self-important one.' She rolled her eyes at the absurdity of it. 'She's an art teacher and you know what they say . . .' I heard the words in my head as she said them out loud. 'Those who can do, and those who can't teach.'

I was pondering if that counted as a tired phrase or a cliché before I stopped myself. I was doing it again. I chalked it up to a tired phrase, which also seemed an unnecessarily mean one at that.

'Maybe she changed her mind because she's not here,' she said in a dismissive tone.

'Could you at least tell her I came by?' I searched in my bag for a business card.

The woman took it and glanced over it disdainfully. 'Writer for hire, huh,' she said. 'What exactly does that mean?'

At this point I wanted to stalk off, but if there was any chance she'd give the card to Maeve, I had to play along. I gave her the rundown of some work I'd done recently, leaving out the love letters. I could just imagine what her reaction would have been since she seemed so arrogant. I wondered if I should tell her about the Derek Streeter book, but I sensed that she would dismiss it as genre writing rather than serious literature.

I mentioned writing pieces for funerals and wedding vows, along with biographical copy for websites. I knew some sort of dismissal was coming next and avoided it by making a move first. I thanked her and backed away from the open door. She wasted no time in shutting it without so much as a goodbye.

I went down the stairs trying to shrug off the bad vibes I'd gotten from her. Before I'd come, I had considered various ways the meeting could go, but never considered that Maeve simply wouldn't be there.

All that nervous energy with nothing to show for it. What a waste.

TWO

I usually handled whatever came along pretty well, but I was definitely upset about being stood up for the appointment with Maeve. When I got home, I tossed my messenger bag on the chair and flopped on the couch. Rocky heard me come in and joined me on the black leather sofa. The big black-and-white cat looked up at me with what seemed like understanding eyes, and once again I was glad to have his company. It really was nice to have someone to come home to.

But I still had a terrible feeling of loose ends. Yes, I knew it was cliché, but I didn't care. What could have happened?

I thought back to my dealing with Maeve. It had all been rather straightforward. She'd contacted me through my website and said she was looking for someone to help with a memoir. Then we'd arranged the time to meet. I had already checked the date and time and both were what we'd agreed on. I'd assumed she might be talking to others. The thought crossed my mind that she had already hired somebody else and simply not bothered to cancel our appointment. Or did she forget? I willed myself to get it together and reached for the plastic bag on the end of the couch that held a half-done crochet project. It was a combination of a hobby and self-soothing technique that always helped me focus.

My mother had taught me how to work a hook and yarn when I was a kid and it felt like an inheritance from her. The time we'd spent together with our hooks and yarn had always been good moments. For a while I had made wearable articles like scarves and hand-warmers and even some blankets, but later I'd settled on making small squares. I used different stitches, motifs and yarns, with only the size staying standard. I liked them because the end was in sight when I began. And when I had enough, I put them together in a crazy quilt sort of mixture. The very first one I'd made hung over the couch I was slouched on. I'd gifted it to my father and he'd hung it in his office at the university. It was just the two of us then.

What was I doing going over all these sad thoughts? I forced myself to sit up straight and made myself keep the hook working through the goldenrod-colored yarn. I glanced around the room which was a hybrid of when my parents had lived there and the changes I'd made since. The artwork that covered the walls was all from them, along with lots of the interesting do-dads like the opera masks hanging by the windows. I'd kept the wing chair adjacent to the couch, but the more modern chairs from IKEA were my addition. The patterned rugs in shades of reds and pink were left from my parents and added a warm feeling to the room.

My surroundings and the crocheting began to work on me and I came up with a plan. There was no way to know if the person I'd dealt with would tell Maeve I'd been there, but on the chance she did, I'd give Maeve the rest of the day to contact me. If I heard nothing, I'd give it one shot and send her a message the next day.

My hopes began to deflate when by seven there was still nothing. I was glad it was Tuesday and that the writing group would be there soon. It was easier to focus on their work instead of thinking about my own.

Ed Grimaldi was the first to arrive. He worked in maintenance at the university and lived down the street. He had his usual impatient manner as he came in wearing track pants and carrying a mug holding an unknown beverage. He had never seemed to feel uncertain about the quality of his writing and had ploughed ahead with what could best be described as fan fiction for one of the TV shows that had one guy with a bunch of women for him to audition as a mate. Ed had taken it a step further and made the women all famous. No one ever said it, but we all thought the main character had an amazing resemblance to Ed. He was very explicit in the intimate scenes and the only person who could read Ed's pages without a lot of embarrassed laughter was Ben Monroe who was a cop. He read all the hot stuff as if it was a police report.

Ed had hooked up with a website and had been contributing his work to them. The success had given him an annoying sense of superiority and he was convinced he only needed our help for grammar polishing. But when I checked Ed's expression this time, he seemed a little grim.

He passed through the entrance foyer and went down the hall to the dining room on his own while I waited at the front to hit the button that unlocked the glass door downstairs. I'd always heard it referred to as the buzz door, probably because that was the noise it made when the button unlocking it was pushed, but the actual term was probably security door. I spent my days putting words together and was always thinking about the right word or phrases to use. I found it fascinating.

There was no use going anywhere until the whole group arrived, so I hung by the intercom poised for the bell to ring again. As my gaze moved from the living room to the long hall and the doors that led off it, I could see why the design had been called a train car. It was hard to imagine that the building was over a hundred years old. Long ago the rental apartments had been turned into condominiums, which seemed like such a modern term to go with such an old building.

It was still a mystery to me what the room I used as my office was originally meant to be. It had a set of frosted French doors that led to the living room and another set of the doors that opened to where I was standing.

The doorbell rang and startled me out of my reverie. Rang was a poor description. It sounded more like a croak. There I was thinking about the right word again. I pressed the button to release the downstairs door.

It was two-for-one this time. Tizzy Baxter and Daryl Sullivan came up together. Tizzy was in the lead and the kimono-style jacket she wore over her jeans fluttered as she waved her arms, showing off the file of papers she was carrying.

Tizzy worked at the business school of the university and lived nearby. We'd become friends outside the group. She was a big supporter of mine and had done a lot to get me writing gigs. She seemed to know everything that was going on in the neighborhood, now and in the past. She was still tweaking her time-travel novel and kept finding out more about the history of Hyde Park.

Daryl's face was locked in a tense expression which was nothing new. It seemed at odds with her outfit, which was probably supposed to look funky and fun. She was the manager of a downtown store that catered to the barely twenty-somethings. The clothes were made to last about as long as the style stayed in fashion. I thought the odd mixture of patterns and prints was an assault on the eyes, and figured it was a sign the designers were really running out of ideas for something new to sell.

Daryl's expression had nothing to do with the outfit. It was all about going public with her pages. She reacted to even the slightest criticism, and if the group tried to placate her by saying it was coming along, she didn't like that either. The result was that the rest of them said nothing and left me to do the dirty work. She was writing a romance novel and tended to have too many details of what the characters did. It was a fine line between making things come alive with detail and being too precise. I thought over the pages she'd left for me to go over from last week.

Karen picked up the teacup with the flowers on the side and the gold trim, took a sip of the Darjeeling tea and then placed the two-thirds-full cup back in the saucer. She wiped a droplet of the amber liquid off the corner of her mouth before folding the delft blue napkin and replacing it in the lap of her dirndl skirt. She looked across the table as Marcus poked through the cucumber sandwiches on the tea tray and picked out one of the finger-shaped snacks. He examined the rectangle of white bread with a layer of cream cheese and cucumber slices so thin they were transparent before placing it on his plate. He took one of the salmon sandwiches next, stuffing it in his mouth instead of putting it on his plate. She noted with disgust that he chewed with his mouth open, sent pieces of the orange fish flying across the table and landing on the white damask tablecloth. Karen ignored his gross behavior and picked through the sweets. She rejected the tiny cup of trifle made with sponge cake and layers of whipped cream and fruit, and the square of white cake with boiled icing, choosing the miniature Napoleon slice made of flaky dough and rich yellow custard.

I had been hard pressed to know what to write on her pages when I went over them. Honestly, I wanted to say that unless Marcus had a knife hidden in his hand and was waiting until he finished the tea sandwiches before stabbing Karen, the scene went nowhere. But I didn't write that. I simply wrote that some dialogue with conflict might make the scene more exciting.

'Where's Ben?' Tizzy asked when I followed the two women into my dining room.

'He must be delayed at his sister's,' I said, reminding them that he always had dinner down there before the workshop. Ben Monroe was the other member of the group. He was a cop, and my downstairs neighbor Sara was his sister. She'd bought him the initial workshop meetings as a gift with two motives. She thought writing might be a better release for him than going out drinking with his cop buddies. And she hoped to play matchmaker and get us together. To further it, she'd come up with a plan to send up a plate of food for me with him. Under the guise of wanting to make sure she got her plate back, she asked him to wait while I ate. It was laughably transparent. Ben had been badly burned by a divorce barely a year ago. His wife had just left with no warning. What seemed to bother him the most is that he'd had no idea there was anything wrong. Personally, I suspected she had gone off with somebody else, but I wasn't about to say anything.

My divorce was ancient history in comparison. I'd been barely in my twenties and an idiot. I somehow thought that everything would be happily ever after once we got married. Ha! He'd felt trapped and had done everything he could to not come home, until one day he let me know he'd decided he needed his freedom permanently and would be picking up his things. I'd been left with doubts about my judgment.

Sara's wish hadn't exactly happened. Taking things incredibly slow by today's standards, Ben and I had gone from being friends to something more. But not too much more. We'd agreed to become each other's plus one for any events either of us had, and we admitted that we liked spending time with each other. We'd tried to keep it under wraps, particularly from his sister. If she knew we were even almost dating, she would be pushing us to move faster than either of us was willing. I had done my best to keep our friendship from the rest of the writers' group, with limited success. The only one who seemed upset was Ed, worried that Ben might be getting extra help with his writing.

While we waited for Ben, the four of us started with our usual small talk. They liked to hear about the projects I was working on. I was glad to share if it was something public, like writing descriptions of menu items. I was considering whether to tell them about my non-meeting. There was no way to take it any other way than rejection. It was important they knew it was part of being a writer and that it even happened to me. But I rethought it and decided the focus was supposed to be on them and not on my problems. 'Nothing much,' I said in a noncommittal tone just as Ben walked in.

Even though the group knew we saw each other outside of the workshops, I felt awkward about it and overcompensated by purposely staring down at the files in front of me instead of looking at him as he pulled out a chair.

'Now that we're all here, let's get started,' Ed said with his usual impatience.

'Then why don't you go first,' I said. It was a replay of what happened every week, but to my surprise, Ed suggested Tizzy start.

'You're always in first position,' Tizzy said, eyeing him with a hint of suspicion at the sudden change.

Ed took a sip from his commuter mug and let out a dissatis-fied grunt. 'Can't I be gracious. You know, ladies first for once,' he said.

'It's out of character,' Tizzy said. 'If I wrote what just happened, you'd all jump on me and say it wasn't believable.'

Ed took another sip from the mug and kept his head bent as he gave us all a sideways glance. 'There's been a change in my situation,' he began. 'I'm not writing for the website anymore.' He didn't give any details, but I saw through it and realized he'd been let go and could probably offer the group a teaching moment on how to deal with rejection if he was honest about what happened. He ran his hand through his salt-and-pepper buzz cut a few times and blew out his breath. 'We'll just say we parted company. I was tired of writing that stuff anyway. Every week it was the same old, same old. I've decided to do what you people have been telling me to do.' He looked around at us, apparently expecting nods of recognition, but all I remember the group saying was that he needed a little emotion in all that heavy breathing. 'I decided to write a romance novel. The same guy will be in it, but instead of him picking someone from a pool of babes on a fantasy TV show, he'll actually date the women.' He held up a handful of pages and I noticed that his hand was shaking.

'If it's a romance novel, I can read his pages,' Daryl said, reaching for them.

'Remember this is something new and it's just a rough draft,' Ed said.

Daryl read two pages and it went fine for a while. The main character was on a plane, flying to Alaska now that he'd gotten out of prison. No one would know about his past and he'd be able to make a new life working on the pipeline. But then suddenly the character was looking at a woman across the aisle and started imagining an encounter with her. All the euphemisms were there, the heaving breath and quickening thrust, the throbbing something. Daryl made it through with only a few nervous titters and then dropped the papers on the table. 'I thought you said it was going to be different. That's not romance.'

'I looked it up and it is romance – erotic romance,' Ed said.

'OK, then next week, Ben should go back to reading Ed's pages,' Tizzy said. We all looked at Ben for an answer and he gave a distracted nod. We had an agreement not to pass judgment on the subject matter, just how it was written. Ed seemed relieved when Tizzy said it was actually an improvement over the website copy in that it seemed to have a plot.

'Why don't you go next,' I said, giving a professional smile to Ben. He stayed in cop mode for the group and usually had an inscrutable expression. But there was a glare in his eyes that made him seem bothered by something.

I was ready to chalk it up to worry about the pages he'd brought. Everyone got tense when their work was to be read and Ben had gone from writing about a terse detective to one who had real feelings. Writing it was hard enough, but then sharing it had to be even harder. He glanced up at the ceiling and shook his head. 'I only have two pages – not enough worth reading.' He started to get up. 'I don't even know why I came.'

They all urged him to stay and he reluctantly sat down. I tried to catch his eye, but he wouldn't look my way. Something was clearly wrong.

I tried to carry on with the workshop and did my best to concentrate on Tizzy and Daryl's pages, but I kept glancing at Ben, wondering what was bothering him. It reinforced my feeling that it was wrong to get involved with someone in the group. My concern about him was distracting me from the others. I was glad that they always left their pages with me so I could go over them with my full attention and make comments.

Ben left with them, which was nothing unusual. The plan was he came back with the plate of food. They probably knew, but we played the game anyway. I was anxious to find out what was up with him, hoping it was just something with his writing. Whatever it was, I was sure he'd tell me when it was just the two of us. I had just dropped off everyone's pages in my office and was coming through the French doors when Ben came in the front door I'd left on the latch for him, carrying a plate covered in plastic.

I expected him to hand me the plate and then go into the living room as he usually did, but he pushed the plate on me and turned back to go. 'I can't do this anymore,' he said.

He'd gone out and shut the door behind him before I could react.

Had he just broken up with me?

If I'd been at loose ends before, now I was comatose. It seemed like there should be a rule that only one really bad thing could happen in a day. Whatever hunger I'd had was gone and I was on automatic pilot as I took the plate back to the kitchen and put it in the refrigerator.

The window in the kitchen looked out on the backyards of the houses on Maeve's street. I came off automatic pilot long enough to be reminded that there had still been no text or message from her.

I went back to the living room, desperate to pick up my crochet project while I tried to make sense of what had just happened with Ben.

While my hook moved through the cheerful colored yarn, I thought back to the first workshop he'd come to. The others had done what they could to make him feel welcome and safe, but he'd sat rigidly with such a flat expression that I barely got a sense of his looks other than the short dark hair and dark brown eyes. It was only when I'd gotten to know him outside the group and he'd let his personality show through that I'd noticed his eyes had a soulful quality and his smile was a little crooked in an endearing way. He'd shown a sense of humor and a vulnerability. All of that had disappeared when he'd handed me the food. What could have happened?

I was crocheting without having to pay attention as thoughts flooded my mind. There was no way to take this other than it was his awkward way of breaking things off. We had both been hesitant about the relationship from the start and now I was grateful that we'd been so slow about getting further into it. But it reinforced what had worried me from the start. My fingers stopped moving mid-stitch and I let out a sigh. I'd had kind of an unwritten rule in mind when I first started the group. I wouldn't get romantically involved with anyone in the writers' group because if something like this happened, he'd feel compelled to leave it. How could I manage to let him know that the end of us didn't have to be the end of his being in the Tuesday crowd.

I'd seen the progress he'd made since joining us. He'd started out with a terse talking detective who seemed like a stick figure, to giving him some emotions and a life outside his job. I dropped my crochet and picked up my smart phone and typed in a text that said: *Just because things have changed between us is no reason for you to give up the group. I can separate my personal feelings from that of leader of the group and I promise it won't be awkward. No questions asked or explanation necessary.* I took a breath and hit send before I could overthink it.

I set the phone off to the side and went back to crocheting. I was pleased to see that, despite being lost in my thoughts, I had managed to stick to the pattern of the single-colored granny square. I was considering changing yarns to give it a black border when I heard a chime on my phone. I forced myself to finish the stitch before I reached for it, sure it was from Ben. When I finally looked at the phone, I saw that I was wrong. The text was from Maeve Winslow. The first line said she was sorry about missing our appointment and I was afraid it was just going to be an apology and then a brush-off saying that she'd changed her mind or hired someone else. Wonder of wonders, I was wrong. There was no explanation beyond the apology, but the rest of the text was about rescheduling and the offer of a time a few days ahead. Grateful for the good news, I started to type in a response without even checking my calendar before I stopped myself. It was close to ten and it might seem a little desperate if I answered right away. And there was the possibility I had something for that day and time.

I was old-fashioned and still used a paper appointment book and took notes with a real pen and paper. When I went into my office to check the black-covered book, I saw the block of time was free. Was it better to wait until morning to respond? But sending an answer now might make it look as if I was on top of things. I chided myself for overthinking again and went with my gut and quickly typed in a text saying yes to the meeting and hit send. My phone chimed just as I set it on the couch. It was Maeve's response that she'd see me then. I scrolled back to my text to Ben, and it showed it had been delivered.

Somehow, I'd hoped that I'd misunderstood and that there would be a response saying that or, even better, that he was coming back. But there was just an absence of words.

THREE

The ringing cut into my sleep and I bolted to an upright position, dislodging Rocky from his spot nestled against my head. It took a moment for me to calculate if the noise had been part of a dream or if it was real. It helped that the ringing continued and I recognized it as my landline.

Was it Ben? I chided myself for the thought as I unrolled the covers and went across the room to find the cordless handset. It was a little too heartbroken teenager instead of the reasonable adult I hoped I was. It would take time but I'd get used to the change in things. I checked the screen on the phone and recognized Tizzy's number.

'I didn't wake you, did I?' she asked in her upbeat voice.

I did what it seemed everybody did and said I was awake. Why did we all do that, as if there was some shame in sleeping when the caller was up and already in their day?

I expected her to ask about Ben's behavior at the group. She knew about the plate of food after the meeting and was probably curious. To use a cliché, Tizzy had a nose for news. I was preparing how I'd give her a noncommittal answer when she surprised me by talking about something else entirely.

'I hope you're free this evening,' she said, not waiting for me to respond before she continued on. 'Alex bought some tickets to an art gallery event and he doesn't want to go. It's a charity thing and he's insisting I go in his place. Theo is coming along. He'll drive and there'll be dinner at the Berghoff afterwards. There's going to be champagne and fancy appetizers. It's a reason to get dressed up and mingle. Say you'll come,' she added in a cheery voice. Alex was her boss at the university's business school. Her title was his assistant and she had an interesting relationship with him. She was very fluid about when she was in the office, and he seemed OK with it. But then I got the feeling that he liked all the news she gathered when she was out and about.

I debated the thought of a social evening downtown. I had been in the neighborhood too much lately and a change would be good. It would get my mind off Ben and the anticipation of the meeting with Maeve. And there was something else – it reminded me of something my mother had always said when she urged me to do something. Nothing was going to happen if I sat home but who knew what adventures might happen if I went out. I let out a sad sigh. There was always a momentary emotional dip when something reminded me of her and how much I missed her even after all this time. I knew in my heart that she would definitely have approved of Tizzy and how she pulled me out of myself.

'Well?' she said finally. I didn't have high expectations for an adventure at a charity reception at an art gallery, but I decided to take my mother's advice.

'I'll go,' I said.

'Good. Then you can tell me what's up with Ben,' she said before she hung up.

As the morning wore on, I tried to fight myself from doing it, but I kept checking my phone expecting to find a text from Ben in response to mine. The clean plate from the food Sara had sent up was sitting on the coffee table in the living room. Once the crochet had worked its wonder, reality had set in and I realized I was starving. It had been macaroni and cheese made from scratch with a side of roasted broccoli and a square of moist cornbread. The least I could do was return the plate and tell her how delicious it was. And maybe get some insight about what happened with Ben.

I could hear the sound of Mikey running up and down the long hall from outside the door. It was lucky the couple on the first floor didn't work from home and have to listen to the thudding sound of his toddler footsteps over their heads. Sara answered the door with a tired look.

'Here's your plate,' I said, holding it out. 'The dinner was delicious as always. Thank you.'

She looked at it and then up at me with a shrug. 'I guess Ben forgot.' Mikey came running down the hall and gave my hand a tug and I let him pull me in the doorway.

'Did he stop back before he left?' I asked.

Sara thought a moment. 'Now that you mention it, he didn't.' I waited for her to elaborate that it wasn't like him or something, but she said nothing. She wasn't making it easy to get her to talk. What would my detective say to get her to open up? Maybe he'd just go for the direct route.

'Did he seem different during your dinner?' I asked. 'Maybe he mentioned having something on his mind.'

She looked at me directly. 'Why are you asking?'

I finally broke down and told her about how he'd acted at the workshop without mentioning that I'd taken it personally. 'I'd hate to see him quit since he has come so far.'

'You and me both. It made me feel good that he had some outlet besides hanging out with his cop buddies. He seemed the same at dinner, but then he's good at holding it all in.'

'Don't say that I said anything,' I said. 'But if he says something about not coming anymore, maybe you can offer him some encouragement.'

'What exactly did he do?' she asked with concern.

I told her he came with barely any pages and seemed upset, and that he'd left the plate of food with me and rushed off. Ben and I had kept quiet about the other time we spent together, but Sara knew about his sitting with me when I ate the food she sent, since she had engineered it, so it didn't seem to be disclosing anything about how far our relationship had progressed.

'Please excuse my brother's rudeness,' she said with a hopeless shake of her head. 'I'll do what I can to keep him coming to the workshops.' She let out a sigh. 'And please don't take it personally. He's got his issues, but underneath it, he's a good guy. Worth the effort.'

But not if he wouldn't talk about it. I suddenly understood how my client Caleb felt.

It was just getting dark when I checked my purse to make sure I had some business cards, just in case. Once I'd agreed to go with Tizzy and Theo, I was glad to have a reason to get dressed up. I even wore a dress.

The Prius was double parked when I came downstairs. Theo

actually got out and opened the back door for me. He smiled and did a mock bow when I thanked him for his gentlemanly gesture.

Tizzy seemed to have forgotten about her interest in Ben and the three of us made small talk on the drive downtown. The streetlights along Lake Shore Drive were bright enough that I got a view of the strip of park that had gone from manicured green back to the natural prairie it had once been. Beyond that the lake was just a dark expanse. Ahead, the impressive downtown skyline of tall buildings dotted with what seemed like a million lights showed our destination.

Theo turned off DuSable Lake Shore Drive and threaded through the downtown streets. People were still going home from work and the sidewalk along Randolph Street was congested with foot traffic. Shoppers were going into the Macy's store and the marques of several theaters were lit up with their offerings. It was such a different vibe than my neighborhood and I was glad to be out in it for a change.

He dropped us off in front of our destination and went to find parking. I let Tizzy lead the way into a tall office building. We walked into a massive atrium with walkways around each floor leading to the various offices. It reminded me of the set-up of some hotels and also prisons, though they had watch towers in the middle.

We took the glass elevator up to the upper floor and, as the doors opened, I heard the din of conversation. The double doors to the Zander Paul Galleries were open, though the entrance was blocked by someone holding a computer tablet checking names. Tizzy got us checked in and we went into a reception area filled with well-dressed people. I followed Tizzy through the crowd, letting her work out the mingling. I wasn't sure if she recognized people she knew or just struck up a conversation, but before I knew it, she was introducing me to a group of people and telling them what I did. I was pleased when someone asked for a business card just as several uniformed servers reached us with trays of hors d'oeuvres and flutes of champagne.

By the time Theo joined us, we'd found a tall table to use as a base for the food and drinks. I'd managed to get a flute of ginger ale and some vegetarian mini quiches.

Once he'd checked in with us, Theo went off to look around on his own. When Tizzy and I were finished with our appetizers, we split up to check out the other rooms. At least I was going to check out the other rooms. Tizzy seemed more interested in checking out the people. I envied the way she could start up a conversation with total strangers.

Someone stood by the entrance to the galleries displaying the art making sure no one was bringing in any refreshments. A table was set up with items for a silent auction with sheets for bids, making it hard to see the artwork. The best I could tell was that there seemed to be a mixture of styles, some abstracts and some landscapes which I glanced over without much regard. But then I saw something that absolutely caught my eye. All the paintings featured the same Scottish terrier in the foreground, which seemed to be looking out from the painting. Only the backgrounds changed. It was hard to see with the constant movement of the crowd, but in one the dog was on the beach, then another had the black scruffy-haired dog in a forest with fireflies around it. Another picture had three Scotties running in tandem with a background that reminded me of Vincent van Gogh's *Starry Night*. I couldn't stop staring at the dog. He, I was assuming it was a male, was soulful, jaunty and simply adorable. I pushed close enough to see the price tag on one. It didn't matter that it was already marked as sold as it was way, way out of my price range.

I heard a voice over a loudspeaker coming from the reception room and went to see what was going on. I hadn't seen it the first time, but now noticed there was a long table with an arrangement of posters, mugs, T-shirts and postcards. I moved closer and saw they all featured the same image of the black terrier with a garden of sleeping flowers around it. It was whimsical, and the bright colors of the flowers made me want to smile. The only item I could afford was a postcard, so I paid for it and slipped it in my purse and went looking to rejoin Tizzy.

'What's going on?' I asked when I caught up with her. A man was standing behind a podium holding a microphone. A small crowd was gathered around him.

'He's Zander Paul Junior and the owner of the gallery. He's

doing a pitch on who they're raising money for. Now I understand why Alex bought the tickets. It's his daughter's school,'
Tizzy said. I checked out the man at the podium. He looked
the part of a gallery owner. Dark collarless shirt under a dark
suit, accented with a scarf worn keyhole style. A pair of glasses
were pushed up on his thick dark hair, a lock of which had
fallen free. My gaze moved to the group standing next to him.
There was something that held my eye on the man in a denim
jacket hanging open over a collarless brick-red shirt. The
sleeves of the jacket seemed to have been folded back with
care, displaying a silver bracelet along with a string of Tibetan
prayer beads. He had longish dark hair and to me had artist
written all over him. When I glanced at the women with him,
I gasped so loudly that Tizzy turned and stared at me.

'What?' she said with a question in her eyes. I debated what
to say. I hadn't told Tizzy about Maeve, so how could I tell
her the woman I'd gasped about was the one who'd given me
the rude brush-off the other day. Even after my mental woman-
versus-girl debate when I'd first seen her, I'd gone with calling
her a woman. Her nasty mood was definitely gone now. Her
shoulder was almost touching the guy I'd decided was an artist
and she seemed quite solicitous. And when she glanced out at
the crowd, she reveled in the attention. Tizzy was staring
at me, waiting for an answer.

'She looks familiar, that's all,' I said, trying to dismiss it,
giving my attention back to the action at the podium. The
gallery owner did a flourish in the direction of the man I'd
pegged as an artist, introducing him as Michael Angel. The
murmur that went through the crowd made it clear they knew
who he was and were impressed. As soon as I heard he was
the painter of the Scotty dog pictures, my curiosity was stoked
and I pressed to hear what the artist had to say.

'Everybody always wants to know about my inspiration.
Monty was my best friend when I was a kid. Dog best friend,'
he said, and everyone chuckled. 'It was a hard time for me.
My parents had just broken up and I always felt like an
outsider in school. Monty was always there for me. Something
in the way he looked at me made me feel that he saw through
to my heart. I carried him in my imagination long after he

crossed into dog heaven and pictured him in different circumstances.'

I kept hoping he would introduce the rude greeter from Maeve Winslow's home, but while she seemed practically glued to one side of him, Michael seemed oblivious of her. He did give a nod to the woman flanking his other side and touched her arm in an affectionate manner. I didn't catch her name, but heard something about her being a filmmaker and very special to him.

Before he could say anything more, a tall, dark-haired woman who'd been part of the entourage at the front stepped in front of him and took control of the microphone. 'I take credit for putting Michael on the map,' she said, gazing out at the crowd. Michael appeared to be miffed, but it was all for show.

'I'm sure you all know Sophia,' he said, taking the microphone back. 'Second Chance Sophia.' There was a sound of recognition from the crowd. Michael stepped back and as Sophia took over, she held up a real live Scottish terrier.

'This is Drexel,' she said and gave the dog a kiss. 'He's my companion on all the adventures on my YouTube channel. I know that Michael Angel was thinking of his dear departed dog when he did the first painting but, as you can see, it looks like he captured the heart and soul of Drexel. The minute I saw the painting of *The Scotty in the Sleeping Garden* at the art fair, I had to have it. And when I showed it to my hundreds of thousands of followers, everyone fell in love with the picture, too.' She gestured toward the display where I'd gotten the postcard. 'And a portion of anything you purchase will go toward the Dupont Academy.' She looked back to the artist. 'So, now that you've been nominated for the National Arts Award, I think you should mention me in your acceptance speech at the gala in January.'

'That's if I win,' he said with a smile.

'You're going to win,' she said. 'Everybody loves your paintings.'

'I'm honored by the nomination,' he said. He seemed to be trying to appear humble, but he beamed as the crowd called out assorted cheers like woot, hear-hear, and a couple of congrats. The only one that made any sense was the last one. What did woot or hear-hear even mean?

'There's more to it, isn't there?' Tizzy said. 'You're staring at that woman like you're a pointer dog who just spotted a fallen bird.

'I didn't realize it was that obvious,' I said, realizing my gaze had gone back to the woman from my appointment that wasn't. 'It has to do with a client. Too bad you don't know who she is,' I said.

'I could probably find out,' Tizzy said, checking out the crowd as she considered her plan of action.

'The artwork is out of our price range and dinner awaits. Let's go,' Theo said, coming up behind us and slipping an arm through each of ours. Tizzy looked at me with a question in her eye.

'It doesn't matter,' I said. 'Theo's right. Let's go.'

'I hope you don't mind walking,' Theo said to me as we exited the building. He said something about it wasn't cost-effective to have to park twice. It was fine with me as it gave us a chance to check out State Street. Now that so many people were living downtown, the stores stayed open late every night and there was a lively atmosphere. Some street musicians were still on the street corners. Theo kept it interesting by adding background information on everything from the permits the street musicians had to have to how State Street had changed over time.

'Don't mind him,' Tizzy said, leaning into me.

Theo is fascinated by how everything fits together and works, but that's the life of an English Literature professor with an insatiable curiosity. When we got to the former Carson Pirie Scott store, Theo had to stop to admire the metalwork on the entryway and go on about how Louis Sullivan had designed the building. The department store had closed a number of years ago and been replaced by a two-story Target store.

'As long as we're here, let's go in,' Theo said, opening the door for us.

Tizzy looked at me with a question in her eye. 'Do you mind? I could pick up a few things.'

'I could too,' I said as we all went inside. Target was a

bright and cheerful general merchandise store, kind of a toned-down version of the department stores that used to line State Street. And they had something the department stores never had – shopping carts.

'That's why he wanted to come in here,' Tizzy said, pointing to Theo, who was pushing a red shopping cart toward the escalators. 'He just loves the way they have a cart escalator.' He pushed the cart onto the moving belt and then rode the regular escalator beside it. A moment later he and his cart were on the way back down. I'm assuming he kept repeating it while the two of us did our shopping.

'That was fun,' he said. He added his opinion that having shopping carts was a subtle way to make people buy more. 'It's human nature to want to fill up available space.' As we continued on our way, he described his take on the reception. 'I don't know if you noticed, but not everything of Michael Angel's was so pricey. There were prints of some landscapes with random nudes that were almost something I might have considered if I'd liked them. They seemed,' he hesitated while he thought of a word, 'nothing special.'

'I didn't even notice them,' I said, remembering my trip through the gallery. 'But I loved the Scotty pictures.' I pulled out the postcard to show them. 'This was all my budget would cover,' I said with a laugh.

'And the prices will probably escalate if he wins that national prize. It comes with a nice cash award, too. No matter that he said all that humble stuff, I think he expects to win,' Theo said as we continued down the street.

'At last,' Tizzy said when we turned on to Adams Street and the Berghoff came into view. 'I forgot you were a vege-tarian when we decided on the Berghoff. It seems like German meat is their specialty.' She sounded apologetic and asked if it was OK with me. The restaurant was 128 years old and served German fare and lots of beer. Tizzy was interested in the place for her time-travel book and Theo just liked the food.

I assured her it was fine. It was never my way to make a point about what I ate or didn't. I always worked it out without making a fuss. It had gotten a lot easier lately as it seemed to have become stylish to be a vegan or vegetarian, and plant-based protein was all the rage.

Tizzy looked around the wood-paneled dining room of the restaurant as we walked in and sighed with pleasure. 'They haven't changed a thing. I bet this place looks about the same as the day they opened.'

It was busy and noisy and the décor did have an old-time feeling to it. The tables were close together and the service best described as brusque, which was supposed to be part of the appeal. Theo and Tizzy ordered Sauerbraten and braised oxtail to share. I chose a newer addition to the menu of a grilled portobello panini with spätzle on the side. They got steins of the special beer, while I stuck with the house-made root beer.

Theo had more to say about the reception while we ate. 'You know that artist, Michael Angel, lives in Hyde Park. And, by the way, Michael Angel is his painting name. His real name is Michael Wolinski,' he said. 'But he signs his work with unintelligible initials anyway.'

'Do you know anything about those two women who were with him?' I asked as the server dropped off our food.

He shrugged. 'One of them was probably his wife.' He looked at the plates piled high with food. 'We can talk about them later. For now, let's enjoy the feast.'

When it got to dessert, we shared apple strudel with ice cream, and were all glad for the walk back to the garage where Theo had left the car after the big meal.

They dropped me in front of my building and I thanked them for the fun time. I wanted to thank them for something else, too. I hadn't looked at my phone once to see if Ben had texted me.

FOUR

'd barely gotten into my place and kicked off my shoes when there was a knock at the door. Sara came upstairs requesting a cup of sugar or something like apple cider vinegar practically daily. It was usually just an excuse to leave Mikey with her husband for a while and get some adult conversation. Though sometimes she did actually need the ingredients.

She was holding a measuring cup when I opened the door, but if she actually needed something she forgot and just said she had news. She noticed I was more dressed up than usual and had that glow people get when they've been out somewhere and had a good time.

'Were you on a date?' she asked, sounding uneasy.

'No, unless you call going out with Tizzy and her husband a date,' I said. My neighbor's face relaxed as she took it to mean I was still available for her brother. She had told me that one of the reasons she kept trying to push us together was that in her ideal life I would be her sister-in-law. I could understand her feeling. My parents had both been only children, and whatever cousins or relatives they'd had had never been part of my life, so I was open to any connections I could get. I hoped I could sell her on the idea that we could be like sisters without really being family.

She went into the living room and sat down fidgeting with the measuring cup. 'How about some cooking wine?' I said, and she nodded an enthusiastic yes. I called it cooking wine because that was how I used it, but since it had become a drink of choice when anybody came over, I'd started buying a good-quality merlot.

I wasn't sure if she'd come up for a change of scene or because she knew something about Ben. I was really curious about him, but didn't want to let on how much. If I'd been hesitant to let her know that Ben and I had been on some actual dates before, I really didn't want her to know about that now, as I was sure it would make her more likely to interfere. One truth about me was that I didn't want somebody who didn't want me. The last thing I wanted was a third party to get in the middle of it and try to patch it up. I would have preferred more of an explanation than him saying that he couldn't do this, whatever 'this' was, before rushing out the door. But I would let it be.

She took a couple of sips of wine and set the glass down, letting out an unhappy sigh. 'I called Ben,' she said. 'I tried to make it just like a normal call to see how he was doing. He kept saying he was fine and asking if you'd said something. I started to say you hadn't, but I'm a terrible liar. I repeated all the good stuff you'd said about his writing and how far he'd come. I said you were concerned he was going to quit the group and hoped he wouldn't.'

'What did he say?' I asked.

'He was quiet for a long time and I asked him if it was something about work. He always gets annoyed when I ask him anything about being a cop. He usually snaps at me and says he doesn't want to talk about it. This time he didn't get angry. All he said was "sure, that's what it is" and changed the subject. I would have expected better of him. He should have realized I'd see right through that and know he wasn't telling me the truth.' She shrugged. 'He finally said he would try to keep coming to the group, but he wasn't doing the food delivery anymore. He tried to hide it, but he sounded miserable.'

She drank some more of the wine. 'I know he's being difficult, but I hope you can give him some slack. No matter what he said, or didn't say, something's bothering him.' She was being serious now and it didn't seem to be about matchmaking.

'Everyone in the group is difficult, except Tizzy, and even she has her moments. I want him to stay in the group. You can tell him that.'

She seemed relieved at my attitude and asked about our evening. It was fun having someone to tell about everything.

When she left, it was too late to go to my computer. I'd

found that working late left me too wide awake and it was hard to fall asleep. I was already keyed up from the evening out and Sara's visit and needed to wind down.

Rocky had come in and curled up on the couch beside me. And once again, I thought of how glad I was to have adopted the big black-and-white cat. He was my first ever pet and I'd had a stereotypical view of cats. I had always thought that they were aloof and kept their distance, but he was all about the cuddles. He slept wound around my head or nestled next to me and he usually settled next to me when I sat on the couch.

He was an older cat and his chances of getting adopted had been pretty close to nothing. In addition to my paid work, I did some pro bono work. I called it that even though it was technically meant to refer to legal work for people who couldn't afford lawyers. Over time the meaning had blurred to cover free work done by any professional. The recipient was a downtown pet store that brought in animals from shelters and made them available for adoption. My job was to write up personality pieces that would make someone want to take them home. In Rocky's case, that person had been me. I'd like to think it was my high-quality writing skills that brought me to tears, but it was really just his story. For some unknown reason, his owners, who'd had him for years, had coldly dropped him off at a shelter. I'd heard that cats chose their humans and it seemed as if he'd picked me. As I went to leave the pet shop the day I met him, he stared at me with big eyes and held out his paw as if to say 'take me with you, please.'

I teared up just thinking back on it. I gave him a hug and reminded him that this was his home forever before going back to the kitchen and making myself a cup of chamomile tea. I took it into the living room and pulled out the square I'd been working on. With Ben clearly gone I was back to being a single woman with a cat who calmed her fragile nerves by drinking herbal tea and crocheting.

I cheered myself by remembering that at least I had another chance with the memoir client. I really, really wanted that gig more than ever now.

FIVE

After the visit from Sara, I felt even more convinced that Ben had broken things off with me, but I also believed there was a reason. Something had happened. It was frustrating not knowing what it was. I really wanted an explanation, but there was no way to make him tell me. For a moment, I thought of sending one of the kind of notes I was writing for Caleb along with a box of cookies or something. But what was I going to say? *Please oh please tell me the backstory of why you decided we're done.* I understood now why people were always talking about needing closure. I was going to have to let it go and act the way I'd said I would when he came to the group. Act like everything was fine.

There was still time before my meeting with my memoir client. I hated to even think it, but what if she stood me up again? I didn't know anything about her. I stopped myself from rehearsing what I would say. When, and if, I was face to face with her, I'd just let whatever was supposed to happen, happen. What good had it been for me to be so nervous the first time? I blew out my breath and simply put it out of my mind.

I opened the Derek Streeter Book 2 folder and clicked on the file marked manuscript. I wondered what my character would have to say about my situation with Ben. Out of nowhere I heard Derek start talking in a Humphrey Bogart voice. *Dames are just a diversion. Better to be a lone wolf, than one with a foot in a trap.* Ewww, really? I stopped writing, unhappy with what Derek was saying. I erased the line and told Derek he needed to come up with something better.

At last, it was time to go. I checked the messenger bag to be sure I had everything and then tucked in some more of the love notes I'd created for Caleb. I'd gotten a frantic call from him and was set to see him after hopefully meeting the memoir client. If I was looking for omens, it didn't look promising. A light rain was falling and the sky was a dull yellowish-gray.

The cool air made me glad I'd worn a jacket and I opened my umbrella as I stepped onto the sidewalk. The coffee shop looked like a port in the storm on the drizzly day. The weather didn't stop the students from their jogging. A group of them went by in matching maroon T-shirts like a herd of gazelles. They looked so young to me now.

A sudden thought hit me: if they noticed me at all, they probably thought I was old. Not that being in your late early thirties was old. It seemed like the time when you started to know who you were. In my case, a long-ago-divorced orphan. I considered if that sounded any better than the singleton with a cat. The marriage had been so short that it almost seemed like it wasn't. The orphan part was true. Both my parents were dead, but I was an adult and I wondered at what age the term orphan no longer applied.

This time I went directly to the house. I marched up the stairs with calm determination, my blue messenger bag loaded with samples of my work. I was ready for anything.

I punched the bell and when no one answered immediately thought it was a repeat of before. I felt a pang of anger starting to rise, but then I heard noise coming from inside. The inner door opened and a moment later the outer one did the same.

A woman wearing jeans and a worried expression looked out at me and then glanced up and down the street with a nervous gesture. 'Veronica?' she said in a tense tone. As soon as I nodded in acknowledgment, she waved me inside. We only got as far as the entrance hall before she stopped short. I noticed a couple of chairs in an alcove to the side of the door, but she didn't offer me a seat.

'And you are Maeve Winslow?' I asked. 'I just want to make sure after last time.' I smiled, trying to soften the moment.

She responded with a sharp nod of her head and stayed anchored to her spot. It seemed a little odd to do our meeting standing up, but she was the client. It was almost funny the way we both looked each other over.

I guessed she was older than me but not by that much. The burnt orange poet's blouse contrasted nicely with her shoulder-length brown hair. The jeans looked comfortable rather than high fashion. She was cute more than pretty, and there was a hint of dimples in her cheeks which probably blossomed when she smiled. I waited to see how she wanted to handle our meeting.

'What did you tell the person you spoke with when you came here before?' she asked, sounding uneasy. The question caught me off guard. I was expecting her to be more interested in seeing samples of my work, and for us to talk about her project. I had to take a moment to think back to the encounter with the unpleasant nameless woman. Since I had no idea of their relationship, it seemed best to say as little as possible.

'I said I had an appointment with you,' I said, waiting to see how she would respond.

'Did you say what it was about?' Her brow furrowed and any hint of the dimples disappeared. I suddenly wondered if she'd had me come over just to discuss what happened the other day.

'I probably said it was about a writing project.'

'Did you tell her what exactly it was?' she asked. I decided to go with the truth, or most of it.

'Honestly, I don't remember if I gave her any details.' I left it at that, not mentioning that I did remember feeling I had to satisfy the woman so she would pass along the message that I'd been there. There had been some other disparaging comments about Maeve that I recalled more by the tone of them than the content. I wasn't about to go into that.

In an effort to move on, I opened the blue messenger bag and pulled out a binder.

'These are some samples of my work,' I said, holding it out to her, but she shook her head.

'Why don't you tell me a little about yourself first,' she said.

I had some basic information on my website, but it was really about my writing experience rather than anything personal. If someone was hiring me to write a bio or some promotional copy, did they really care where I grew up or what my hobby was? She sensed me hesitating.

'The job will require us to spend a lot of time together,'

she said by way of an explanation. 'Will our personalities jibe?'

I would have preferred to do this sitting, but she made no move to another room, so there was no choice but to do the best I could in this awkward situation. 'I grew up in the neighborhood and I live nearby.' I waved my arm in the vague direction of my place. I gave her a rundown of the schools I'd attended and told her that my father had been an English professor at the university. I didn't know how personal I should go and finally added that I was single, was a vegetarian, and liked to crochet. 'Just in case eating meat is involved,' I said, trying to make it sound like a joke.

I was relieved when she smiled and I saw I was right about the dimples. 'The fact you're local is good and bad,' she said. 'Good because it would be easy for us to get together . . .' I waited for her to add the negative. 'You know how this neighborhood is. It's almost like a small town within the city and gossip spreads fast. It's extremely important that anyone I work with is discreet. I mean the person has to keep the project totally under wraps until we're done.' Her expression lightened a bit. 'It's meant to be a surprise.'

'I can do that,' I said. 'A lot of my clients require secrecy.' I thought about Caleb and how he'd insisted I not share what I was doing for him.

I tried again with the samples, but again she stopped me. 'That won't be necessary,' she said. 'There is something else, though: the project would have to be completed in six weeks.' I waited to see if she was going to add some explanation, but she just looked at me. 'Would you be able to manage that?'

'Oh,' I said, a little surprised at the short amount of time. 'It's a little hard to say for sure until I know more about what's involved.' I hoped she might give me some more details, but when she didn't, I decided to go for it. 'But since I only have one other client at the moment, I'm sure I could manage it.'

She seemed to be considering what I'd said. It was hard to know where to go from there since she was telling me so little. 'I could give you a proposal,' I said, in an effort to ask for the job, 'though until I know more about what's involved, it would be hard to set a price for the work.'

I heard her phone ping and, as she glanced at it hurriedly, her body stiffened. 'I'll be in touch.' She opened the inner door and almost pushed me out the outer one, urging me to hurry.

SIX

The rain had stopped and the air felt close as I reached the sidewalk. I looked back at the beautiful old house, totally confused. I had no idea if she intended to hire me or not. Though the fact that she seemed to have panicked when I mentioned the proposal made me think it was more likely *not*. Weird that it seemed more based on me personally than my work. And where I lived. I couldn't help but feel deeply disappointed. Rejection was part of writing, and the advice was always not to take it personally, but it was impossible not to this time.

I let out a sigh, reminding myself of my resilience and the spring that bounced me back up when I seemed to hit bottom. I'd get past it, tomorrow could bring something even better, and for now, I needed to get myself together to meet with the math professor. I was glad that we were meeting at a doughnut shop on 53rd. It would give a walk to clear my head.

The doughnut shop was his choice and I thought it had more to do with giving him an excuse to indulge in some sweets than anything else. The mixed smells of sugar, grease and coffee hit me when I walked in. My client was sitting at a table by the window, scribbling something on a napkin.

'Hey Caleb,' I said approaching the table. He looked up with a blank expression and then his eyes came into focus and he said hey back. The counter person called out a number and he got up and went to pick up his order. I was a little surprised when I saw that he'd gotten coffee for both of us, along with a plate of doughnut holes. My impression of him was that he was too 'out there' to consider the person he was meeting might also want coffee. It was as if his head was so full of numbers and formulas that he didn't have room to think about ordinary stuff. But then that was why he needed me. He had been short on details and I'd had to fill in the blanks myself. I gathered he'd done something to make his wife angry

enough to push him out of their house. The closest to details
he would give me was that it was really bad and then he'd
hung his head. He wanted to get back with her, but she had
cut him off so completely that she wouldn't even talk to him.
My job was to write something that would get her to speak
with him. It would have helped if I'd known something about
her, such as what she liked, what she didn't like, and did she
have soft spots for kittens or love crossword puzzles, etc. I
didn't like working this way, but he had been adamant about
it and I needed the gig.

Just to be sure he had no ill intent, I'd done a little checking
on my own about him. I hadn't told Tizzy why I was asking
about him, but with all her university connections, she'd had
gotten me assurance that he was the mild-mannered, socially
awkward person that he appeared.

He set down the tray and I took everything off it. He was
already eating the fried balls before I took a sip of the coffee.

He was a very ordinary-looking man. His dark brown hair
might have had waves if it was a little longer. Seeing the
plaid shirt and green cotton pants, I had the feeling he just
reached in the closet and wore whatever he happened to
pull out first. I always checked out footwear and he seemed
to favor old-fashioned loafers. He always had a faraway,
unfocused expression, as if he was juggling formulas full of
numbers in his mind.

'So, any response from the last note?' I asked, already
knowing the answer. If there had been, I wouldn't be there. His
shoulders did a slight drop and he put down the sprinkle-covered
doughnut hole he'd been working on.

'No, but I'm sure she's reading the notes. I'm thinking we
need to up things a little. Think of something you could say
so she'd have to call me. If she won't talk to me, we can't fix
this.'

I eyed the doughnut holes and took one that was dipped in
cinnamon sugar. Despite everything he'd said, I made another
attempt to get some info on the situation. 'If I knew what the
problem was, I might be able to come up with something.'
He looked panicked.

'I can't tell you. I'm too embarrassed. I didn't intend for it to happen,' he said, getting wound up and upset. 'I can't apologize or make it right if she won't even talk to me.'

I pulled out a file from the messenger bag and showed him a selection of notes I'd written for him. While he looked them over, I started to ask him questions about what his wife might react to.

'Would she call if she thought you were sick?' I asked.

'Hardly, since she seems to wish I'd drop dead.'

'What about money? Maybe you could say you got a refund of sorts and she was entitled to it.'

'She wouldn't believe it since she handles all the money,' he said. 'I like this wording.' He pushed the paper across the table to me and I read it. *My heart is broken into pieces too vast to count. Nothing adds up without you.* 'I could pick up some of those little heart-shaped cookies at LaPorte's.'

'Sure, that sounds good,' I said. 'You're getting the hang of it.' Up until now I'd had to suggest what to include with the notes. 'I wrote up the description of those cookies when they added them to the bakery.' I looked for his reaction to my comment, thinking he might be interested in hearing about the work I'd done for them. LaPorte's was a family-owned bakery and café. Every time they added a new menu item or bakery treat, they had me do the description. It was my work that described a sandwich as *imported brie cheese slathered with flavorful cranberry chutney on a freshly baked croissant.* Just recently, I'd described the cookies he'd mentioned as *dainty hearts enrobed in red buttercream icing.*

He clearly wasn't impressed as his forlorn expression didn't change. 'If your boyfriend or husband did something terrible, you'd forgive him, right?'

It made me think of Ben and how shut out I felt. 'How about this card?' he said, picking one out of the group I'd brought. It had a big heart made up of tiny flowers on the front. I gave my approval to his choice and he began to copy my words onto the blank interior.

He had small handwriting and all the letters were the same size. I wondered what a handwriting expert would say about it.

When he got to the end, he held the pen up. 'I could just write in *call me.* Maybe if I just said it directly, she would.'

He shook his head. 'That wouldn't work. She hates it when anybody tells her what to do.'

I promised to think about something we could add to a note that might inspire her to pick up the phone. He popped the last doughnut hole in his mouth, saying something about not letting it go to waste, and we walked outside together.

It was crazy, but I'd noticed the same thing about him every time we met. He started out feeling depressed and hopeless, but left with an optimistic expression and a bounce in his step. Was it my notes or the doughnut holes?

I had been ignoring my cell phone, but when I got home I scrolled through the messages and junk emails, wondering if there'd be something from Maeve or Ben, but there was nothing from either. I had taken Maeve's weird behavior as a brush-off, but in the back of my mind I was hoping that I was wrong or at least that she would give me closure by saying she'd decided on somebody else. And with Ben. I wanted to throw up my hands with frustration.

Rocky had greeted me when I came in the door and followed me to the couch as I checked through my phone. I reached over and stroked his back and he let out a loud purr. There was something about having this little soul waiting for me when I came home and always being so glad to see me. It made me feel good to have someone to love. 'How did I manage without you?' I said, giving him another pet before I went back to scrolling through the messages on my phone, wondering if I'd missed something. I hadn't.

The phone rang while I was holding it. It always startled me when that happened and as usual caused me to drop the device. It was like grabbing a slippery fish as I tried to retrieve it and as soon as I saw the call was from Tizzy, I hit accept.

'You have to come over for sherry,' she said after I'd said hello. 'I found out who that woman was. The one you were staring at. And Theo has become obsessed with that artist and he needs another ear besides mine to bore,' she said with a chuckle. 'I don't know if you understand how he is. He's interested in everything and does endless research to deal with his curiosity. I'm fascinated, but at a certain point, I'm glad to have some reinforcements to listen to it all.'

I didn't want to tell her that I didn't care who the woman was anymore. I knew the best thing I could do was to put Maeve out of my mind. As for the rest of it, I liked Theo's boundless curiosity. I thought he was interesting and fun. The company of the two of them was just what I needed, so I agreed.

'Wonderful,' Tizzy said. 'I'll tell Theo to mix up a special drink for you.' Tizzy had developed a ritual of having a glass of sherry when she got home from work. She used it as a way to transition into evening and as a social moment. I had a standing invitation to join her and had taken her up on it before. She knew the sherry part didn't work for me. I liked the idea of the sherry and had tried having a tiny bit of the amber wine in a glass, thinking it might be OK. By the second sip, I'd felt a buzz in my head and an unpleasant sensation of what I could best describe as feeling like there was velvet stuffed in my brain. The most I'd managed was having a tiny bit of sherry mixed with a lot of sparkling water. I enjoyed the fragrance and a hint of the taste with none of the bad feeling.

When I hung up, I smiled at having something to look forward to.

The angle of the sun was lower now that it was fall, and the late afternoon had a golden glow as I walked up the block to Tizzy's. I called her house a twin house – actually it was more of a conjoined-twin house. Two identical houses with a shared wall in the middle. The exterior was red brick with aqua painted around the windows. Tizzy opened the door and we passed through a small entranceway that was meant to collect boots and umbrellas and keep the cold air from the inside of the house. A second door led into an airy room in front of the staircase that Tizzy called the parlor. She led me into the adjoining room that looked out on the front yard and the street which she referred to as the living room. Both rooms had fireplaces with pretty tiles around the openings. No surprise Tizzy had eclectic taste, and seemed to prefer old things that she thought were somehow touchstones to the past.

She was on all the neighborhood committees, arranging

events like the twice-yearly garden fair and the used-book
sale. She was on the board of the Hyde Park Historical Society
and wrote pieces for their newsletter. She loved being in the
middle of things and it was a way for her to be in the know
about everything going on in the neighborhood.

As soon as we sat down, she started right in about a garden
club meeting she'd gone to and the fuss over what sort of plants
they should offer. 'Of course, we'll have pots of chrysanthemums,'
she said. 'I love the way they smell.' She paused with a smile,
as if remembering the scent. 'But I thought we ought to have
plants that can be brought inside and grown on a windowsill
like herbs. I'd like to get one of those set up, with the lights
and watering systems, so I could grow tomatoes year-round
and maybe lettuce too.'

Theo came in with a tray. He set down coasters and sherry
for the two of them and the special concoction for me. He'd
brought some nuts and olives as well as some pub cheese and
crackers. He took a seat and suggested we toast to the end of
another productive day.

Maybe for them, but my day didn't feel like it had been
very productive. After my meeting with Caleb, I'd tried to get
back to working on the Derek Streeter book but got nowhere
and released the frustration by cleaning my apartment.

'Now that we're all situated, I'll tell you all about that
woman.' She took a sip of her sherry before she began. 'It
was fun solving the mystery,' she said. 'Since Alex was the
one who gave me the invitation, I figured he might know who
all the players were.' I still found it unnerving that she called
her boss by his first name, but then it worked for them so who
was I to say. 'He didn't know, but suggested the art gallery
might have some information. I had to kind of make up a
story, but as soon as I explained that she'd been with the star
artist, the person on the phone was able to narrow it down to
two women, and when I said she appeared to be in her twenties, she knew exactly who she was.' Tizzy did her impression
of a trumpet flourish before a big announcement. 'Her name
is Suzzanna Angel.'

'What is she, his much younger wife?' I asked.

'That's what I thought, too,' she said. 'No, she's not his

wife. His daughter. I don't think she was exactly popular with the person I was speaking to either. Her tone sounded forced when she explained that Suzzanna worked very closely with the artist. The woman on the phone referred to her as Michael Angel's assistant.'

Then her behavior to me wasn't anything personal, just her manner. It didn't explain her relationship to Maeve, though.

'The other woman with him is making a documentary about him. Her name is Jennifer Soames. And just judging by the way she had her hands on him, there's probably something personal with him too,' Tizzy said.

'I wonder if she'll include what the art critics say about him,' Theo said. He put down his sherry glass and looked at me. 'I did some research and those art critics really tore Michael Angel to shreds. His art wasn't serious. It was too whimsical and more suited for a child's bedroom than an art gallery.' Theo nodded. 'They hate it that he's so commercially successful. And that he's connected to a YouTuber. And that he seems pretty sane. No ear chopping off for him. And he loves the spotlight.' Theo seemed pleased with himself. 'You know me, I always like to find out the story behind the story.'

Tizzy went on to add some more about the artist's daughter. 'It sounds to me like she's riding in on his coattails and has gotten a position of power out of it.' She turned to me with a smile. 'I know it's a cliché, but I didn't feel like coming up with something better.' She swirled the wine in her glass and took a sip. 'Why are you so interested in her, anyway?'

I thought about what to say. The truth was after the disappointing meeting with Maeve, I didn't really care anymore who the rude woman was. But Tizzy had gone to a lot of trouble and I didn't want her to feel she'd wasted her time, but also, on the slight chance that Maeve came through, I didn't want to mention her. I kept it vague and said that she'd looked familiar and that I thought she was connected to a client.

'Maybe you saw her around Hyde Park. Michael lives in the neighborhood. He started out showing his work at the art fair,' Theo said. It was a tradition that on the first weekend of June, 57th Street was blocked off for artists and craftspeople to display their work for sale. Then we got in a discussion about which art fair, since there were actually two that went on at the same time. There was the famous 57th Street one that had been around for over seventy years. That was juried, which meant a committee that Tizzy wasn't on got to choose who would be allowed to have a booth displaying their art for sale. Some artists and craftspeople who were unhappy at being excluded had organized a community art fair across the street that was open to anyone who wanted to sell their artwork or crafts.

Tizzy and Theo had gotten into a tense back and forth, each giving their reasons why they thought Michael had been in one art fair or the other. I finally stepped in.

'What's the difference, anyway?' I said. 'And if you really want to know, I bet Suzzanna knows.' They both laughed at how intense they'd become and dropped the subject.

'Are you going to tell me what got Ben into such a mood at the last gathering?' Tizzy said. Theo rolled his eyes and got up. I assumed that Tizzy had told him all about everyone in the writers' group and, by the roll of his eyes, I guessed that Tizzy had said there was something going on between Ben and me.

'When you start talking about boys it's time for me to leave. I'll be in my study,' he said, heading to the staircase.

'Well?' Tizzy said expectantly when we were alone.

I shrugged. 'He never explained,' I said. 'He seems to have cut me off.'

Her expression dimmed. 'It seems a shame. I thought you two would make a nice couple.' I knew she was being diplomatic by appearing to go along with the ruse that Ben and I were just student and teacher.

I had kind of thought that too, but I really didn't want to talk about it and finished off my drink before getting up to leave.

It was well after dark when I got home. The socializing had done me good. I spent too many hours alone with my computer. Rocky was company, but our conversations were one-sided.

I put the last of the leftover vegetable stew on to heat up and went to check my messages and emails. I stopped, stunned when I saw there was a text from Maeve. It was noncommittal and asked me to call her. I dithered for a couple minutes, thinking about whether it was good or bad news. It was only a little after seven, so hardly too late to call – and why leave it hanging? It was better to get the news and then deal with whatever it was.

I punched in her number and hoped when she saw the ID on the screen she would answer. It seemed to have rung a bunch of times and I prepared for a recording asking me to leave a message, but a voice answered in a whisper.

'Maeve?' I said, not sure I'd gotten the right number.

'This is not a good time,' she said so softly I could barely hear her. 'The job is yours, if you want it.'

I was dumbstruck by the offer and I mumbled a yes without even thinking.

She seemed to be picking her words carefully. 'I will text you the day and time.' She was very curt, and I didn't know what to say beyond an uh-huh. Then it seemed as if she was talking to somebody in the room with her. All I heard was something about hiring the cleaning person they'd requested before she clicked off.

Rocky looked up from his bowl and I gave him a quizzical shrug. 'I think that was good news.'

I poured some of the stew in a bowl and, as I carried it into the dining room, there was a ping on my phone announcing the arrival of a text. All it had was *Friday 3:30. Come to back door.* I suddenly wondered if she'd hired me to help write her memoirs or to clean her kitchen.

SEVEN

All this mystery with Maeve had intrigued me and I couldn't wait until our next meeting to see what would happen. It was a relief when Friday finally arrived but then the hours until the appointed time seemed to drag. There was no getting into the flow of work on anything because I kept checking the clock. There had been no more texts from Maeve with any additional explanation. I was past worrying about how I was dressed and decided the long sweater over comfortable jeans would have to do. I even stuck with sneakers. The only professional touch was the peacock blue messenger bag and I put on some lipstick.

I was keyed up by the time I'd reached the front of the lavender house, wondering what was going to happen this time. She'd offered me the gig and I'd accepted, but clearly there were things that had to be worked out first before it was official.

It felt strange, but she had instructed me to do it, so I went up the driveway and into the backyard. I gave the yard the once-over just long enough to note that the grass was still green but had a layer of fallen leaves. Beyond the grassy section there was an area of dirt that had a garden with some flowers and what looked like vegetables. A short staircase led up to a deck and a door. I didn't see a bell and knocked lightly. When no one responded, I thought it was another dead end. I had just turned to go when I heard the door open and a whispered voice called my name.

'This way,' Maeve said, taking my arm and hustling me inside. I barely got a chance to check out the roomy kitchen, which had a nice combination of updated and old-fashioned touches, before she pointed at a few stairs leading up. It turned at the landing and more stairs led up to the second floor. A lot of these old houses had two sets of stairs. The front one was carpeted and impressive, with a fancy wooden banister and several landings. A window halfway up bathed the stairs in light. The back stairs were meant for the help, which apparently was common to have in the late 1800s when these houses were built. It was like a steep, narrow tunnel.

As we stepped out on the second floor, she stopped and took a moment to listen; when she seemed to feel the coast was clear, she had me follow her to a door at the back end of the hall. There were more stairs. She sent me up first and closed the door behind us. I heard her let out her breath and she appeared to relax a bit.

'I'm sorry for all the sneaking around. I'll explain in a moment.' As I expected, the stairs led to the attic which had been turned into a charming room. Light filled the space that had windows to the east and the south. She showed me the little balcony at the front and I imagined sitting out there and looking at the stars.

Inside there was a bookcase and some comfortable chairs. A long worktable was set up in the middle of the room. A counter along one wall served as a kitchen area. She saw me looking at a short hall off to the side with two doorways. 'A bathroom and storage,' she said, answering my thoughts.

'This might sound a little strange, but would you mind doing an art project with me while we talk.' I must have looked a little wary because she smiled, showing off the dimples. 'It's like a ritual I do whenever I have a visitor up to my sanctuary. I promise it will be fun and easy.'

'I'm more of a word person,' I said. 'How much is my art talent going to count in considering me to work on your memoir?'

She actually laughed a little. 'Not at all. Well, it's in your favor for being a good sport. I'm an art teacher at the Dupont Academy. Believe me, there's no talent required for this project. It's just fun. You'll forget all about your worries about being good once we get started.'

For the first time I noticed what she was wearing. The long navy-blue dress with tucks to give it shape looked like something an art teacher would wear to work. The colorful necklace with patterned beads made from Fimo clay gave it an arty touch.

I looked at the long white table littered with art supplies and wondered what I'd gotten myself into.

'So you call this your sanctuary?' I said, taking in the space again as I tried to stall.

'It is,' she answered. 'It's off limits unless you're an invited guest.' She seemed to sense my hesitancy about the art project. 'You'll like it, I promise.'

She pulled out one of the chairs on wheels for me and I sat, rolling it close to the table. 'Along with the art project, I always offer visitors a drink. Coffee or tea?' she asked. We narrowed it down to tea and she suggested Masala chai.

'Chai actually means tea in Hindi,' she said. 'Sorry, it's the teacher in me. I can't help myself from offering extra information.' As she created the drinks, the fragrance of spices filled the air with a wonderful scent. She brought two blue patterned cups of the creamy-looking tea mixture to the table along with a sugar bowl. I had the same old cups and thought of mentioning it, but I was afraid it would sound like I was trying too hard to show how simpatico I was.

'Cheers,' she said, holding up her cup from across the table. I joined her in the toast and took a long sip.

Her manner and the drink were beginning to work on me, and all the confusion of my previous visits there faded away. There was something infectious in her manner as she pulled off paper from a long roll at the end of the table and set down a sheet in front of each of us. She seemed to have a sense of fun as she pulled out a palette with pots of colors. 'I promise you are going to like this.' Her dimples were on full display as I asked about brushes and she held up her finger and said, 'This is all you need. These are ink pads, not paint.'

She proceeded to demonstrate and I was mesmerized as she made colorful shapes on her paper. She showed me how to wipe my finger between colors and finally how to use a pen to add details to enhance the marks. The shapes became pumpkins, witches on a broomstick and a caterpillar.

'OK, it's your turn,' she said, giving the palette a subtle push toward me. As soon as I made my first mark, I realized she was right. It was fun and easy. I had a thought as I made a red heart. Maybe instead of the store-bought cards I'd been offering Caleb, he could make his own. The handmade touch might finally cut through to his wife's heart. I'd think about it later. For now, I wanted to get things straightened out with Maeve.

I was trying to think of what to say to focus in on why I was really there, but she started without any help from me.

'Now that we have drinks and something to do with our hands, we can get down to the real reason you're here,' she said, taking a deep breath. 'I don't remember what I told you, so please forgive if I repeat. The first thing that is essential is that you don't disclose even that you're working on the memoir with me.' She stopped and her face clouded. 'I thought I could write it myself, but I'm not a word person. I wrote the beginning, but then I got lost and it started going all over the place. I have notes and sort of an outline, but it needs a professional to put the rest together and to make it interesting.'

I continued making marks on the paper as she talked. Making a memoir interesting about a private school art teacher sounded like a challenge, but I knew how to make ice-cream flavors sound exciting and paint colors sound poetic. I was sure I could find a way to inject something fascinating into her notes. I did wonder about all the need for secrecy, but thought it might be her way of making the whole thing seem more exciting.

'I think I covered this before, but since it's really important, I need to ask you again. It would ruin it if news of what we're working on got out. This neighborhood is like a small town. All it takes is telling one person and then it's all over.' I smiled at her comment, thinking of Tizzy and she continued. 'I need your word that you will tell no one about the memoir or what's in it.'

'Absolutely,' I said. 'I've had other clients who have asked for anonymity and it's never been a problem.'

'OK then,' she said with a smile. 'The way I thought we could work is that you and I would get together and go over sections of what I have and then you would turn it into chapters. I'd sign off on what you'd written and we'd move on. Everything is in the notes except the ending. I plan to tell you about that when we get to it. I don't want to take a chance on it getting out. It's a bit of a surprise.' She looked at me directly.

'Though in your case, you might figure it out on your own. I read your mystery and you seem good with clues.' I waited to see if she'd add something about my book, as in that she liked it, but she left it at that.

'What exactly is the endgame you want for these memoirs?' This was the sticky part. I hoped that she didn't think I had connections to get it published.

'I have a deal with a small publisher. They want the release timed to an event.'

'That's why the six-week deadline,' I said, remembering she'd brought that up before. I was intrigued that she had a publisher. Since she appeared close to me in age, I had to wonder what could be so compelling about her story that she got a publishing deal based on a pitch?

'Now that I have more of an idea what you want, I can put together a proposal,' I said. It was my way of opening the door to a discussion of money. It was going to be a consuming job and I had no idea how difficult she would be to please. I might have to write and rewrite portions numerous times. People tended to think that having the idea or subject matter had all the value and what I did was like filling in a template. I usually had to build up my importance to a project as the client tried to diminish it. In the end both sides needed to feel it was fair. And there was something else. I'd had clients who'd claimed to be unhappy with the final work and simply reneged on our agreement and paid me less, usually with some unkind comments to go with it. Yes, we had an agreement, but I wasn't going to sue and they knew it. The best I could do was try to work with people I thought were honorable and to get a good-sized deposit.

'I already talked to my publisher and they know I need help finishing the book. The credit will read "by Maeve Winslow as told to Veronica Blackstone".' She'd gotten out a laptop computer and, after a moment, turned the screen to face me. 'It's a contract with the publisher.' She let me read it over and it spelled out what she'd already said, including the time frame and the credit. There was also an amount at the bottom. It was more than I would have asked for by several thousand dollars.

'All you have to do is sign it electronically and we're ready to start.' Her face softened. 'I'm sorry for rushing you around and being a no-show for our first meeting. I was actually up here. I'd thought I'd be home alone and when I wasn't, I panicked.'

I read the agreement over again and hit a key to sign it. We both seemed relieved that we'd settled our deal and she encouraged me to go back to the artwork as she showed me how to make Christmas trees and Easter bunnies.

'Now we can officially start,' she said. 'The first thing I should probably tell you about is my husband. He goes by the name of Michael Angel and he's an artist.'

My first impulse was to jerk my head up and mention the reception, but this was really about her talking and me listening, so I let it go by. But as she did, I tried to put the pieces together. Tizzy had found out that Suzzanna was the artist's daughter. Did that make Maeve her mother? I looked at the art teacher and again realized she was just a little older than me and remembered that Suzzanna appeared to be closing in on thirty. OK, so she had to be the second wife. I stopped the artwork and took out a notebook and pen, scribbled down some notes.

'It's my memoir,' she said, 'but he's really the story. He's far more interesting than I am,' she said.

Ah, now it made sense.

'What a coincidence,' I said, before mentioning my attendance at the reception. 'Were you there?' I realized since I hadn't met her yet, she could have walked right by me and I wouldn't have known.

'No. I used to go to everything, but well . . .' Her voice trailed off and she shrugged. 'Things have changed, and his daughter has anointed herself as his side person. She's not exactly a fan of mine.' I almost nodded in agreement, remembering Suzzanna's tone as she talked about Maeve. 'We'll get to all the relationships with the people who have come into our life when we work on the manuscript. Just a hint, they aren't as they seem – except for with my stepdaughter. With her it's very clear. She would like me out of the picture.' Maeve's lips curved in a sly smile. 'There's a certain irony to that.' She glanced at me. 'You'll understand when we get to the end.'

'I love the Scotty dog pictures,' I said. I thought of the postcard that was still in my purse and considered bringing it out to show her.

'You and everybody else,' she said. 'They seemed to have touched a common spot in different kinds of people. I think the paintings speak to the heart.'

I remembered Tizzy and Theo's argument over which of the local art fairs he'd gotten his start in. I might not be able to tell Tizzy and Theo how I found out, but I could at least settle the dispute between them, so I asked about it.

'The community art fair. The committee for the 57th Street fair rejected us. We were so disappointed, but . . . I guess it turned out OK,' she said with a little laugh at the obvious understatement. She'd continued with the ink pads as we talked and added some details to a bumblebee she'd created. 'Who knows if the painting would have been noticed in the other art fair?'

Her expression grew wistful. 'I wish I'd been there for the kismet moment when Sophia saw the painting and the Scotty looked just like her dog. Michael was so excited at the sale and even more that her companion owned a prestigious art gallery.' She let out a sigh. 'If only I hadn't gone out to get sandwiches, everything might have been different. Michael threw in the copyright when they offered him some extra money.'

'What does that mean?' I said. I knew what a copyright meant with writing, but not with art.

'It means she could make all those posters and T-shirts and stuff. But it was really a win for Michael. All that exposure put him where he is today.' She finished making a set of tulips with the ink set and pushed the paper away. 'I didn't expect to start talking about anything until you'd looked over what I have.' She got up and came back with a stack of papers held together with oversized rubber bands, handing it to me.

'Oh,' I said, taking the hefty pile. I glanced at the top page and saw it was handwritten.

'I didn't want to use a computer,' she said. 'So be careful with it. That's the only copy.'

I was barely able to get the thick wad in the messenger bag. 'And the check,' she said, putting it on the table in front of me. We hadn't discussed it, and I assumed it would be a deposit, but it was the whole amount. I started to say something, before she stopped me. 'I wanted to make sure you got paid even if there are some snags.'

'What do you mean *snags*?' I asked.

'I'm sure there won't be, but in case anyone tries to stop the project.' Her expression darkened as she said it. 'That's why all the secrecy. It's about family and well, they might not like what I'm going to say.'

She froze at the sound of a car door closing outside. 'You'd better go,' she said. I rushed to gather up the paper I'd covered with colorful markings, realizing too late that I hadn't cleaned off my finger from the bumblebee I'd just started; I left a mark on the teacup. I went to wipe it off, but Maeve seemed more concerned with my speed at leaving. She walked me down the attic stairway, holding a finger to her lips to signal me to be quiet and sent me on my way.

I tried to be as stealthy as I could as I went down the dark back stairs, only catching my foot once on the matting meant to make them less slippery. As I turned onto the last few steps ending in the kitchen, someone came in through a swinging door. I found myself face to face with Michael Angel.

'Who are you?' he demanded.

I had to think fast. I remembered Maeve's phone call and what I'd heard her tell someone in the room. 'I'm part of the cleaning crew,' I said in a rush of words as I slipped my messenger bag behind my back. I saw his gaze go to my empty hands. 'I'm just the labor. You supply the cleaning supplies.'

His eyes narrowed as he looked me over and I was glad that I hadn't worn one of my so-called professional outfits. The jeans and sneakers were perfect. Even so, I slipped out the back door before he could ask any more questions.

What had I gotten myself into?

EIGHT

Rocky came out from his nap place and greeted me as I put my keys down. 'It'll be fancy cat food tonight,' I said, waving the check at him. I had spent the walk home basking in the glow of officially getting the job and getting paid up front, but it was fading already as I thought of the short time I had to complete it. I dropped my jacket on the chair by the door and took the messenger bag into my office. The sun had disappeared behind the buildings across the street and, even with the French doors open between the living room and my office, I could barely find the switch on the glass-shaded lamp on my desk.

I was anxious to look at the notes she'd given me. I pulled out the wad and, as I peeled off the rubber bands, a photograph slipped out and fell to the floor. I glanced at it as I went to stick it back with the papers. It was a kid sitting next to a Scotty dog. I stuck it back in, remembering the story Michael told at the reception about his dog Monty being his best friend.

There was a rumbling feeling in my stomach. I had been so focused on the meeting, uncertain of what the outcome was really going to be after all the false starts, that I hadn't thought about eating. Now that my hunger had returned, I needed to eat something before I did anything else. When I checked the kitchen, I remembered that I needed to go to the store. Peanut butter and jelly on bread that was past its prime made tasty by a few minutes in a frying pan would have to do.

I had brought the wad of papers to the dining room before I made the food and, once I'd eaten the sandwich and there was no danger of me dripping jam on anything, I took a quick tour through the unwieldy stack and saw there some neatly written sheets, but a lot of pages ripped from a legal pad and a soft-sided notebook that seemed like a journal. I was glad that she would be able to shepherd me through them all.

It was a little overwhelming to think of reading everything at once, so I did the obvious and started at the first page, relieved to note that her handwriting was precise and easy to read.

Five years ago, nobody knew who Michael Angel was and the only time the masses thought of Scotty dogs was probably when they chose the game piece for a Monopoly game. I didn't even know who Michael Angel was. I did know that Michael Wolinski managed the coffee house and gallery I liked to stop at after work.

We'd become conversation buddies since we both were interested in art. If I'd known he was married, it never would have gone further and I certainly wouldn't have taken him up when he jokingly offered to show me his etchings. But I was to find out that Michael bent the rules to suit himself in different aspects of his life. I overlooked it all and even helped him cover it up.

He had a room with southern exposure above the coffee house that he used as a studio and 'etchings' location. It was furnished with an old magenta-colored chaise he'd rescued from a thrift store. The walls were brick and covered with his paintings. Folding doors opened on a compact kitchen that fascinated me with the way the pieces fit together. Two burners above and a refrigerator tucked below, a little bit of counter space and a bar sink. To me the place was romantic and it became our rendezvous spot.

To say we understood each other, was an understatement. Yin and yang, fingers in a glove, we fit together. I tried not to think about his family and to believe what he said about his wife not being supportive of his artist soul. The divorce was contentious. His wife even threatened me and that was before our fortunes changed.

I didn't want to be the evil stepmother and attempted to make friends with his daughter Suzzanna to no avail. She was an adult anyway and, simply put, she hated my guts.

I had to live with being a home-wrecker, though I

*convinced myself that I had saved Michael. That is what
he told me over and over.*
      But life has a way to come back and bite you.

The next page had a title which I glossed over and went right
to reading the content. It was a bit all over the place, but it
was about the day that changed everything for them. It needed
to be rewritten, but it seemed like most of it was there.

The next page seemed to jump back in time and I gathered
it was about how they got together.

> *We'd already met before, but it was just as customer and
> coffee-house manager. Small talk when I came in. But
> then I was left with a cup of steaming coffee and no
> place to sit. He invited me to a chair in the back. I saw
> his sketchbook and we started to talk about our art. And
> he told me about a concept he had for a series of
> paintings.*

It was a good set-up, but would need some details. I began to
think of questions I'd ask her so I could make it into a scene.

I flipped to the next page and found something about a party.

> *It was the first fancy party we'd been invited to. No wine
> in paper cups or an open box of pizza. The house in
> Highland Park was a mansion and the guests were art
> collectors more than art lovers. It was all champagne
> and canapés before an elegant buffet. Michael's first
> time being the honored guest. The artist who did those
> wonderful paintings. Did he ever eat it up. So funny how
> people hung on his every word. How many times did he
> tell the story about Monty? All anybody wanted from me
> was to hear what he's really like.*

It ended as abruptly as the first page had. Both were begin-
nings, but needed some filling out. It was obvious to me now
how she'd gotten the deal for a book. He was a hot artist who
was nominated for a national prize. It seemed like a rags-to-
riches kind of story and, as she said, it was mostly about him.

I planned to tell her, there ought to be more about her. I sat back and took a breath to let it all settle for a moment.

A sharp rap at my front door startled me and I went to gather the papers up and put them in the sideboard before I answered it. I assumed it was Sara. She was always curious about my work, so if she saw a pile of papers, it would be awkward not to tell her about the project.

She was dressed in mom clothes and had Mikey with her. With my Sherlock Holmes skills of deduction, I knew that meant she wasn't looking for an escape with some cooking wine and girl talk. As an extra incentive, she was holding a plate covered in aluminum foil. I couldn't see what it was, but whatever she'd brought smelled delicious and a lot more appealing than another round of peanut butter and jelly.

I brought them inside and she let Mikey loose. I wondered what he thought about being in a place that looked just like theirs but different. He went right back to the dining room and an old doll house. It was handmade and more of an art piece than a toy, but I let him have fun rearranging the toy furniture.

Sara took a seat on the couch in there where she could keep an eye on Mikey while she and I visited. I put the plate of food on the dining table. 'How about some coffee?' I said.

She leaned back and let out her breath as she thought it over. 'Coffee is good, but wine is better. I don't usually have it when Mikey's with me, but since there are two of us to keep track of him . . .' She looked at me expectantly.

As soon as I handed her the glass of dark red liquid, she urged me to eat while the food was still warm. I uncovered the plate to find spaghetti in a thick marinara sauce with a piece of garlic bread. I dug in and discovered it was as delicious as it smelled. 'This is great, thank you,' I said as I twirled more of the noodles on my fork.

'Somebody had to make sure you didn't starve. It's hard when you're cooking for one,' she said with a smile. Between my living alone and being a vegetarian, she was always concerned about my eating. If she'd seen how empty my refrigerator was at the moment, she would have been frantic.

'I think I know what happened to Ben,' she said. And suddenly I understood the reason for her visit was more than the spaghetti delivery. 'He's been incommunicado. I finally called his landline and a woman answered.' She let the tension build for a moment before she continued. 'I went right for it and asked who she was.' There was another pause, this time punctuated by an unhappy sigh. 'It was his ex-wife, Ashleigh, or as I call her Assleigh. She was all friendly and saying how we had to get together. She wanted to see Mikey and how much he'd grown. No mention that she'd abandoned my brother with no explanation. I wanted to grill her about that and what she was doing there, but she got off the phone fast.'

Oh. I suddenly had a hard time swallowing and my appetite disappeared. Ben had never given me too many details about the demise of his marriage, just that his wife's leaving had been a total surprise. He'd had no idea there was anything wrong, which had to do with why he'd taken it so hard. He didn't say it exactly, but I took it to mean that it made him lose confidence in himself. The way she'd left him without a word had devastated him and probably left him vulnerable to taking her back. I wondered what she'd told him. But did it really matter? If she was back, it meant that the break between us was irreparable.

'Have you talked to him?' I said.

'Not yet. It just happened.' She drank some more of the wine. 'I'm so upset with her. How can she just drop back in like that and expect us to act like nothing happened?'

Mikey seemed unconcerned with our conversation and had moved all the furniture out of the doll house and dropped a car in that he'd brought with him and was driving it around the rooms.

She saw that I'd stopped eating and her face fell. 'I should have let you finish eating first before I told you. I'm sorry.'

I felt bad that she felt bad and forced myself to have another forkful. 'What about the writing group?' I asked. She shrugged.

'I hope he doesn't leave it,' she said. 'No matter what you said or really didn't say, I know there's something going on between you. I hope he doesn't mess that up.'

'If his wife is back, I don't think she'll approve of our friendship.' I had tried to say the words calmly, but I still choked a little.

When Sara left, I tried to go back to Maeve's pages. I looked through more of them. I sincerely tried to read them over, but the words didn't register. My mind was stuck on the news about Ben. I was about to call it a night and give up trying to get through anymore when the tone on my phone notified me that a text had arrived. It was from Maeve. She was anxious to get started and asked me to come the following afternoon so we could go over everything from the beginning. It forced me to pull myself together and stop thinking about Ben, which is what I wanted to do anyway.

I spread the papers out again and took the beginning that Maeve had written into my office. I found the postcard of *The Scotty in the Sleeping Garden* and propped it up next to the computer for inspiration.

There was just something about the image that made me want to look at it. The expression in the dog's eyes looked out at me, seeming to see into my heart. The way he seemed to almost smile gave off a message that everything would be all right. Gazing at the reproduction, I understood the appeal of the paintings. It was more than a stylized rendition of a dog. It stirred the viewer's emotion. I laughed at myself, thinking I was starting to sound like an art critic.

I read the page over again and, rather than attempt to rewrite it, I wrote down a number of comments about things to ask Maeve before stopping for the night. I was keyed up by it all and spent a long time crocheting – long enough to finish the black border on the sunny yellow granny square and to begin another. With the combination of stitches and colors, it would look like a sunflower in a square when I was done. The hook moving through the yarn worked its magic again, and when I went to bed I fell into a deep sleep.

The weather had grown gloomy again, but I barely noticed. After all the ups and downs with Maeve, it was settled. She had hired me to help her with the manuscript. She had a publishing deal, had paid me up front and she was even giving me credit. All was good. I was excited about getting started. I loaded up the pages I thought we'd discuss and headed out.

I'd probably be retracing these steps a lot, I thought as I turned on Harper. Even with the drizzle that had started to fall, I could feel myself smiling. I was embarking on a writer-for-hire dream job. I liked Maeve, was fascinated by the dog paintings and interested in finding out more about Michael. And there was the tantalizing thing she'd said about a surprise ending.

The drizzle had almost stopped by time I reached the rambling lavender house with the fish-scale siding. I rushed up the front stairs and rang the bell. When there was no answer, I began to think I might have gotten her instructions wrong. It was no wonder with all the secrecy and confusion. A gust of wind blew across the covered porch, pushing against the door, and it slipped open. So maybe the plan was for me to let myself in. It felt strange to just walk inside, but if that was what she wanted, who was I to say. Though, honestly, I didn't like it. I called out hello a few times with no answer.

I assumed she was up in the attic room and expected me to join her. I was glad to go up the front stairs. They were carpeted and easier to navigate. My footsteps were silent as I went up to the second floor.

It felt a little eerie and almost like I was an intruder as I went down the hall to the closed door leading to the attic. But, I reminded myself, Maeve had set up the appointment and must be expecting me. When I stepped on the first stair, I called out hello a few more times so I wouldn't startle her when I suddenly appeared in her sanctuary. I hated to call it an attic. It was such a charming space. When I reached the top stair, I walked right into the main area. The light coming in the windows was low due to the gloom outside, and the room was lost in shadows. There was no sign of Maeve and I continued to check around. The door was open to the bath-room, making it obvious she wasn't in there. I opened the door to the storage room, calling out hello again. The shade was pulled down on the window in the room, making it even dimmer than the main room. Everything in there seemed covered by sheets and it appeared to be a room of ghosts.

Then it occurred to me that she had probably heard me and been going down the back stairs as I was coming up the front ones. I walked through the main room again, pulling out my phone to take some pictures to keep for reference when I was working so I could add some specific details when I described it. In the process my messenger bag clipped the table and hit a cup. When I checked for damage, I saw the handle had broken off. I was embarrassed at my clumsiness and remembered how much she liked the vintage cups. Breaking one was hardly the first impression I was going for.

I noticed a bottle of glue on the table and thought I could stick the handle back on but, in my haste, the squeeze bottle slipped from my hand and landed on one of the wheeled chairs. I panicked and came up with a new plan. I'd get rid of the broken cup, take another from her supply and put it on the table. I had the same exact cups and would bring one of mine on a subsequent visit and slip it in with the others. Unless she had a lot of people up there at once, she would never notice that one was missing. The point was to get rid of evidence quickly. To keep it all together, I pulled the sheet of paper it was sitting on around it, careful not to spill the liquid in the bottom. Feeling frantic, I stowed the mess at the back of one of the cabinets against the wall. I quickly grabbed another cup from the counter and put it on the table, relieved that it now looked just as I'd found it.

Thinking she'd pop up at the top of the stairs, I gave it a moment. But when she didn't, I went to look for her. I took the back stairs, expecting to find her waiting for me in the kitchen, not realizing I'd gone to the front. The back stairs were even darker than before, thanks to the gloom outside, and I took my time going down them. I was relieved when I got to the landing with no mishap. Calling out more hellos, I turned to descend the last few stairs that went into the kitchen.

I stopped with a start. There was something draped over the short staircase. A floral blanket maybe? I stepped around to the side, preparing to pick it up, and then saw it wasn't a blanket at all. Maeve was sprawled over the landing with her head where the last step met the kitchen floor. I dropped the messenger bag and rushed to her side, calling her name and asking if she was all right. There was no answer, not even a moan. Then I saw the gash on her head and a small amount of blood on the step. It gave me hope she'd just been knocked unconscious by the fall. I pulled out my phone and punched in 911.

Everything became a bit of a blur as I let the paramedics in the front door and the place suddenly swarmed with uniforms. I showed them where she was and hung out in the corner by the sink. I expected them to do something like wave smelling salts in front of her and then help her to her feet, but it wasn't happening. Something about how slow they were moving seemed ominous.

A pair of cops came over to me and started to ask for information. The adrenalin was still pumping through my body and I was on automatic pilot as I explained who I was and why I was there. They took me into the dining room and told me to stay there.

It was hard to tell how much time had passed when I heard someone come in the front door yelling for Maeve. Michael Angel rushed toward the kitchen with his daughter following close behind.

His gaze stopped on me sitting at the table. 'Who are you?' he demanded in a surprised tone. He looked at me hard and there was a flicker of recognition. 'You're the cleaning person from yesterday.'

Suzzanna had been eyeing me the whole time and shook her head. 'Cleaning person, hah.' That was all I heard before one of the officers escorted me back to the entrance hall and sat me on a bench looking out on the front porch.

As I sat there looking out the window, and saw the paramedics loading an empty gurney back into their rig, I realized Maeve was dead.

NINE

The man in the suit was clearly trying to place me as he approached, but I recognized him right away. Detective Jankowski and I had met several times before. It was late in the day, but I suspected he always had that worn look about him. His eyes lit with recognition after he looked at the clipboard that one of the officers had handed him. Instinctively I stood, wanting to be on the same level he was. It was a power thing.

'Veronica Blackstone,' he said with a tired smile. 'So, we meet again.' I waited for him to add a comment about my mystery writing, but he said nothing more.

'We need to talk.' He looked around the entrance hall and through to the dining room and kitchen beyond. 'Where shall it be?' He offered his car or the precinct, neither of which sounded appealing.

'Or there's my place,' I said. I reminded him I lived nearby and I watched his expression dim.

'Right, the third-floor walk-up with no elevator,' he said with a weary sigh.

He looked like he needed a jolt of java, I thought, chuckling at the phrase. It sounded like something out of a 1940s movie. 'I've got some fresh ground French roast and cream,' I said, noting to myself that what I'd just said would never have been in one of those old films, where the coffee was probably described as strong and bitter.

'OK,' he said finally.

He drove the short distance and parked in the spot in front of the no parking sign that it seemed was always parked up with cops going to the corner coffee shop.

I was glad the vestibule was empty because I wasn't thrilled at having all my neighbors knowing I was once again being questioned by a detective. That relief ended when we got to the second floor. Ben was standing outside his sister's door. He covered any awkwardness he felt with a flat cop expression. His gaze went from me to my escort, recognizing him from before. Jankowski gave him a cursory glance and then pushed on across the landing.

As we went upstairs, I heard Sara's voice as she opened the door and brought her brother inside.

I let the detective in my place and he stopped in the entrance hall, looking around. 'I remember this place now. They don't make buildings like this anymore. The new apartments are like boxes.' He sounded appreciative and I agreed. He looked down the hall. 'I suppose there's a dining room and then the kitchen with a small bedroom.'

'I didn't know you were into local architecture,' I said.

'I see a lot of interiors,' he said. 'Not always under the best of circumstances, but it helps me to have an idea of the layout. So I know where someone might be hiding.'

I considered offering him a tour, but it seemed like a better idea not to offer up anything I didn't have to.

'As I remember from before, you said you inherited it and you live here alone,' he said. Was this small talk or was he looking for information?

'Except for him,' I said, gesturing toward Rocky, who had just walked into the living room.

'Right. It's just you and the cat,' he said. I knew what he was thinking – single woman of a certain age with a cat as a companion. I had thought as much myself. It had a whole connotation that went along with it – implying I was fussy, a control freak and probably love-starved. I wondered if any of it was true.

'All right if I sit on the couch?' he asked.

'Sure, go right ahead,' I said a little too quickly. It was probably a little too desperate of a move to show that I wasn't some sort of tense singleton. While he made himself comfortable, I went to make the coffee. I carried it in on a tray along with a small pitcher of cream and a bowl of sugar. He used both generously. He even repeated the excuse he'd offered the first time he'd had the highly adulterated coffee – that it was the afternoon slump.

'I see you're still old school,' I said as he took out a notebook and pen.

'More dependable than trying to type on screen. Everything slips around and that presumptive type changes stuff.' He shook his head dismissively. 'Now then . . .'

It started with what I expected: asking why I was there, what I'd seen, etc. Since it seemed like this was a formality and that her death would be chalked up to an accident, I wasn't worried about being a suspect, or person of interest, which it turned out was another way of saying suspect.

I explained what I'd been hired for and that I'd only met her a few times. 'We were really going to get started when we met today,' I said. Figuring that was it, I sat back and waited for him to gather up his things, but he looked at his empty cup instead. 'Is there any left in the pot?'

Then we weren't finished, I thought, wondering what else there was to say. I got him a refill and watched him fix it up and drink off some before he spoke. 'What exactly was her condition when you found her?' he asked.

I explained that I had not realized it was a person at first. 'I thought it might be a blanket. Then I assumed she'd knocked herself out in the fall and called for help. I didn't check her pulse if that's what you mean. I thought she was still alive.'

He didn't ask me why I'd thought that, but I began to wonder myself why I'd expected her to come to and be OK. I didn't get very far with my thoughts before he asked me a jarring question. 'Do you know of anyone who would want to harm her?' He watched my expression change. 'The cause and manner of death hasn't been determined. We just ask for more than we need.' He'd made quick work of the second cup.

'I barely knew her,' I said.

'How did you get into the house? It's just a little strange that you were there and her husband thought you were part of a cleaning crew.'

I explained going to the front door and that the wind had blown it open.

'And you just walked inside a stranger's house?' He leveled his gaze at me, waiting for my response.

'What we were working on was supposed to be a surprise for her family. She didn't want him to know why I was there,' I said.

'A good surprise, or a bad one?' he asked, trying to appear casual, but I could tell his attention was heightened.

There was no secret about who her husband was or that he was nominated for a big award, so I told Jankowski what Maeve was creating with my help. Jankowski didn't know about the Scotty dog paintings, at first anyway, but as I described them more, he nodded with recognition. 'So that's who he is. One of my kids got one of the posters.'

It was the first time he'd mentioned anything about his life outside of being a detective. 'How old?' I asked and he gave me an odd look.

'Grown,' was his answer. He flipped the notebook closed and stood.

Got it. He wasn't about to start giving details of his family. Seeing that he was ready to leave was a relief anyway. I wasn't so sure that he believed I wasn't there when she fell.

He thanked me for the coffee. 'I may want to talk to you again.'

After he left, I filled my mug with the last of the coffee and dumped in the rest of the cream from the pitcher and threw in some sugar. I too was in an afternoon slump, to put it mildly.

I wanted to zone out for a while and let everything that had happened settle, but Caleb called. I'd forgotten that I'd told him I had an idea for him to make the cards he was sending to his wife. I hadn't mentioned there was artwork involved for fear of scaring him off. I still had the paper full of flowers, pumpkins and everything else. It had been exactly as Maeve had said. Fun, easy and the end result nice. The thought of her brought back the last image I had of her sprawled on the stairs. Something seemed off. Caleb kept talking and I couldn't pursue the thought. He wanted to set up a time to see what I was talking about . . . Actually, he wanted to come right over and get started. The coffee had helped a little, but the events of the day had left me drained, and under the circumstances I wasn't up for doing an art project. We agreed to a time in a few days, and I scribbled it down on my calendar, glad to have gotten off the phone.

I needed something to pull myself together. I didn't have it in me to work on any complicated crochet stitches and started one that was the plainest of the plain. Just rows of single crochet in a wheat-colored yarn. I had to make two of them before I could function. It was simply too much to think about.

It was dark by now and the wind was rattling the windows. I could feel swirls of chilly air that snuck around the edge of the balcony door and came inside. Leaves were flying off the tree out front and landing on the balcony. I shivered both from the cold and from all I'd been through. The best I could do was wrap myself in an old shawl I kept around the back of my office chair before I went back to the kitchen to survey my options for dinner.

There was a rap at my front door and my first thought was that it was Sara. I didn't know how much she'd seen of Jankowski, but I was sure she'd wonder who he was. I was hoping she might have a plate of food, too. As I pulled open the door, I sniffed for food smells, but only caught a whiff of lemon hand soap. Instead of Sara, Ben stood back from the door frame.

'Oh, it's you,' I said. After what Sara had told me and the way Ben had acted at the last meeting of the writers' group, I hadn't even considered that it might be him and, judging by the way he was standing halfway across the landing, he wasn't sure about being there either. I was surprised, glad to see him and confused all at the same time. 'I think that came out different than I meant it,' I said, referring to my greeting. 'I just didn't expect it to be you.'

He seemed to be trying to keep an inscrutable expression, but there was a hint of concern. 'I saw that detective. I wanted to check if everything was OK.'

'No leftovers,' I said, looking at his empty hands. It was an effort to lighten the moment and cover the hodgepodge of emotions I felt.

His expression stayed serious and he dropped his voice. 'I didn't want Sara to know I was coming up. She thinks I went home.'

I opened the door wider and stepped aside. 'C'mon in anyway.'

He stepped into the entrance hall. 'So why was a Chicago PD homicide detective escorting you home?' he asked.

'Before we get to that,' I began – this was my chance to say my piece to him in person, 'I know there's been a change in your status. But you should stay with the writing group. You have really been making progress and, besides, we need you to read Ed's copy.'

He seemed relieved that I was keeping things light. 'I don't know about that. Ed seems to have toned things down,' he said, almost cracking a smile. 'You were going to tell me about the detective.'

'I recognize the cop trick,' I said. He was trying to keep the conversation going in the direction he wanted it and off anything personal. 'And I don't want to keep you from whatever.' I knew there was an edge in my tone. I really needed to learn how he managed that unemotional cop tone.

'I understand how you might be angry,' he said. His shell was beginning to crack. 'Tell me about the cop, and then I'll try to explain.'

'Are you staying by the door so you can make a fast escape?' I said, noting that he hadn't made a move to sit.

'The idea did cross my mind.' The shell was dissolving and his expression was turning him into the person I knew. It had taken a long time for him to let his personality show through. He even looked different when he had the cop persona. It was as if the lights were off inside.

'Would you like to sit?' I asked.

'It's kind of late and Mikey wore me out with piggyback rides, so sitting would be good.' I gestured to the living room and he took his usual seat on the couch. It had gotten that we'd shared the couch, but it felt wrong now, so I went back to the armchair where I'd originally sat.

There were a few moments of awkward silence and then I began. Since I'd told the group nothing about the possible job with Maeve, I had to backtrack and tell him who she was and that I'd been doing some work for her. The whole episode from earlier came tumbling out with all the pent-up feelings.

It was the first time I'd seen a dead body. Despite my best efforts, I began to cry. I hated to cry in front of anyone; not so much because I felt uncomfortable, but because it made the viewer feel awkward and like they had to do something, or talk me out of crying.

As a cop, he must have had to deal with all kinds of emotional outbursts, and I wondered if there was special police training on how to deal with tears. He must have aced it if there was. He handled it perfectly. He got some tissues to hand me and didn't seem uncomfortable as the tears continued to roll down my cheeks. If anything, his behavior seemed totally impersonal. I had to admit that a hug of comfort would have been nice. He listened as I gave him the details of finding Maeve.

'It sounds like an unfortunate accident. You said yourself that you caught your foot on those stairs and they were steep.'

'Or maybe not,' I said, having contained my tears. Ben sat up straighter as I told him that something seemed off.

'Can you be more specific?' he said.

'That's just it. I can't quite figure it out.'

'Did you bring it up to the cop?' he asked.

'No. He hardly views me as a colleague and it's just a vague feeling. Can you imagine how he'd react to that?' I said. 'Besides, I didn't want to stir things up with him, since I was the one who found her and—'

'He could tag you as somehow involved,' Ben said, finishing my thought.

'Yes. He was already implying that I might have been there when she fell.' Crying had left me with a stuffy nose and I used some of the tissues he'd given me to blow it.

'You sure know how to handle tears,' I said. 'It's probably another of those things you learn in police school.'

'It's called an academy, and the closest they came was talking about how some people used tears to try to talk their way out of a traffic ticket.'

And then there was a grand silence as he seemed to be collecting his thoughts. I probably should have left it alone, but I thought it might help if he knew he didn't have to start from scratch.

'Sara told me your ex is back,' I said.

His eyes flashed with upset. 'Sara shouldn't have said anything,' he said. 'Not without knowing the whole story.' He took a deep breath. 'She called me out of the blue.' He shot a glance at me, knowing he'd used a cliché, but I withheld any reaction. It wasn't the time to talk about word choices. 'She came over and did a whole number on me.' There was a pause and I wondered if he was going to go into detail. Thankfully, he didn't. The last thing I wanted to hear was about some hot reunion between the two of them. 'She had a whole story about what a mistake she'd made and then she dropped the real bomb.' He shook his head with disbelief. 'She'd never signed the divorce papers.' I noticed that he was having a hard time making eye contact with me, which I could kind of understand. I wouldn't have wanted to look at me either if I was telling that story. 'I was careless and didn't pay attention that I'd never gotten the final documents. It was a sore spot and I was glad to ignore it.' I was trying to keep my calm, but in my mind I was going *what?* An ex-wife showing up was bad enough, but a still-wife was a whole other thing. I forced my voice to stay even. After everything I'd been through with finding Maeve and being interrogated, I was operating on fumes.

'So then you got your happy ending. You were confused and devastated when she left, and now that she's back, probably makes it all good.'

He put his face in his hands. 'You got it right, except for the happy ending part.'

He looked up at me and his eyes were filled with emotion. 'I didn't know what to say to you or Sara and I took the easy way out, saying nothing. I hoped to sort things out first, but my sister never knows when to leave things alone. I hadn't bargained on her talking directly to Ashleigh.'

'This is what I worried about when we became *friends*,' I said. 'If things didn't work out with us, you would feel too awkward staying in the writing group.'

'And you wouldn't feel uncomfortable?'

'I'm a professional,' I said. 'And I know how to separate my personal feelings from my work.'

'Really? You really wouldn't suddenly look at my work in a new perspective? Suddenly make a federal case out of a misplaced comma.' I appreciated that he was trying to inject some humor to keep it from being maudlin.

'I just let a cliché slide,' I said with a smile. I suddenly felt drained from the day, the crying, and now dealing with his news. He picked up on it and got up to leave. I walked him to the door. There was an awkward moment on how to say goodbye. It had always been with a hug, but it suddenly seemed inappropriate. He finally gave me a salute as he left. I noticed that he'd never answered about continuing with the workshops.

By now, even the fumes were running out, and I was too exhausted to think about anything. I settled for a peanut butter sandwich and fell asleep on top of the covers with Rocky cuddled behind my head.

TEN

I tried to have my Sunday morning ritual of a nice breakfast and read the Sunday paper. I still read the print edition. A nice breakfast was not another peanut butter sandwich on bread that even a few minutes in a frying pan wouldn't help. I usually had something like waffles or an omelet, but I didn't have the fixings for either. The best I could do was the French press coffee and apple slices spread with peanut butter. There was already a piece about Maeve in the newspaper. A small article, which was mostly about Michael, stated that she'd been found at the bottom of their staircase and that the police were still investigating the details. I stared at the article, trying to read between the lines. Did that mean that the police were questioning if it was really an accident? Had something seemed off to them, too? I wished I'd been able to squeeze some information out of Detective Jankowski, but he'd been pretty clear that he was there to get information, not give it. He wouldn't even offer any details about his kid, other than that he or she was grown.

I didn't want to think about what all this would mean for the manuscript. What were the ethics on the situation? Thanks to the ease of mobile deposit, I had put the check Maeve gave me into my account the day I got it. I'd already used some of it to pay bills. I thought of what she'd said about *snags*. She couldn't possibly have foreseen this. I had left my messenger bag untouched. I needed to give everything a little time to sort out.

Sara came upstairs looking for a cup of sugar. Even though she actually did need the sugar for something she was baking, she stayed awhile. Ben hadn't been as stealthy as he'd thought and she'd figured he came up to my place when he claimed to be leaving to go home. She was relieved to hear that I'd tried to get him to continue with the workshops. But she really lost it when she talked about his situation.

'Quentin doesn't want to hear about it anymore,' she said, referring to her taciturn husband. 'He urged me to come up here and vent. He was so desperate to get me to go, he offered to turn off the game he was watching and sit with Mikey while he watched kids' shows. How can my brother let that woman back into his life? I call her Assleigh for a reason. She's a real pain in one.' Sara gritted her teeth as she shook her head.

Sara seemed so upset, I felt as if I had to smooth things over for her even though I was pretty much in the same place. I didn't know Ashleigh's personality first hand, but it seemed to me if she'd left him without any explanation, she couldn't have really cared that much for him. Despite the cool professional air I'd tried to put on with him the previous night, I was upset too. I'd liked Ben and it was nice to have a plus one and to actually go on a date. But what I'd told him was true. I had thought ahead to something like this happening and vowed not to let it interfere with him being in the group.

It was useless to try to calm Sara, so I let her continue to vent. 'I never liked her from the first time I met her. You should hear her voice. She always sounds snippy. Her nails are like decorated claws. And she has sharp features like a ferret and those eyebrows . . .' she said, looking skyward. 'Doesn't she know when to stop with the tweezing?'

I asked Sara if she wanted some cooking wine. 'I know it's kind of early,' I said, leaving off that she seemed a little wound up.

'Yes, thank you. How different is that than having a mimosa with your brunch?'

'Sorry, I don't have anything in the brunch department to offer. I do have apple slices with peanut butter.' She surprised me by taking the food offer. I guess she needed some sustenance to keep up her energy to trash Ashleigh. Quentin sent her a text finally telling her to come home.

I gave up on my plans to do a big shopping and went to the little grocery store around the corner. It was expensive but convenient. I grabbed some fresh bread, more peanut butter, a few cans of soup and some frozen food to keep me going until I could do a real shopping. I heated one of the cans of soup and lost myself in an old Thin Man movie on the TV while I ate it. When I saw Myrna Loy's thin eyebrows I thought of Ashleigh, and Sara's rant. I laughed at how far Sara had gone in trashing the woman. I hoped I'd never get on her bad side.

It was back to reality on Monday. In all the ups and downs with Maeve, I'd neglected to look over the pages the group had left the previous week. After having them read aloud to the group, they left their work for me to give them a second read and make comments. I took the pile into the living room, planning to go through them, when my landline rang. Most of the calls were trying to sell me some 'sure thing' invest-ment opportunity or threaten me with arrest if I didn't pay up some back taxes with money put on gift cards, so unless I recognized the number I let it go to voicemail. When I checked, there was a message from someone named Fredricka Stanhope and she asked me to call her on an urgent matter. The name sounded vaguely familiar, so I returned the call.

'Fredricka Stanhope,' an efficient-sounding woman announced when she answered the phone.

I explained getting a message and gave her my name.

'It's so sad about Maeve,' she said in a somber voice. The comment caught me off guard and then I realized why the name was familiar. I'd seen her name on the contract that Maeve had given me. She was the publisher.

'Yes, it's terrible,' I said, wondering what was coming next.

There was a little throat-clearing on her end and, when she continued, her tone had changed from sympathetic to business-like. 'Regarding the book you were working on with her,' she said. Here it comes, I thought. She's going to say they're canceling it and they know that Maeve paid me out of her advance so they'll be asking for the money back.

'I don't mean to be cold, but we've invested a lot in the project already. It's a change for our publishing company. We've only done art books rather than those about the artists until now. Everybody loves the Scotty dog paintings and, with the award nomination, we found there was a lot of interest in the person behind it all. Actually, we already have a commitment for copies to be distributed to the whole audience at the award event.' She stopped for a breath. 'My point is that we want the manuscript.'

'Oh,' I said, surprised.

'We understand that it won't be exactly as we'd originally agreed on, but I believe that Maeve gave you a rough draft.' I thought about what I'd seen. Calling it a rough draft was too generous. There seemed to be some beginning entries and then random notes and a journal. 'We want you to finish it on your own. Do whatever you have to, to flesh it out. Interview people and, if need be, take some poetic license. Maeve said you were an experienced writer, so I'm sure you can figure it out.' She stopped talking and it was my turn to say something. There really wasn't anything to say. To be crass, I needed the money, and didn't even have all of it to give back anymore. I felt a sense of commitment to Maeve since she'd seemed so determined that the manuscript be completed. And there was a part of me that loved a challenge.'

'OK,' I said finally. I wondered if I should tell her that Maeve had mentioned a surprise ending and that she would give me the details when we got there. But what was the point, since it wasn't going to happen? Something else Maeve had said floated through my mind. That I might be able to figure it out on my own. It might be true, but I didn't want to promise something I might not be able to deliver, so I said nothing and let Fredricka continue on and remind me about the deadline before she ended the call.

I had to take a deep breath and let it settle for a while as I thought over what had just been laid in my lap. At least, I didn't have to keep it a secret anymore.

I fought the urge to dive back into the stack of papers from Maeve; I owed it to the group to finish going over their work. I'd left Ben's for last. It was only two pages and wasn't even a complete scene. The last line seemed to be more of a note to himself and read: *Oh, s—t.*

I was considering how to comment when my landline rang again. I might have just ignored it and let it go to voicemail, but I thought it might be Fredricka calling back and went to check the screen. When I saw it was Michael Angel, I felt my stomach clench as I clicked the green button.

I let him identify himself even though I knew who was on the phone. The first thing I did was offer my condolences. I barely got the words out before he launched into the reason for the call.

'I'm trying to make sense of it all,' he began. 'Tell me what happened.' It wasn't surprising that he should ask. The police had rushed to keep us separate and, other than a few comments when he first arrived, he had no idea of my story. There was no reason not to tell him, so I recounted what had occurred from my arrival to when I called the paramedics. I didn't offer any extra comments about my feeling that there was something more to what had happened.

'And you were there because of a writing project with my wife,' he said. 'I am shocked that she didn't tell me about it.' I was surprised that he knew. Then I realized that Suzzanna must have filled him in, based on what I'd told her the first time I'd gone to the house.

'She meant it to be a surprise,' I said, hoping that would smooth it over.

'What exactly was it? Tell me the details,' he demanded.

'She was calling it a memoir, but the plan was that it was really about you and your art.' I wondered if I should tell him how much I personally loved the Scotty paintings, but I wanted to keep the conversation impersonal, so didn't mention it.

'Well, you can consider the whole thing cancelled now,' he said. 'You can keep whatever you were already paid.'

'It's not quite that simple,' I began, before explaining that Maeve had a publishing deal for it and there was a contract which committed me to finish it.

'That's ridiculous,' he said, and demanded to know the name of the publisher. I gave him Fredricka's number. 'I'll deal with them directly.' He didn't even say goodbye before he ended the call.

His call made me glad that I hadn't rushed into working on the pages. He'd sounded determined to end the project and I didn't know if he could manage to get Fredricka to bend to his wishes.

I'd barely made it to the kitchen to make myself some lunch when the landline rang once more. I rushed to grab the phone and saw it was Michael Angel again.

'I understand that you have a rough draft,' he said in an angry tone. 'I'd like to see it.'

'You talked to the publisher?' I asked.

'Yes, and she's refusing to stop the project.' He sounded upset, probably on a lot of levels. I could even understand his request, but there was no way I was going to agree. I remembered Maeve's comment that she was concerned family members would want to make changes, which I was sure was correct. I had to somehow sell him on the idea of the book and tell him no to seeing what Maeve had given me, without actually saying it.

'You do understand that it's all about you and how wonderful your art is. The publisher told me how they already have marketing plans for the book. It can only help broaden your presence.' I was throwing in verbiage that sounded good. 'You'll be able to make appearances at art museums and galleries to sign books, since you are more important than the writer.'

'Hmm,' he said, seeming to be softening.

'I'd appreciate it if I could meet you in person. You could give me the story from your perspective,' I said.

'And you could hand over the draft you have,' he said. His insistence made me think of another possibility. Once he saw that most of it was handwritten, he could literally rip it up in front of me and make it disappear.

'It's not in any form to let you read it,' I said. 'Maybe just before I turn it in to the publisher.' I wasn't refusing him, just holding off. If I did actually let him look at it at that point, then I would have it on my computer and he could rip up all the papers he wanted to and not make it go away. But why would he anyway?

He didn't sound happy with my answer, but he seemed to realize there was nothing he could do. I was glad that he backed off on his demand. I didn't want to have to get tough and say that he had no claim to the pages. Everything was between Maeve, me and the publisher. He agreed to meet in person and wanted to do it right away, but I got him to push it to the following day. I tried to get him to agree to a neutral place, but he insisted on our meeting being at the house. He said he wanted to show me his studio.

ELEVEN

Once again, I was going to the Victorian house on Harper. There had been so much strangeness connected with going there, the meeting with Michael Angel fit right in. I wished he would have agreed to meeting in a public spot. His almost threatening manner about the writing project had made me feel uneasy. To be on the safe side, I'd made a copy of the draft I had and left it hidden away at my place. There'd been no delay in him answering the bell and we'd stopped in the entrance hall.

He was unshaven and appeared distraught. I'd repeated my condolences and he'd said he was doing the best to hang in there. It was a non-contentious moment, but then he went right back to being adversarial. 'I still don't understand how you got in the house,' he said in a hostile tone.

I repeated that while I'd gone to the kitchen door before, I'd gone to the front door this time. 'I rang the bell and no one answered. The door slipped open.' I stopped there rather than explaining the rest, that I'd gone up to the attic and then down the back stairs. I didn't want to relive the whole thing again, particularly when I was in the location where I'd found her. I did what I could to get him to move on. 'You were going to show me your studio,' I said.

He led me through the living room to a doorway into what had probably been built as a sun porch. With all the exposure, the light was wonderful. 'Is this your work in progress?' I said walking over to a big easel with a partially done canvas. This time the Scotty was wearing a beret in a garden of flowers with the Eiffel Tower in the distance.

'It's not the *Mona Lisa*, but people seemed to love the Scotty,' he said. I moved on to taking in the whole room. Since the room had windows on three sides, the back wall was the only place to hang anything. I noticed a couple of landscapes and a still life. The landscapes all had a nude woman rather randomly placed in them. There was a moveable stand with trays of art supplies, and a number of places to sit. It seemed to me that either Maeve had said – or I'd seen it in the notes – that he liked to entertain in his studio.

'As soon as I finish a Scotty picture, it goes right to a gallery,' he said. He offered me a seat on an unusual-shaped sofa that was covered in chartreuse suede with colorful throw pillows. He slid into a tall director's-style chair that I gathered he used when he was painting.

He seemed to have lost some of the hostile attitude and I sensed that he was trying to be more like the person I'd seen at the reception. 'I don't know what's with the police. At a time like this, you'd think they would show some compassion, instead of asking me the same questions over and over. It's almost as if they think it was more than it was.'

'Did they say why?' I asked.

'No,' he said in a tired voice. 'I've been nothing but co-operative with them. I don't understand why they sent people out from the medical examiner's office to investigate.' He looked at me directly. 'Why can't they settle that it was an accident and release her body so I can arrange the cremation? Anybody who looks at those stairs can see they're dark and steep. I warned Maeve about them from the day we got this house,' he said, sounding frustrated.

'The medical examiner usually investigates an unattended death, particularly in someone young and in good health,' I said. But what I didn't say was if the investigation was as intense as he said it was, it was because something didn't add up. They had the advantage of knowing what seemed out of place, while I had only a vague feeling. I didn't share any of that with him. Since he had brought up the incident, I decided it was my turn to ask some questions.

'Then you weren't home Saturday afternoon?' I said. 'I suppose the police asked you to account for your time.' It was a nice way of asking if he had an alibi.

'I don't know why it should matter,' he said, still in the tired voice. 'I left in the late morning. Maeve probably told you that we're doing a short documentary; there was a brunch with some of the first people who recognized the value of my art. The filmmaker wanted to get some comments.'

'I'm sure a lot of people saw you, so you don't have to worry,' I said.

'Why would I have to worry?' he said as his eyes flashed anger. 'Do you think I had something to do with what happened to Maeve?'

'No,' I said, quickly. 'I was thinking about the police. In case they determine there was foul play. You must know that the first person they look at is the spouse.'

'I thought the point of you coming here was to discuss things for the book.'

'Yes, that's right,' I said, hoping to calm his flare of anger. 'Why don't you begin?'

'What did Maeve tell you about us?' he asked.

I didn't want to tell him that I'd barely gotten past their first meeting. 'She certainly was in awe of your talent,' I said.

'She really said that?' he peered at me, seeming surprised.

'Maybe not exactly, but in so many words,' I said.

'All couples have their moments,' he said. 'She probably said some negative things about me, about our relationship.' He seemed to be trying to be cordial now. 'The sudden success might have gone to my head a bit.' He looked at me expectantly. So, he was hinting that things hadn't been exactly perfect between them. I had nothing to pass on to him since I'd only met with her briefly and had only given her notes some cursory examination. Even if I'd known what he was hinting at, I certainly wouldn't have told him and given him the chance to squash it. When he finally spoke again, it was all about the Scotty paintings. 'The paintings make people smile. That's far more important than anything about Maeve and me,' he said.

He talked on a bit after that, mostly about how much the nomination for the award meant and his hopes that he would win it. It was on the boring side, and the only way I could use it in the manuscript was if I needed to talk about how pompous he'd become.

I felt unsettled when I got home. The way the police had repeatedly questioned Michael, and the fact it hadn't been ruled an accident yet, made me believe I was onto something with my feeling that something hadn't added up. I'd read a book once about how a judgment made in the blink of an eye was often more correct than one made after a long study. Maybe I was right. I tried going back over the moments when I found Maeve. I remembered that I hadn't thought it was a person first because all I'd seen was the pattern of the kimono jacket she'd been wearing. I'd expected her to be OK. But why? And then an image appeared in my mind and I knew what felt wrong. I started to do research and then I had an a-ha moment as I realized something startling. I wanted to check it out and there was only one person who could help – Ben.

TWELVE

Between the call with the publisher and then meeting with Michael Angel, I felt overwhelmed with figuring out how I was going to extract a book from the sheaf of pages that Maeve had left me. Added to that was the realization I'd come to after my research. If my conjecture was true, it changed everything. Ben was the only source I could think of to discuss it with, but I didn't want to call or text him about it as I thought he might take it just as a silly excuse for me to contact him.

If he showed up for the writers' group, I could ask him then.

As it neared seven, I started to pace, knowing I'd have my answer soon. The doorbell went off, sounding more like the croak of a frog than a bell, startling me. I knew it wasn't Ben since he would be coming up from dinner at his sister's and always knocked. I hit the button that unlocked the downstairs security door and opened the upstairs one in anticipation. Tizzy stepped onto the third-floor landing, slipping the shawl off her colorful kimono top. She looked like she was busting to tell me something.

'Did you hear what happened on Harper?' she said in an animated tone. She gave me a hug as she came through the door. Of course, I should have known that she would have heard. Tizzy was like a magnet for gossip and news. Thanks to all the committees she was on, she knew everybody, and her work at the university put her in the middle of things there. And her boss had been the one to give us tickets to the reception.

But this was one time that I had more news than she did. She was bubbling over with details that the artist's wife had fallen down the back stairs. 'We have a set of those in our place,' she said. 'Theo is always saying that we should do something to make ours less treacherous. They're so steep

they're almost like a chute. I don't know if carpeting would
help. I guess when they built the Rosalie Villas, they figured
the servants would figure out how to navigate those stairs
without taking a tumble.'

'I know all about those stairs from experience,' I said.

'You do?' Tizzy said in surprise. 'Tell me everything.' The
doorbell interrupted and I went to push the button to unlock
the downstairs door.

'We'll have to talk about it later,' I said, as I heard someone
coming up the stairs. I knew that once I started telling Tizzy
about it, it would take over and pull the whole group into the
conversation. It wasn't fair to them to take up their workshop
time with neighborhood news.

The door was still open as Ed reached the top landing and
came inside. He looked from Tizzy to me. 'I've got some great
pages tonight,' he began. 'I hope Ben's up for reading them.
They're so hot, the pages practically sizzle.'

He missed our eye rolls and went on back to the dining
room. I suddenly remembered that I hadn't cleared the table
for the group and rushed after him. Tizzy offered to man the
door for Daryl and Ben.

I didn't tell her that I wasn't sure if Ben would show. It
would open a discussion about what was going on with him,
and I wasn't about to share his situation and how it had
disrupted our relationship.

Ed took his usual chair and looked over his pages again,
smiling as he mouthed the words to himself. I deliberately
didn't try to read his lips as I moved the placemat and fruit
bowl off the table. I had all the stuff on the sideboard when
Tizzy came back with Daryl and Ben. I swallowed the
surprise at seeing him and nodded a hello to both of them.
Whatever he was feeling was hidden behind the neutral cop
face.

I got their pages from the previous week with my comments
and handed them out while everyone settled in. Tizzy was
practically twitching in her seat and I knew it was all about
wanting to hear the rest of the story that I'd teased.

Ed noticed that Daryl had a tattoo of a butterfly on her wrist
and seemed fascinated by it. 'I think I'll give one to my

character,' he said. 'Something that starts someplace visible and continues on someplace private.' He took a sip from his commuter mug and his mouth slid into a lascivious grin and asked her if she had anymore that didn't show.

His comment was just enough to pop the cork on Daryl's emotions. She literally sputtered air as she glared at him. 'This is it,' she said with distaste. 'I got it under pressure from work.' As the manager of a downtown clothing store that catered to twenty-somethings, she had to dress the part.

'Your boss can't force you to do that,' Tizzy said, getting indignant.

'No, but peer pressure can. I couldn't take them all showing off their tattoos anymore and then looking at me like I was some kind of outsider, so I got the butterfly.'

'Time to read,' Ed said, holding up his pages and handing them to Ben. There was the slightest raise of Ben's eyebrows as he glanced down at the first words and began to read. Ben kept to the flat police report sort of tone, but he still had trouble. Ed's romance novel was turning into one explicit sex scene after the other. His attempt at making the characters seem more developed was hearing their inner thoughts as they were going at it.

Ben set down the pages, letting out a breath of relief.

'Well?' Ed said expectantly. We all looked at each other and I suggested we just be concerned with the grammar.

Ben had brought some work, though only a few pages. I was disappointed to see that he'd gone back to the bare-bones style he had started with. Tizzy had brought a rewritten scene and everyone agreed it was improved. The fuss about the tattoo had only increased Daryl's tension, and she was biting her lip as Tizzy read her pages. She had written a love scene with no details other than something like *her heart swelled with love as they made contact.*

'You call that a love scene?' Ed said. 'What about the rest of their body parts?' He shook his head in disbelief. 'You need some throbbing, heaving, pumping stuff going on.'

Because she was so overly sensitive, no one wanted to make a comment, and it usually fell on me to say something. I was always careful to say something that wouldn't set her off.

Certainly nothing like what Ed had said. We all looked at her, expecting an outburst.

She turned to Ed and surprised us all as she said, 'I'll see what I can do.' I think we all let out our breath collectively, so shocked that she didn't have a meltdown. And we all probably had the same thought. We couldn't wait until next week to see what she brought in.

There was a little small talk at the end and everyone headed to the door. Tizzy turned back to me and mouthed *call me* as she mimicked picking up a phone and dialing. She knew that Ben had been coming back after everyone left. I knew it was driving her crazy to have to wait, and nodded in agreement.

Ben was taking up the rear. 'I need to talk to you,' I said, coming up close behind him. I watched as his shoulders hunched. 'It's not personal,' I quickly added, and his shoulders relaxed. He went out with the others, giving me a nod as he did. I left the door on the latch and went back to the dining room to gather up the pages they'd left for me to go over.

'I'm back,' Ben called out as he came in the door. I was on my way out of my office, having dropped off the group's work.

He showed off a plate of food covered in foil. 'As long as I was coming up here, I brought this. It made my sister's day when I told her I'd bring it to you.' Even with the cover on the plate, I could smell the spices and garlic.

'An added bonus,' I said. 'Thank you for bringing it and for coming back. I need to run something by you about my client who died.'

'Any time,' he said. 'Where shall we do this?'

'Here's fine,' I said, gesturing toward the couch. It felt awkward, and I'd only turned to him because he was the sole resource I could think of who might help.

'Would you like a beer?' I offered. I'd been keeping it on hand for his visits and still had one left. He accepted my offer of it stiffly. Neither of us quite knew the parameters of our dialed-down relationship. I left him to sit down while I went to the kitchen.

When I returned with the drinks, he was sitting on the couch, stroking his forehead as if he was upset. He sat up as I came in and resumed his non-expression expression.

'I need your professional opinion on something,' I said, hoping that hearing that would lessen the tension.

He took the beer and flipped open the bottle and offered a thanks before taking a sip. 'OK, shoot,' he said, leaning back against the cushion.

'It's about the other day.' I told him how something had bothered me about how Maeve had looked when I found her. 'She had a gash on her head and my first thought was that she'd knocked herself out and would be OK. I was shocked when the paramedics weren't able to revive her. I kept thinking back to when I first saw her and wondering why I'd thought that. After hearing that the medical examiner wouldn't sign off on the cause of death as being accidental from the fall, I did some research. Head wounds cause a lot of blood because the scalp has blood vessels close to the surface of the skin. I remembered that while there was the gash on her head, there had been almost no blood. There was no way there would have been so little blood for the size of the gash on her head . . . unless—'

'She was dead when she took the fall,' he said.

I nodded. 'It takes a beating heart to push all that blood out.' I leveled my gaze at him. 'It could mean that someone killed her and then pushed her down the stairs.'

'You were right about it not being anything personal,' he said with an almost chuckle. 'But what do you want from me?'

'Could you use a favor and find out if that's what Jankowski thinks?'

'I'd have to call in some favors and it might take a bit of time, but sure,' he said. 'Off the top of my head, your thinking sounds good.' I reached for the covered plate and pulled off the foil. Tomato sauce with what looked like ground meat oozed over thick lasagna noodles and he made a face. 'Sorry, I'm afraid my sister didn't know what we'd be discussing. And if you're worried, the crumbles are vegetarian. Some people have meatless Mondays. Sara has decided on meatless Tuesdays, even if it doesn't roll off the tongue as well.'

True I'd been talking about blood, but I was also starving

and that latter won out. I dug in. 'Tell your sister a thousand times thank you for the food. It's delicious.' I cut another piece off and speared it with the fork.

He cracked a smile. 'I'm sure she'll be glad to know.' There was an awkward silence after that. He looked at the beer bottle in his hands and rolled it back and forth, seeming uncomfortable. 'I owe you more of an explanation.'

'No, I just want to know if they think it was murder,' I said. 'It makes a difference in how I look at the notes she gave me. I mean, will I be looking for a suspect?'

'I didn't mean about that, but I see your point,' he said. 'It's about my wife.' He let out a sigh. 'She showed up without warning, and I'm confused, to put it mildly. For a moment I fell for her saying how wrong she was for walking out and that she wanted to make another start. I think it's human nature to want something like that. But, well, I'd moved on.' His voice faltered. 'With you.' He rushed to say that he knew that it was just being each other's plus ones and spending some time together, and was casual. 'The problem is . . .' He stopped and blew out his breath. 'I can't just tell her to go. Since she didn't sign the papers, she's still my wife. I need to get this cleared up first.'

He left it hanging, but I understood what he was saying. It was confusing for him to suddenly have a wife again and a sort of girlfriend. 'I don't know what constitutes cheating in this situation. Am I cheating on you to be with her, or vice versa? Who's the other woman?' he said as he set the empty bottle on a coaster. 'The only way I can deal with it is to keep a distance from everyone, including from my sister. She really tore into me, but I told her the only way I'd come over was if she let me work it out without her comments. And that's without her knowing that we're still married.'

I had set down the fork. The blood talk might not have dented my appetite, but this sure did. When I turned back to look at him, I melted when I saw the look on his face. His eyes were dark and his mouth had settled into a sad expression. 'I really appreciate that you made such an effort to keep me coming to the group. And that you're not angry at me.'

'Upset maybe, but not angry,' I said. I debated how much

to say. It was not my way to run after someone who was rejecting me, but he wasn't exactly rejecting me. I wasn't sure what he was doing, so I flat out asked him what he wanted. This time he smiled. 'Well, I'd like to have my cake and eat it too,' he said, watching me react to the cliché. 'In noncliché terms, continue to see you while I work things out with her.'

I made a face. 'That sounds like I get to be the other woman,' I said. 'Not my style.'

'I said it poorly. Yes, when she first showed up, I did have that feeling that she realized she was wrong and wanted me back. Nobody likes to lose. But something happened when she left. I don't really want her back. She says she wants to move in and resume like nothing happened. I told her I'd have to think about it. It was more of a stall while I sort things out.'

I couldn't fault him for not being honest, and now I had to think what I really wanted. No matter what he said about how he felt, they were still married, and whatever had brought them together in the first place could do it again. But much as I'd tried to be so controlled and rational, I missed his company.

'I don't usually do things like this,' I said, with a smile to keep it light. 'But I'm OK with us being friends while you sort this out.'

'I was hoping for more,' he said, looking a little dejected. 'But I can work with that. Is a hug OK?' he asked and held out his arms.

'I guess even friends give hugs,' I said.

THIRTEEN

By the time Ben left, it was too late to call Tizzy, so I sent her a text suggesting we meet for coffee in the morning. It might be too late to make a phone call, but still was early enough that I could do some work. There was a feeling of peace in the building, as if everyone had gone to bed, and it seemed like a good time to give the pages another look to see what I had to work with.

I made myself a cup of tea and set up the stack of papers on the dining-room table. I'd seen the first few pages several times. I had the sinking feeling those few pages were the only ones that could be called a draft as I looked at some random pages beyond. On one, she had drawn an arc and had scribbles coming off it. I knew what a story arc was. There were seven points on it: inciting incident, rising action, crisis, climax, falling action and resolution. Her arc was a little different. She'd written *the change, how life changed* on the ascent of the arc and *so good, award nomination* on the top of the curve. Next to the portion of the arc that descended, she'd written *I was a fool, Michael up to old tricks, not usually a vengeful person, but.*

I gathered from the arc that she planned the beginning of the book to be about Michael's rise from a nobody artist to being in the running for a big award. The rest of the book sounded like it was going to include some unflattering observations about him, and it implied she was angry about something.

The next page had a list. *The wedding, Michael's baggage, first gallery, Michael's dream studio, third wheel.* I let it all settle for a moment and realized that the pages weren't going to be much help without Maeve to decipher what everything meant. I made a list of people to talk to, figuring I could get enough from them to create a story. I wasn't going to worry about whatever Michael had done to upset her. The publisher just wanted a book about Michael, and she'd made it clear that I was free to create whatever was needed. I didn't want to make it too saccharine, and would put in just enough controversy to make it interesting. I'd already decided to include more about Maeve and who she was. Michael had seemed a little hostile to me and I wasn't sure if I'd be able to talk to him again. While he probably knew the most about Maeve, I had sold him that the book was about him and his art. He seemed pretty full of himself, and I wondered how forthcoming he'd be about her part in his success anyway. I thought about the school where she taught. I would reach out to them.

I started to go through the journal that was stuck in the middle of the papers. Most of the entries were notes about her day, reminding her to pick up the cleaning and such. There were a couple of short entries describing events they'd gone to and then I found something strange. It was in the middle of a page and said, *He underestimates me. The power I have and when pushed will use.* I had no idea what that meant and chalked it up to something to deal with later.

I was anxious to have something to show for my time. I found something with the title *D Day, That's D for Dog*. Under it were some notes about what was described as the day when everything changed. I'd heard enough about it from the reception, what Theo had told me and from what Maeve had said at our one meeting that I thought I could write it.

I took the page and went to the computer and knocked out my first writing for the book. When I was done, I sat back and read it over.

I can't believe that I missed it. If only I hadn't gone for the sandwiches, I would have been there when our world changed. Michael thought they were just another couple going through the art fair. After a day of too many people going by without giving the paintings a second look, he was happy someone had stopped. Even better, they really loved the painting of the Scottish terrier and the sleeping flowers, showing off that the dog they had with them seemed like the image of the one on the canvas.

There was no way to guess that simple moment would

lead to Michael going from obscurity to being the darling of the art scene. The woman was Sophia, who had a YouTube channel with hundreds of thousands of followers who would instantly fall in love with The Scotty in the Sleeping Garden *and scoop up posters, T-shirts and mugs. The man was Zander Paul, who owned an art gallery. He wanted to see more of the Scotty paintings and bought a number of them. In no time, Michael would get his dream of being featured in a major gallery.*

I was going to suggest that the publisher include color plates of some of the paintings.

I sat back satisfied that I'd finished something. Then I looked at the time. It was already tomorrow.

When I left to meet Tizzy, the sky was a thick gray and the only brightness was coming from the bright yellow leaves on a tree I passed. It was a coffee day for sure. Double so for me after my late night.

I thought over how much I would share with Tizzy. I wasn't going to tell Tizzy anything about the Ben situation. It was too confusing to describe. It was too confusing for me to figure out. I meant it when I told him I didn't want to be the other woman, or even *an*-other woman. Despite what he'd said, there was always the possibility he would decide to give it another try with Ashleigh. For now, I was glad that he was continuing to come to the workshops and that we were talking.

I also wasn't going to share that I thought Maeve was dead before she went down the stairs. Telling Tizzy would guarantee that it would spread around the neighborhood, and I didn't know for sure if it was true, and didn't want it to get back to Jankowski that it had come from me.

School was in session at Ray Elementary and the crossing guard was just leaving her post as I passed. For once I didn't pass any student joggers. I walked through the pedestrian gate to the campus and noted a scattering of students were on the sidewalk. A girl was sitting on the bridge over Botany Pond wistfully looking down at the water.

Tizzy's office seemed bright after the gloomy exterior. Her

red patterned kimono added to the cheer. She was staring at her computer screen, with her boss looking over her shoulder. He turned his gaze over at me and smiled. 'Your coffee date is here,' he said to Tizzy. She was one of the lucky few who loved their boss, but then he was highly indulgent about her taking off for one of her many committee meetings or, like this, a coffee date.

'Can I get you anything, Alex?' Tizzy asked.

'The usual,' he said with a nod to her.

'Right, an Americano and all the news I can gather.'

Alex was a tall, dry-looking man, probably in his late fifties. He seemed a little embarrassed that she had spelled it out as he glanced at me. 'It's always good to know what's going on.'

She grabbed her purse and jacket and we went out the door.

She eyed the tables in the small food hall next to what passed as a student center for UChicago. I knew when she picked the one in the center of the others, she had chosen the spot where she could pick up on the most conversations, while at the same time hearing what I had to say. I left her to settle in while I went for our coffees.

'OK, I want to know everything you know about what happened on Harper,' she said as soon as I handed her the steaming mug.

'Why don't you tell me what you know first,' I said. I was curious to hear what story was circulating on the street. All she had heard were the bare details that Maeve had fallen down the back stairs and died.

'She was an art teacher at Alex's daughter's school. He's the one who told me. That's all I know,' Tizzy said, offering me the floor.

'I was the one who found her,' I said, and Tizzy's eyes looked like they would pop out of her head. 'She was a client and I'd gone there to meet with her.'

'A client? For what? You never mentioned anything to the group about her,' she said.

'I was hesitant to say anything before I had the gig, afraid it would jinx it, and then when she hired me, she swore me to secrecy.' I shrugged. 'It doesn't seem to matter anymore, though since she seemed mostly worried that her husband would find out. He knows now and has already tried to cancel the project.'

'You didn't let him, did you? What's the project?' She did a scan of the area around us to check for anyone interesting.

'She hired me to help her with a memoir and already had a publishing deal in place. I couldn't have cancelled it if I wanted to. The publisher is anxious to get it, and the fact she's dead doesn't seem to make a difference. I thought she had a rough draft for me to work from. Only there isn't. I'm going to have to create something around what I have and talk to people who knew her to fill in the gaps.' I took a moment to take a breath and a sip of my coffee. 'I don't know how I'm going to end it. She said the final stuff wasn't in the notes – that she'd give me the details when we got there.' I remembered Maeve's offhand comment. 'She said that I might figure it out on my own.'

'Wow, a mystery.' Tizzy's eyes lit up with interest. 'Maybe it wasn't really an accident,' she added. I thought about what I should say. I didn't want to lie and insist that Maeve's death was absolutely an accident, but I didn't want to start any rumors yet either.

'Who knows?' I said finally.

Tizzy's phone pinged and she checked the screen. 'I have to go. Alex needs me to take care of something and he's anxious for his coffee drink.' She started to gather her things up. 'Come for sherry tonight. I know Theo would love to hear about everything.'

As soon as I left Tizzy, I started my walk to the Dupont Academy. I'd called the headmistress before I'd left to meet Tizzy. As soon as the head of the school heard what I was working on, she was open to my visiting, and when I explained the tight schedule I was on, agreed to setting it up that very day.

Before I'd called the school, I'd done some research on it. It was a small, exclusive private school, housed in a Kenwood mansion. I was fascinated by the pictures I'd seen of the building online and couldn't wait to see it in person.

I technically left Hyde Park when I crossed 51st Street, also known as Hyde Park Boulevard, and entered Kenwood. It was an elegant old neighborhood, with houses that were mostly mansions featuring grounds and old carriage houses.

When I reached the school, I took a moment to admire the exterior. The rectangular gray stone building had a massive feel. I'd checked and the style was called Italianate Revival. I walked through what seemed like a mini park with lots of mature trees on the way to the entrance. The front was flat with no porch, just a few stairs leading to the wooden double door with an appealing half-moon window above.

As soon as people knew that I'd be writing about our encounter, they tended to give me special consideration. It was definitely true here. The headmistress welcomed me like an honored guest and, to use a cliché, rolled out the red carpet for me. I could have said that another way as in 'she was accommodating', but that didn't say it as well. Her name was Renee Faulkenberg and she looked like what I'd expect of a headmistress of a private academy. She wore a suit and shoes with low heels.

Before I'd cleared the foyer, she had already told me that the school curriculum was based on a combination of philosophies, mixing some Waldorf with Montessori added to the traditional learning style. I saw that the kids were wearing uniforms, and she explained that they had a lot of scholarship students, and they didn't want them to feel different than the students who came from wealthy backgrounds. I was instantly in love with the place, and so grateful that she gave me a tour, even though I wasn't sure how much of it would really be about Maeve. Nothing about the place felt remotely institutional. We stood at the back of several of the common rooms where lessons were being taught. The students' desks were in the former bedrooms and arranged so they each had their own space around them. There was a library with comfortable chairs, and a science room with a metal table and Bunsen burner.

'We let the students use this as a lounge and a place to do homework,' she said, taking me into another room. I had to keep my mouth from falling open at what I saw. It looked like the inside of a log cabin and had a stone fireplace. A Native American print rug covered a part of the pine floor. It seemed like a room meant for dreaming.

The top floor was taken up by a ballroom with a dark blue domed ceiling. The recessed lights looked like stars. She smiled as I oohed and aahed over it. 'We use this for dance classes and events.'

'The students prepare the meals,' she said when we reached the kitchen. 'And as much as possible we use produce from the garden. We even have an indoor garden for the winter.' We hadn't even gotten to the art room, and I wanted to go back in time and go to this school.

'And this was Maeve's classroom,' Ms Faulkenberg said, opening a door and inviting me in. The walls were painted a soft brick red and the French doors opened onto a large terrace that looked out over a beautiful flower garden. It was filled with blooms even now. 'The students are all very upset,' she said with a sigh. 'Everyone loved her. Her smile with those dimples lit up the room.' She invited me to have a look around and to feel free to open any cabinets or drawers I wanted.

'Did you know her husband?' I asked.

The woman nodded. 'Maeve was so excited when they got together. Before he became so important in the art world, she was always trying to promote his work. Some of the parents are art collectors and, whenever there was a fundraiser for the school, one of his paintings was always included in the auction.' I looked at the easels around the room as she continued. 'Unfortunately, the attendees' sense of value was less about how they felt about what they saw and more about whether it was done by an "important" artist. Of course, all that changed after he was discovered. His recent donations of his artwork have made it so we could offer more scholarships.'

The headmistress pointed at a traditional-style teacher's desk. 'Maeve used that as home base. You can look through it if you like.'

It felt strange pulling open the drawers and seeing her personal items, including a pad with her notes and doodles. Flipping through it, I saw that she had made notes with nicely done rough drawings of projects for her classes. The drawer held some of Michael's sketches as well. She had written comments about composition on them that seemed meant for the students.

'Maeve was first and foremost a teacher. She loved helping the students find means of expression. She never used the words "good" or "bad". She was the perfect helper to her husband. She was so happy to let him shine.'

'How did you feel about him?' I asked.

Her expression faded. 'You know the saying that "love is blind"? Well, I didn't have the same view of him she did.' I wanted her to elaborate, but she seemed ready to end our visit and took me back to the foyer. She looked down at the notebook in my hand. 'Is there anything else you need?'

I had written down a few notes and felt confident I'd be able to flesh it out into something that gave an impression of Maeve. I would have to figure out how I was going to present it because the information had come from an outside source, but I'd figure that out later. 'I think I have what I need.' I dropped the notebook in my purse and thanked her for her time and the tour. 'This is a wonderful school,' I said, taking a last glance around.

She seemed very pleased with my comment. 'You might be just what we're looking for. We want someone to teach writing and we like to bring in people working in the field.'

'I would love to,' I said, handing her a card. I hoped I'd hear from her. I already knew the room I wanted to use for a classroom. The one with logs on the wall.

Sara opened her door when I was on my way up the stairs. I heard Quentin in the background trying to convince Mikey to watch ESPN instead of a kids' show. Sara pointed upstairs with a question in her eyes and I told her I'd get the cooking wine ready.

I'd barely gotten inside my place when I heard her knock. She followed me back to the kitchen as I went to get her the drink. I expected her to go right into talking about Ben, but she surprised me.

'Did you hear what happened on Harper?' she said. There was no space for me to answer before she continued. 'Some woman fell down the stairs and died.' I poured the wine and grabbed some sparkling water. We took the glasses and went back to the front. She chose one of the chairs in the bay windows and I sat in the other. 'I took Mikey to the playground this morning and it seemed all anybody could talk about. I guess her husband is some well-known artist who paints pictures of dogs.'

'Did they say anything about how it happened?' I asked.

'I gather it was an accident, at least sort of. Someone said they thought she was on pills or drunk, maybe.' She turned toward me. 'The women at the playground kept going on about her husband. Apparently, women love artistic types. They find them passionate and intense.' Sara shrugged. 'Not me. I'd take a quiet pharmacist like Quentin any day.' She was thoughtful for a moment. 'I know who that artist is,' she said, sitting forward. 'I saw him on that morning talk show, Windy City Live. I think he had one painting of a dog, but the rest of them were all landscapes. The show had to blur out part of them because there were nudes amongst the trees,' she said with a smile. 'If I were him, I'd stick with the dogs.' She fiddled with the wine glass for a moment and then she got to the real reason she'd come up.

'I don't know what I'm going to do about my brother. If our parents were still living around here, maybe they'd get involved. When I told them Ashleigh was back, they were like *whatever*,' she said with a shrug. 'He'd better not bring her over.' She turned toward me. 'I know he's been up here. What has he told you?'

No way was I going to mention that Ben had told me they were still married. 'Not much really,' I said, trying to be vague.

'I guess he didn't tell you how hard-looking she is and about the short tight dresses she always wore. I was always afraid what would happen if she bent over to pick something up. You know, offer more than anyone should see. I didn't really have to worry. She expected someone else to pick up whatever she dropped anyway. She's a real princess type. She manages a nail salon, or that's what she was doing. Every time I saw her, she had some elaborate nail decorations.' Sara set her empty glass on the table between us. 'She kept offering to do the same for me.' Sara punctuated her comment with a laugh.

I looked down at my 'good' jeans and then at my plain-looking nails. I'd tried nail polish, but it virtually rolled off my fingers right after I put it on.

'And like I told you, her eyebrows are too sparse and too arched. I think they make her look like a Disney villain.'

'I guess you're not a fan,' I said facetiously. Maybe she wasn't, but Ben must have been if he married her. If she was his type, there wasn't much chance for us.

'Do you think they'll get back together?' I said.

'Don't even say it.' She shook her head. 'I thought my brother was smarter than that.' She turned to me. 'Remember how I said the reason I kept trying to push you together with him was because I wanted you as a sister – well, I never said that to her. If you care at all about him, do what you can to make sure he doesn't take her back.'

I was really glad I hadn't mentioned their marital status, but thinking about it brought up my feelings about being the other woman all over again. Then I chuckled at myself. I'd been so worried about seeming dull and spinsterish, living alone with a cat, set in my patterns and fussing about clichés. *Other woman* sounded at least more interesting. But maybe not when it was really *other woman friend.*

FOURTEEN

As the afternoon was fading into evening, I went over to Tizzy's. I liked being included in her sherry ritual. Theo answered the door and seemed more enthusiastic than usual. 'It really seems like synchronicity the way we all went to the event at the art gallery featuring Michael Angel and you were meeting his wife about a writing job.' His voice dropped as he brought me into the house. 'It's really too bad what happened to her. The back stairs at these old houses are really dangerous. I'm always telling Tizzy to be careful. I guess they expected servants to be nimble of foot when they built these places.'

I shouldn't have been surprised that he knew everything that I'd told Tizzy. I hadn't said anything about keeping it to herself. He continued talking as he ushered me into the living room. 'Tizzy told me about the memoir you're working on and how you're going to have to create more copy. I might be able to help with that.' He offered me a seat and said Tizzy would be down shortly. He left me and went to the kitchen for the drinks and snacks.

Theo had been mostly a mystery to me. I'd only seen him as an associate of Tizzy's; since she had such an outgoing personality, he'd seemed to fall into the background. His looks didn't help. He had sort of an everyman appearance, hidden behind a pair of horn-rimmed glasses. He would have been a great detective – in real life, not fictional. No one would notice him tailing them.

But as I was getting to know Theo more, I realized he was much more interesting than I'd thought. His curiosity seemed boundless and he was as enthusiastic as his wife. I liked being around them and hoped some of their liveliness would rub off on me. Their relationship was an inspiration. With so many couples falling apart, it was good to see one that worked.

Tizzy came down a few moments later, and joined me just

as Theo came in with a tray. 'I've upped my game,' he said, pointing out the metal shaker. 'I've switched to a martini. There's Tizzy's sherry and I brought a glass of sparkling water for you.' He asked if I wanted him to add a touch of sherry to my drink, but I declined since I had noticed I could feel even the small amount of alcohol in the drink. I caught a whiff of his martini. So odd, I couldn't manage even a taste of the cocktail, but I loved the smell of gin.

Theo took a sip of the martini and set it on a coaster. 'After the reception, I got curious about what gave an artist's painting value. It turns out who owns some of the art matters. It helps if someone famous has an artist's work in their collection. That Sophia woman is a celebrity of sorts, and it appears she introduced his art to a huge number of people. It's interesting that her boyfriend owns an art gallery,' Theo said.

'What's your point?' Tizzy said.

'It's not exactly a point,' he began. 'I was just thinking that the painting that put Michael Angel in the spotlight happened to belong to her. And then I started thinking: what if it was a plan? We know they found the painting at the art fair, and probably bought it really cheap. What if they figured out they could make him a sensation by plastering the picture all over her YouTube channel, and maybe her boyfriend bought a few more paintings on the cheap and planned that when they made Michael into an art star, he could sell them for a big profit at his gallery?'

'That's a lot of supposing,' Tizzy said. She turned to me. 'You probably are beginning to figure this out about Theo,' Tizzy said, giving her husband's arm an affectionate squeeze. 'He's always thinking about whatever crosses his path and looking for information. I'm surprised he hasn't worn out the Internet with his endless researches.'

'You can't wear out the Internet,' he said with a surprised smile. He turned to me. 'Tizzy's always joking that Alexa or Siri is going to say "you again" one of these days. I just wondered how Michael Angel got where he is. I was curious about Sophia as well, and so I researched influencers. It's all about them sharing their lives with the public. They need to have something that makes them stand out. Sophia seems to have a certain amount of charisma, but the draw is her relationship with the Scottish terrier. She has made him into her co-star on her show. When she first started doing the YouTube thing, she would let the dog size up potential dates. If he let out a low growl, it was his way of saying "lose this one". Apparently, one time she didn't listen and the guy turned out to be a super creep. It was all put out there for the world to see and she gathered a lot of followers.

'She must have realized she couldn't sustain that, or maybe when she met the guy who owns the art gallery, he wasn't so happy about it. She changed everything except the dog. Now her channel follows her turning something trashy into a treasure sort of thing. I wonder what the deal is on all that merch with *The Scotty in the Sleeping Garden* on it that she sells from her website.'

Tizzy gracefully stepped in. 'Theo, the plan was to give Veronica information she could use in what she's writing.'

'So sorry,' he said, holding his hands in a prayer-like posture and bowing his head. 'I get carried away. You know how it is – one thing leads to another. I meant to see what I could find out about the woman who died, but I got detoured,' he said. 'I forgot to mention that Sophia has a sponsor. Sukey's Super Stick. It's some kind of super-glue she uses to fix the stuff she finds.'

'That's OK,' I said. 'I was going through her notes and talking to people who knew her. I already talked to Michael Angel.' I thought back on how unpleasant our encounter had been. 'He didn't give me much since he's against what I'm doing. I got some nice stuff from the school where she worked.' I turned to Tizzy. 'And maybe a lead on some work for me.' Tizzy knew the school because her boss's daughter went there.

'That would be wonderful,' she said, and then wanted to know what the place looked like. After my description, the conversation went off on a tangent, with Theo looking for examples of Italianate Revival architecture, which led to us talking about a mansion on Michigan Avenue downtown in that style, which had been turned into offices and a restaurant with a puppet theater.

Theo had a guilty look and typed something into the laptop

he'd brought out. 'Here's something about Maeve . . .' he said, and we all leaned over the screen to read.

The article was from several years ago and detailed a confrontation between Maeve and Michael's first wife at a gallery event. Rina Wolinski had apparently thrown a glass of champagne in Maeve's face and said that she was Michael's real muse and inspiration and that Maeve was just collecting the gravy.

'I'm glad the ex didn't make an appearance at the reception we went to,' Tizzy said.

'Maybe that explains why Maeve wasn't there. She was afraid of a repeat performance.'

'Do you think the ending of the memoir she alluded to had anything to do with his first wife?' Theo asked.

Wow, Tizzy really had told him everything, even about the missing ending.

FIFTEEN

It was dark when I went home. It had been a fun evening with all the talking and conjecturing. It was nice to feel that I had some allies in helping with Maeve's memoir. We'd ended up ordering a pizza and moved off talking about Maeve. Theo had gotten into doing research about the 1893 World's Fair, which had been held in the area. I didn't know that the first Ferris wheel had been just a few blocks from where we were, or that a remnant had been found buried in the ground. His research was in support of Tizzy's time-travel novel. It was sweet the way he wanted to help her.

As I started up the outside stairs to the front porch of my building, I sensed someone suddenly come up behind me, making me feel uneasy. I rushed up the last few steps and positioned my key between my fingers as an impromptu weapon to poke an assailant. Just as I got to the door to the outer vestibule, I turned with the key showing.

'You?' I said in surprise as I recognized Detective Jankowski.

He looked down at my hand with the key pointed toward him. 'How about you stand down with the key,' he said. I couldn't tell if he really felt threatened or amused. Either way, I lowered my hand.

'To what do I owe the pleasure?' I said. Yes, it was a cliché, but it didn't count because I was being sarcastic.

'If you recall, I did say that I might need to talk to you again since you were the person to find the victim.' He left it hanging to imply that it somehow made me a suspicious person. 'And there have been some new developments,' he said.

'Really?' I said. 'Like what?' He gave me a tired look.

'It doesn't work that way. I get information, not give it.' It didn't matter because I knew what the development was. He'd just confirmed what I thought about Maeve being dead before she went down the stairs, which changed it from an accident to murder. Technically, since he didn't actually say those words, it probably didn't count as actual confirmation, but to me it was. It was probably not a good thing for me, since now he was looking for a killer. I knew that sometimes killers tried to act as if they'd found the body as a way to cover what they did. From what I'd heard, they usually tried to have a witness with them when they 'found the body', but Jankowski probably looked at that as only a sometime detail.

He gestured for me to proceed through the door. As we got inside the outer vestibule, he glanced through the glass door to the stairway and I heard him let out a tired-sounding sigh. 'How about we go to the coffee shop on the corner?'

I knew there was the possibility that his suggestion was just based on his not wanting to climb the stairs, but it also could be his way of making it seem more relaxed so that I'd be more likely to say things that might not be in my best interest. And since I could get up and leave, anything I said could and would be used against me without him having to warn me first. I wondered if he knew that I knew that.

It was already late and the coffee shop was empty. He led the way to a back booth and took the seat that gave him a view of the door and the whole place. A typical cop move. A man had just brought out a pail and mop and started cleaning the floor as the waitress came with menus. She recognized me and gave Jankowski the once-over. Did she think it was a date?

He told me to order food if I wanted, complimentary of Chicago PD, and told her he'd just have coffee. I declined the food and watched amused as he checked the metal cream pitcher on the table to make sure it was full.

The waitress dropped off the coffee and I could tell by the smell that it had been sitting in the pot for a long time. It didn't matter to Jankowski because he dumped so much cream in it that the cup almost overflowed. As far as I was concerned, my cup was just a prop. I took one sip and set the cup down, not expecting to lift it again. And I was right, the coffee had that thick bitter taste it got from sitting on a heater for too long.

The waitress came back and dropped off a couple of dishes of rice pudding on the house, explaining it was the end of the day and they never kept it over. Jankowski looked at it for a moment and then dove in. I loved their rice pudding, and under normal circumstances would have joined him, but his presence had killed my taste buds. I took a polite spoonful and it seemed like tasteless glue to me.

I really wanted to get to whatever he was going to ask. The tension was putting my stomach into a knot. I knew that I would be cautious about what I said, but even so I could say the wrong thing. Not talking wasn't an option unless I said I wanted an attorney. Hah, like I could afford an attorney, anyway.

'OK, what is it?' I asked, not being able to take the suspense any longer. I saw his dark eyes narrow, not happy that I had tried to take control.

'I wanted to ask you some more about your visit to Maeve Winslow,' he said.

'I'm just going to tell you the same thing again. She'd hired me to help her write her memoir and we were supposed to talk over the first section. When I got there, the front door opened on its own and I went inside.' I noticed he was watching my face intently, lifting the coffee mug without looking at it.

'You're sure the door was unlocked?' he asked, and I nodded. 'Didn't it seem strange to you that it just opened on its own?' I thought about what I should say that wouldn't stir things up. Best to keep it simple and just on what he'd asked. I would not bring up the first appointment and my encounter with Suzzanna. I'd already told him she wanted to keep what we were doing to be a surprise. After talking to Michael Angel and seeing his reaction to the project, I thought there was more to it. But that was all conjecture, and I didn't want to share it with Jankowski, figuring he would accuse me of trying to play detective.

'There was some confusion about which door to go to. She'd had me come to the back door before, probably because it was a more direct way to get to her private space.' I reminded him that the back stairs ended right before the door leading to the third floor.

'What made you go to the front door this time?' he asked. I debated what to tell him, and then made something up that could have been the truth.

'Her husband thought I was a cleaning lady when I went out the kitchen door. She didn't give me any instructions the second time, and I didn't want to be mistaken for a cleaning lady again.' It sounded kind of lame when I said it, but he seemed OK with my reasoning.

'And then what?' he said. He took his eyes off me long enough to check his empty coffee mug and waved the waitress over. She poured the last of the pot into his mug.

I shrugged as I thought back over it. 'I called hello a few times and, when there was no answer, went to look for her. I found her sprawled on steps in the kitchen. I called nine-one-one and they took over.' I was aware that I'd condensed my going up to her attic room into 'went to look for her', thinking that the less I said, the better.

He looked down at his notes. 'Last time we talked, you mentioned the memoir was a surprise for her husband. I notice you left that out this time.' He let the words hang in the air while I tried to think of an explanation. Finally, I gave him a helpless shrug.

'I guess I forgot.'

I couldn't tell if he bought it or not. I had a feeling that he had an agenda in his questioning and wondered where he was headed.

'Maybe there's something else you forgot,' he said leveling his gaze at me. 'Like maybe you did meet with her and had words?' he said. 'About this writing job you have mentioned.'

'No,' I said, feeling uncomfortable.

'My understanding is that she fired you and insisted on the check back.' If he was looking for a reaction, he got it. I was shocked.

'Who told you I was fired?' I demanded.

He kept the stone-faced expression and I blathered on. 'You must have misunderstood. Her husband told me to forget the project. She didn't fire me.' Then the pieces fell into place. 'You think she fired me and I killed her when she asked for her check back?'

'What about the check? Do you still have it?' He'd done the detective trick of not answering my question and instead asking one of his own.

'I already cashed it,' I said.

'You probably were depending on that money. Maybe you already spent some of it,' he said. He nodded toward the exterior of my building, which was visible through the window of the coffee shop, and his meaning was clear, I had a big place. 'When people are in a corner, they sometimes do things in the moment.' He waited to see what I was going to say.

I considered offering to show him the notes that Maeve had given me, as proof that I hadn't been fired, but it might backfire. He could say that I still had them because I'd killed her rather than giving them back. I didn't want to let on that I'd figured out that Maeve was dead before she went down the stairs. It's the kind of information that the killer would know. I knew exactly where the story had come from. Michael Angel was determined to stop the project and must have thought that if I was being investigated, it would fall apart. There was another possibility: he was the one who killed Maeve and was trying to pin it on me.

I also knew if I was too vehement in denying it, it could make me look bad as well. I managed to keep my cool and simply told him that whoever had given him that information was wrong. He kept an inscrutable face throughout it all and I had no idea if he believed me or not.

It was a relief to finally go home, and nice to find Rocky waiting for me. He was acting more and more as I would have expected a dog to behave, and I loved it. While the cat cuddled and I stroked his back, I kept going over the meeting with Jankowski in my head. Now on top of worrying about creating a memoir out of thin air, I had to worry about being implicated in her death. Jankowski couldn't really believe I had done it, could he? A bunch of questions floated through my mind. The first was, how did she die and the second was, how strong did someone have to be to drag her from somewhere else and launch her down the stairs?

The extra-strong coffee and the conversation with the detective – along with my thoughts afterward – left me tense all over. It would have been nice to call Ben and talk it over, but

I talked myself out of it. Chamomile tea and crochet would have to suffice. I didn't even want to think about the image of myself connected with that.

I was hardly in the best shape to deal with Caleb on Thursday morning, but he'd called me verging on hysteria. It was seven a.m. and, after the previous day, I had been planning to treat myself to a little extra sleep. I was already putting on the coffee while I talked to him.

'It's not working,' Caleb said in a frustrated wail. 'Still nothing. I saw she was inside when I brought the last note over. I tried hiding when I rang the bell so she wouldn't know it was me, but she got one of those doorbells with a camera and I couldn't evade it.' He let out an unhappy sound, sounding hopeless with some anger. 'We have to up the ante,' he said.

I reminded him that we had an appointment and I'd planned to show him an idea I had. It had come from the art project I did with Maeve and wasn't just for Caleb, but for any love-letter clients I got in the future. A handmade card could make the missives more appealing and, in his case, might be the thing that would push her to talk to him. I had already ordered one of the palettes with all the colors of ink and it had arrived the next day. It was still sitting waiting for its inaugural use. I told him about the art project and I heard rumbling at the other end.

'Art project? I'm not an artist. It'll make things worse,' he said. I did a whole pitch on him that not only was it easy and something I was sure he could do, but it was more about the effort than the outcome. 'I get it,' he said, sounding calmer. 'If she thinks I made a card for her, maybe she'll melt the deep freeze.'

'Yes, that's it exactly,' I said. As an afterthought, I asked him if his wife was afraid of him. He laughed at the absurdity of the thought.

'I crunch numbers, not my muscles.'

We'd always met at his favorite doughnut shop, but I couldn't picture him doing the artwork in public, so I suggested he come to my place. I had made it a point to try to keep my meetings with clients somewhere else, but I already knew him and I couldn't imagine it being a problem. Once he agreed, he wanted to do it immediately, so we set up a time for that afternoon.

On the dot of two, the croaky bell went off, and I buzzed the security door to let him in. I walked out on the landing and looked over the railing as he came up. He seemed a little perturbed by all the flights and took a deep breath when he reached the top landing. 'You probably save on a gym membership with all these stairs.'

He stopped in the entrance hall, waiting for instructions. I pointed him back to the dining room and led the way. 'This is one of those railroad-car-style apartments,' he said. 'I like these old places, even if they don't have amenities like elevators.'

'I never asked you where you live,' I said. I had the dining-room table all set up for him, with some sheets of paper for him to practice on and some nice cardstock to use for the final product. He stopped behind the chair and looked everything over.

'I'm renting a studio apartment in a new building until I get back with my wife. She lives on Harper with my daughter.'

'Harper?' I said. My ears perked up when I heard that. 'Where exactly?'

'The area is called the Rosalie Villas?' he said. 'They're all old houses built in the late 1800s. Ours – well, hers – is in the middle between 57th Street and 59th.'

'Do you know the neighbors?' I asked. He looked surprised at the question as I continued. 'I've always heard that the people all know each other. They make arrangements for Halloween and such.'

'My wife is the one into that. I never paid much attention.' He seemed to think of something and his face brightened. 'I know that the house next door still has fish-scale siding and the woman who lives there does yoga in the backyard. The one with a series of connected poses. Sun salutations,' he added, seeming pleased that he'd come up with the correct name. He caught himself, realizing it sounded weird. 'What I meant is, my office faced their backyard, and when I happened to look up from my work, I noticed that she was doing sun salutations in their yard.'

'Was the house painted lavender?' I asked, remembering that Maeve's house was one of the few on the block that still had the Victorian-style siding.

He had to think about it for a moment. 'I thought of it as more a blue with some gray, but I suppose you could call it lavender.'

'Did you know that woman died?' I said.

'No, I didn't,' he said in a flatter tone than I'd expect for that type of news. I expected him to ask for details, but instead he suggested we get started because he had allotted only an hour for this and he had an appointment.

I showed him samples and then demonstrated how to make hearts and flowers. He was a little put off about getting the ink on his fingers, but after making a few marks that pleased him, he got into it. He practiced making hearts and flowers using a pen to add definition. Then he found his inner artist and moved on to making caterpillars and bugs. I used the time to see if I could elicit any more information about Maeve that he might not realize he knew, but he shrugged off my comments.

I knew mathematicians had a reputation for being in their own world of numbers, but Caleb's lack of interest still struck me as odd.

SIXTEEN

Caleb forgot about his other appointment and stayed for a couple of hours. He moved on from playing around to making the actual cards, but even so went through a lot of cardstock before he'd made a couple of cards he was satisfied with. I had some content ready to put in them and he copied my words into them. He was going to drop one off right after he left. Relieved that it had turned out so well, I walked him to the door and followed him out onto the landing. As he reached the second-floor landing, he passed Ben. Caleb paid no attention to Ben, but Ben's eyes were locked on Caleb. My client continued down the stairs and Ben looked up at me.

'I have the information you requested. OK if I come up?'

I was surprised to see Ben and for a second I didn't know what he was talking about, but then it came back to me and I nodded.

'Replaced me already?' Ben said as I ushered him inside.

'He's a client,' I said. 'Love notes.'

'I'm not surprised. He looks a little too buttoned down and zipped up to be someone who could write mush.'

'It's not mush,' I protested. 'He needs help expressing his feelings.'

'As long as they're not for you,' he said with a smile.

'I didn't take you for the jealous type.' I wanted to add that with the current circumstances he had lost that right anyway.

He didn't offer a hug or any form of affection, but kept his hands at his side, as if to remind himself that PDA were off limits for now.

Thanks to Jankowski's visit, I already knew what he was going to tell me. As I'd thought, Maeve was double dead. But I didn't want to ruin Ben's reveal. 'You could have just called,' I said.

'Your Highness Mikey requested my presence for dinner,

so I was coming here anyway.' He glanced toward the living room. 'Can I sit?'

'Sure.' I pointed the way, which of course he didn't need. 'I actually found out more than you'd asked. I figured you'd be in a hurry to know, so I thought I'd come up before dinner, but if you want to wait I'm sure my sister will want me to bring you some leftovers.'

'Now, please,' I said. His tease of more information had worked and I was impatient to know what else he'd found out.

'I want you to know that I had to go through a lot to get all these details, including claiming that my sister knew the victim and I might have some information.' His eyes flickered over my face, waiting for a response. I thanked him profusely, anxious for him to get on with it. He paused for a moment longer and I wondered if he was enjoying building up the suspense.

'Well?' I said finally.

'As you thought, they believe the victim was dead before she fell. Do you want all the technical details or just what they think may have been the cause of death?'

'Everything,' I said quickly.

'Her eyes were bloodshot and there was a high level of carbon dioxide in her lungs.' He looked at me to see if I understood.

'So, you're saying she suffocated?' I knew a bit about forensics from writing the Derek Streeter books. 'What about the signs of a struggle?'

He shook his head. 'No signs she tried to fight anybody off. She might have been drugged before she was suffocated. They didn't find any evidence at the scene, but took samples from her. The results of the tox screen won't be back for at least four weeks, maybe longer.'

My mind was clicking as he talked. 'That means it was someone she knew,' I said. 'I wonder how they suffocated her. They probably thought it wouldn't be detected and the fall would be considered the cause of death,' I said, and Ben agreed.

'Did they say where they think it happened?'

'No. They are still investigating as far as I could tell.'

His phone made a sound and he looked down. 'I hate to
break up this cheery topic of conversation,' he said, 'but Mikey
awaits.' He got up and went to the door. 'I'm sure you'd be
welcome to join us. I heard my sister made an apple pie.'

My mouth was watering at the thought, but I shook my
head. It was too awkward with things being the way they were.
'No thanks, but I wouldn't say no to some leftovers,' I said.
'Or it's peanut butter sandwiches again.'

He did a mock bow with a smile. 'At your service.'

'And don't forget the apple pie,' I said before I shut the
door.

I was left with plenty to think about. Someone had gone to
an effort to take her out. It meant planning, premeditation, not
something done in a moment of anger. She had seemed a
pleasant person with a sunny disposition, from what I'd seen
of her. Why would someone want to kill her? I remembered
the strange comments in the notes, seeming to plan some kind
of revenge. There were no names named, but I had to believe
the 'person' that she referred to was Michael Angel.

I was still thinking about Maeve and the notes when Ben
came back with some delicious-smelling leftovers and a piece
of pie. He didn't even come in, just handed it all to me at the
door, saying he had to get home. I couldn't help but wonder
if there was someone there waiting for him.

SEVENTEEN

My mind was heavy with thoughts the next morning as I drank my coffee. Ben had reconfirmed what I'd already figured out from meeting with Jankowski, but he'd added details about how Maeve had died. It made me feel short of breath to think of her being suffocated. If I'd had the slightest doubt that it was murder, I didn't anymore. I was guessing that the police had put the case on hold until they got the results from the tox screen.

How could I create the manuscript without knowing who killed Maeve and why? At the same time, I couldn't wait around while the police figured it out. There was also the issue of me being implicated in her death. Jankowski had come up with a motive and I had been at the house in the vicinity of the time she died. I couldn't believe that he really saw me as a suspect, but who knew? It seemed my only alternative was to find out everything on my own.

All of the above left me stuck in neutral with no idea how to proceed on anything. I knew the best antidote was to leave it all behind or go for a walk to clear my head. I threw on a jacket and headed west on 57th, thinking I had no destination in mind, and yet I walked directly to the campus and the business school building.

I suppose Tizzy's office was in the back of my mind all along, though I still was surprised when I ended up there. She was doing something on her computer and looked up when I came in. I worried about bothering her at work, but she seemed happy to see me.

'I hate to interrupt you, but there's been a development with that client of mine and I need someone to talk things over with,' I said. 'I thought maybe we could get coffee.'

'Of course. Is it about the artist's wife? She's the only client of yours I know about, so I suppose it has to be about her,' Tizzy said. As she was talking, her boss Alex walked in. He nodded a greeting at me and then stopped next to her desk.

'Are you talking about Maeve Winslow?' he asked. I was a little taken aback by his question, meaning that he was admitting he'd been eavesdropping, and I nodded as an answer. 'She was my daughter's art teacher. The kids are having a hard time processing that she's gone.'

He looked at me with new interest. 'She was a client of yours? I suppose what you want to talk about is what you were working on for her.' Alex knew that I was a writer for hire and led the group that Tizzy was in. I didn't want to say any more about what I'd found out – or that I was sort of a suspect – in front of him.

Tizzy picked up on my hesitation and turned to her boss. 'Veronica gets very involved with her clients. She's still processing her loss. It helps when you have someone to talk to,' she said. 'It's time for my coffee break anyway.' She picked up her purse and jacket.

'I'm so sorry,' Alex said in a somber tone. 'Of course, there is nothing like the comfort of a friend at a time like this.'

As soon as we were outside, Tizzy turned to me. 'I hope that was OK to say, but I had to give him something.'

'What you said was perfect. It's hard to keep up with how connected everyone around here is,' I said.

'The usual place OK?' she said. I knew she meant the coffee stand in the food court we'd gone to before. There was the issue of people overhearing what I had to say.

'It's fine, but can we sit outside?' I said, thinking the wind would keep my words away from any nearby ears. She agreed and this time she got the coffees and brought them out to me.

I'd already found a bench, not concerned that the others around it were taken. There was a bite to the air, but the sun was shining, drawing people sit in the pleasant courtyard.

'Whenever you're ready, I'm all ears,' Tizzy said. A gust of wind blew a paper cup across the stone patio with a rattling sound.

She'd splurged and gotten us cappuccinos, and I took a sip of foamy coffee drink. Though I had kept some of the information back before, I'd decided to tell all now. 'To begin with,

I have reason to believe it wasn't an accident, and since I'm the one who found her, it makes me a suspect or person of interest, which is just a nicer way of saying the same thing. The detective has even come up with a motive that she fired me from the job of writing the memoirs.'

'Where did he get that from?' Tizzy asked.

'I know Michael Angel tried to stop the project, and I think this is another attempt of his. He could think that if the police are investigating me, I won't have time to finish the manuscript even though there's a contract. I'd also like to find out who killed her, in case Detective Jankowski decides that his gut tells him it was me.'

'And you want my help,' Tizzy said with an expectant look.

'Of course, I'd be glad to. I can be your wing person. We can shoot ideas back and forth. Theo will probably want to be involved. He really enjoyed the other night. You saw how he loves delving into things.'

'I don't know about Theo,' I said. 'I was hoping to keep it kind of quiet.'

'He won't tell anyone. I'm the blabbermouth in the family, but when I give my word to keep it quiet, I do.' She played with the lid on her coffee cup. 'You saw that I didn't tell Alex about anything.'

I had to admit she was right, and I knew from before that she could keep something to herself.

I told her everything I knew about the detective's visit and what Ben had told me. As soon as she heard his name, she sidetracked into wanting to know what was up with him.

'I know that you want the group to think you're just friends and that his delivery of food after our meetings is just an attempt to get extra help, but I know there's more.'

I could see her point. She had run into me a number of times when Ben and I had been out together in the neighborhood. 'And I also know that something happened. He's been all weird lately. The way he had so few pages and his bristly mood.' She looked at me, waiting for an answer.

So far, I hadn't been honest with anyone about how far my relationship with Ben had gone. Both Ben and I wanted to keep Sara in the dark because it would put pressure on a future for us. That seemed like old news now. I hadn't wanted the group to know because of exactly what happened. If Ben and I had a falling out, they might feel awkward and like they had to take sides. It was hard to define our relationship any way other than tentative. We'd been taking it very slowly, since we both were nervous about anything with too many expectations. Since Tizzy had obviously seen through my efforts to make it seem that Ben was just my student, I decided to tell her the truth.

'His ex-wife showed up?' she said, incredulous, after I'd explained. 'No wonder he was out of sorts the other night.'

'There's more. You really have to keep this quiet. He hasn't even told his sister.' I stopped to take a breath, thinking the situation over again and shaking my head in exasperation. 'She never signed the divorce papers.'

'Wow,' Tizzy said as her eyes opened wider. She forced herself to recover quickly. 'The important question is what does he want.' She offered me a sympathetic nod.

'I don't really know. He claims to want to end it with her, but I know there's that part of anyone who has been dumped that wants another shot with the person who dumped them.'

'And you?' she asked.

'It might make me seem less dull, but I'm not cut out to be the other woman.'

She insisted that I wasn't dull at all, and that I really led a very exciting life. I used my wits to make a living, had solved mysteries, and could handle Ed and all his salacious copy that he brought to the group. And then she agreed about my not wanting to be the woman on the side.

'But the thing is, I like him,' I said, feeling as if I sounded like a silly teenager.

'And I'm sure he will pick you,' she said in a reassuring tone. 'Now what makes you think it was murder and what should we do?'

Tizzy listened wide-eyed as I told her about Maeve already being dead when she fell down the staircase. I could have just given all the credit to Ben for the information, but I was proud of the way I'd figured it out, so I shared the head wound and lack of blood with her. She was duly impressed.

'Double dead,' she said with a nod. 'I like that.'

'I thought we might start with Michael Angel's ex-wife. You remember Theo found that article, which described Michael's ex throwing the champagne in Maeve's face? It's pretty clear she wasn't a fan of Maeve's, and for good reason. And another reason why I don't want to be the other woman. What's that quote – *hell hath no fury like a woman scorned.*' I thought about how Sara had described Ashleigh and wondered how far she would go to hang onto Ben.

By the time we'd finished our coffee drinks, we'd come up with a plan.

Saturday morning, Tizzy was waiting for me downstairs. She had dressed down for the occasion. No fluttery colorful kimono top, but a trench coat over what seemed to be black jeans and a black sweater.

'We look like a couple of ninjas,' I said, showing off my similar outfit, though I didn't have a trench coat, but instead a long cardigan-sweater.

I'd found out that Rina Wolinski worked at a downtown art supply store. I'd checked and made sure she was working that day. 'Wolinski is Michael's real last name,' I explained as we rode downtown on the Metra train.

'I can see why he goes by Michael Angel. It's a lot more poetic and memorable,' Tizzy said.

We got off at the last stop and as we came up the stairs from the station were immediately in to the hyperactivity of downtown.

We joined a throng of people walking down Randolph. When we got to State Street, a group of musicians were performing on the corner; it was impossible not to start walking to the beat of the drums. Farther down the block, a preacher with a portable sound system was offering to save everyone from the fires of hell if they acknowledged their sins and gave up a few things.

Tizzy looked at the street ahead of us and brought up how much she missed all the department stores that used to be there. 'It's a bygone era,' she said wistfully. Macy's was the only one left. The plaque on the building still said Marshall

Field's, but the other signs all said Macy's. Chicago people had a loyalty to their sports teams, their pizza and to their stores. There had actually been protestors when Macy's insisted on changing the name.

Art World was on the other side of State Street. I'd passed it before, but never paid attention until now. It was two stories, and I had a sign touting that it was an artist's dream. Inside it smelled faintly of oil paints and clay. We stood at the front and looked at the two stories, trying to figure out how to proceed. Since it was supposed to be a chance encounter, we couldn't ask for her by name, so instead we began to wander through the maze of easels and paints, pens, and boxes of clay.

Luckily, all the clerks wore nametags and we kept going until we found her hanging out in a corner looking at one of the books on display. I guessed Rina was somewhere at the end of her forties and had an arty look with chopped-off hair that had a rainbow tint. Her neck was decorated with a tattooed necklace and her ears were full of piercings. Tizzy and I had a story ready. We were shopping for a new art student and wanted to know what we should get. It seemed like it would keep her with us long enough to get some information.

'She'll need a box to carry her paints and brushes,' Rina said. She showed us a selection of what looked like plastic toolboxes. We stood looking at the different colors, seeming to be debating which one to pick. I winked at Tizzy and she nodded to show she got the message.

'I certainly hope Geraldine takes my advice and goes into commercial art. Fine arts leads to starvation, or having to have another job to pay the rent,' Tizzy said with a nod for emphasis.

Rina's ears seemed to prick up and I knew she was listening as we fumbled through the paint boxes, finally picking out a royal blue one.

'You must know about artists,' Tizzy said, looking at the middle-aged woman. 'Am I right or what?'

'Yes, but then there are artists like Michael Angel,' I said before she could answer. 'His paintings are selling for a bunch and now he's nominated for a national award that will only up the value of his art. I just love that Scotty dog.' I mentioned the reception and all the attention he'd gotten.

I heard Rina sputtering as she led us toward the tubes of acrylic paints. 'Let me tell you about him . . .' she said, trying to contain her tone. 'I should have been the one with him at that event.' We both feigned surprise at her comment. 'He's my ex,' she added with distaste. 'Just like you said, we were starving fine artists, doing other jobs to pay the bills so we could do our art. And then, after he left me, he becomes the toast of the town.'

She opened the blue box and started dropping tubes of paint in, which hit the plastic with an angry clatter. 'And he's full of himself being an important painter. It was all luck that the Scotty dog stuff got noticed by that influencer. And now the same paintings that nobody noticed are hanging in a fancy gallery with a big price. If he hadn't dumped me for that boring art teacher, I'd be in on it all and getting those eyeballs on my sculptures, thanks to being the spouse of the dog painter. Instead, I'm doing this . . .' she said with disgust.

We moved on to brushes and she grabbed what she said were basic ones and threw them in the box with the paints. Then she gave me one of the hand-held baskets for the rest of the supplies and dropped in pens, pencils, sketchbooks and a set of watercolors.

She looked at me. 'Never hook up with an artist. They're bad news. Always looking for their next nude model. That's their line, you know. I looked the other way when it seemed like a revolving door of different women, but I should have known when he focused on one, it was trouble.' She threw in a mixing tray into the basket. 'But then the same would prob-ably have happened to her.' A managerial-looking person stopped next to us to pick up a box of fallen colored pencils. As he stood, he gave her the evil eye, obviously having heard her angry rant.

'Rina, weren't you supposed to take your break?'

He took over for her and it became awkward, because we didn't want to buy all the art supplies. I finally said it seemed better to get Geraldine a gift card so she could pick out what she wanted on her own. Then Tizzy rushed in, improving on it by saying that we really should talk to her mother first. The man gave us the evil eye now, and then I saw a display of multicolored ink pads like the one Maeve had introduced me to. It had been such a success with Caleb, I'd thought it could work for other love-letter clients. I grabbed one that had a different selection of colors than the one I had and some more cardstock. Tizzy looked at me as if I'd lost my mind.

'I'll explain later,' I said under my breath as I went to pay.

As a treat for our efforts, we went back to Macy's. The Walnut Room still had the same elegance and trademark Frango ice-cream pie from the days when it had been Marshall Field's. We were seated by a window in the wood-paneled restaurant. Water trickled in the fountain in the center of the place, though not for much longer. It would be drained and draped before they put up the two-story-tall Christmas tree that was a tradition left over from the original store. The only thing that had changed was how early it was put up. They barely waited for Halloween.

It made me momentarily sad to think of it. Just like a lot of other Chicago people, it had been a tradition to have lunch by the Christmas tree. Well, with my mother. My father had tried to keep it up, but it wasn't the same. It was like a duty for him, but had been somehow magic with her. I thought of the snowmen made out of balls of vanilla ice cream rolled in coconut, and Santa Claus making the rounds.

Tizzy looked at the plastic bag on the empty chair. 'So, what's the story with the art supplies?'

I had made it a point to keep my love-letter clients on the down-low since I was basically fronting for them, but I decided to tell Tizzy about Caleb because he lived next door to Maeve.

'This is one of those things you have to keep quiet,' I said.

'All you have to do is say that, and it will go no further. You have no idea the secrets that I've kept.'

'Like what?' I said, suddenly interested.

She gave me a helpless look. 'I'd blow what I just said if I told you.'

'I see your point.'

'So you can trust me with anything,' Tizzy said, mimicking zipping up her lips.

'I'm afraid it's going to be a disappointment after all that,' I said before telling her about Caleb, his silent wife and the art project. She remembered that I'd asked her about him, but not given her an explanation. She nodded with understanding.

'So, that's why you wanted information about him.'

'It turns out that his wife lives next door to Maeve's and, before he did whatever he did to get his wife so angry, he lived there as well. He told me that he watched Maeve doing yoga in the backyard.'

'It sounds a little creepy, but about right. Those numbers guys are in their own world.' The server came and we ordered finger sandwiches and a piece of the chocolate mint pie to share.

'So, what do you think about Rina?' I said while we waited for our food.

'She certainly could have done it,' Tizzy said. 'She sounded pretty angry.'

'So her motive would have been revenge. As for how she could have done it . . .' I said, taking a moment to think over what I knew. 'Suppose she told Maeve that she wanted to smooth things over. She could have said she wanted it just to be between the two of them, without Michael being involved. Maeve seemed to feel guilty about taking up with Michael while he was still married, so the idea of making things right with Rina might have appealed to her. Rina would have had to know that Maeve would invite her up to the attic. She certainly looked like somebody who would know how to get hold of some pills that knock people out. If Maeve was dead to the world, suffocating her would have been easy. Even a trash bag over her head would have worked.' I looked at Tizzy. 'You saw Rina's hands with all those calluses. I bet she's really strong from squeezing all that clay; she could have managed to get her down the stairs. She could have thought it would be chalked up to an accident. The perfect crime. All because Maeve was willing to mend fences with her.'

Tizzy's eyes widened and she laughed. 'Caught you in a cliché,' she said, shaking her finger in mock scolding.

'Guilty,' I said. 'But back to Rina as the killer. Thinking it could be her is a start, but we need proof to show it was her.'

EIGHTEEN

'I did a little research,' Theo said, 'and most murders are committed by people close to the victim, and spouses are the number one suspects.' Theo seemed so excited about offering the information he found, that I didn't want to tell him that was pretty much a 'duh' to anyone who read mysteries or worked in law enforcement.

'You mean, Michael Angel?' I said, and he nodded.

Tizzy and I had gone our separate ways when we got home from checking out Rina, with a plan to regroup at their house at sherry time. She was anxious to include Theo, and I really enjoyed getting together with them, particularly since it was Saturday night and I didn't want to sit home alone.

Theo knew without me having to say anything that I was back to drinking straight sparkling water and that I liked to get a sniff of his martini. He had his laptop ready to do research as needed.

'He would be the number one suspect, but I'm not sure what the motive would be,' I began. 'I looked through more of the material she gave me and, from all that I've read, it seems that Maeve adored him and was always promoting his art.' I mentioned what the headmistress at the school had said about Maeve trying to get Michael's paintings seen by parents at the school who were art collectors. Theo asked if they were all Scotty pictures. 'No. I don't know. The headmistress just talked about before and after he'd gotten famous.'

'Did it work?' Theo asked.

I shrugged, trying to remember what the woman had said. 'I'm not sure. But what's the difference? She was still trying to help. Who kills somebody who does that?'

'There's always the old standby,' Theo said. 'He found somebody else and it was the easiest way to make himself single.'

Tizzy and I looked at each other, remembering our meeting with his first wife. 'Isn't that what Rina implied? That Michael would do the same thing to Maeve that he did to her,' I said. Tizzy nodded in agreement.

'When he left Rina, he had nothing, but it's a different story now,' Tizzy said. 'People do crazy stuff when money's involved.' She looked at her husband. 'Veronica figured out how it could have happened, and that whoever did it probably thought it would be ruled an accident. Anybody who has back stairs knows how steep they are. And dark and uncarpeted, so it would be believable that someone could fall hard and hit their head.'

She had me tell Theo what I thought might have happened. I had to backtrack and tell him about her workroom and my visits there with her hospitality.

'That sounds very plausible,' Theo said. He went back to looking up things on the laptop and seemed to have found something useful. 'If that's what happened, it's too bad your client didn't have one of these . . .' He turned the screen so we could see it. There was a product on Amazon that tested drinks for the presence of drugs that made people black out. They weren't very expensive, and Theo was curious so he ordered a kit.

By now we'd long finished our drinks and they had plans for their evening, so I went home. I was busy mulling over everything we'd talked about to keep myself from thinking that I was going to be home alone on a Saturday night. Michael really did seem like the best suspect. But best suspect didn't mean he did it, and all I had was conjecture. I decided to put it to rest and spend the time working on the manuscript. I had changed my mind on how I was going to write about the school. Instead of making it impersonal, I'd figured a way to make it so it seemed like it was coming from her. I sat down at the computer and began to type.

I believe that there is no good or bad in art. Just personal expression. That's what I have always told my students. It's been a dream come true to teach at the Dupont Academy. The environment is wonderful for the kids.

Everything is offered to them in a way that makes learning
exciting. I like that there is a diverse group of students
and, because they wear uniforms, they seem equal.
  I knew that some of the parents were art collectors
and hoped getting Michael's paintings in front of them
would help his career. He was frustrated that the only
place he could show his work was in the coffee house
he managed. Every time there was a fundraiser with an
auction, I made sure Michael donated a painting.

I stopped here, not sure how to continue. I was creating this
out of what I'd heard. I realized it would be more interesting
if I described the paintings that had been in the school auction.
Were they pictures with the dog, or something like the ones
I'd seen on the wall in his studio? I made a note to find out.

I decided to stop after that, and I used the last of the bread
to make myself a peanut butter sandwich. Toasting the bread was
the only thing that made it palatable. Sandwich in hand, I
looked through my collection of old movies, hoping for some
entertainment to get my mind off everything. I pulled out
Indiscreet, which turned out not to be the greatest distraction.
It was a very funny movie, but the plot centered on Cary Grant
pretending he was married to keep himself from having more
than a fling with Ingrid Bergman. It made me think of Ben.
The only difference was that he was really married.

And then it was Sunday again and there was nothing to
make a special breakfast. I tried to convince myself that it was
a good thing. It showed that I wasn't stuck in a rut. I ended
up with the good coffee and a bunch of packets of saltine
crackers that had come with the to-go soup I'd gotten at the
coffee shop weeks ago. As soon as I read the paper, I looked
over at Rocky who was snoozing on the couch. I might have
been reduced to eating saltines, but he'd never come close to
running out of cat food. I was a responsible pet parent. 'I'm
going to the grocery store,' I announced. The cat opened his
eyes for a moment, as if to say it's about time.

I grabbed the folded-up shopping cart and went out. I'd
tried to do mindful walking and notice every crack in the
sidewalk, but I slipped into mindless walking as I went back

to thinking about Maeve. I knew the route by heart and paid no attention to the contrast of the newer box-shaped town houses on one side of the street to the more interesting vintage ones on the other. I thought back to our meetings. Once we'd gotten past all the 'will she, won't she' hire me, I liked her. It made it even worse about what had happened. I wanted to do justice to the memoir. I thought back on her tease about the ending, thinking over if there was any hint in what I'd found out so far. I also wondered if her death was connected to it. A momentary shudder passed through my mind. What if her death was connected to that and the killer thought I knew whatever the secret was? I pushed away the thought and forced myself to think about how beautifully the trees formed a canopy over 56th Street.

Pulling out one of the red shopping carts at Trader Joe's forced me to stay in the here and now. It also reminded me of my obsession with clichés as I pondered whether *here and now* counted as one. It absolutely caught the meaning of being – well – where I was and the current moment. I chuckled to myself as I decided to let it slip. I'd eaten saltines for breakfast and I was letting a cliché slip. Didn't that mean I was loosening up and becoming a real *whatever* sort of person, I thought with a smile. Didn't *whatever* say it so well? Like no matter what happened, you'd go along with it and be OK.

I was reaching for a jar of peanut butter to replenish my dwindling supply when a cart smacked into mine.

'Sorry,' a voice said. I looked to see who the offender was and was surprised to see Caleb. He was already rearranging the items in his cart that had been knocked around during the crash. I was always curious about other people's groceries. I'd even played games making up stories about the people in line ahead of me, based on what they'd bought. You could tell a lot about people by what they shopped for. Caleb's cart was easy to read, even if I hadn't known his circumstances. He had a lot of frozen entrées, two bags of cookies and a selection of chips – both corn and potato – and a six-pack of pumpkin ale. It screamed guy living alone with no sense of food groups like vegetables and fruit.

'That card-making we did was brilliant,' he said. 'But there's a problem. The ones I left were so professional looking, she won't realize I made them. We need to make more, and whatever you come up with to put in the cards has to make it clear that I did the artwork.'

Inwardly I laughed at how he never made small talk, but just got right down to business.

'I bought some more supplies. I have ink pads with interesting colors and more cardstock,' I said. 'When do you want to come over and do it?'

He didn't pause for a breath before suggesting the current afternoon. I had planned to go back to writing about Maeve's school, but he seemed so eager that I agreed.

I put away my groceries, which had plenty of fruits and vegetables along with some cookies and popcorn. I wasn't averse to some non-essential food groups. Without thinking, I'd picked up a six-pack of the pumpkin ale, thinking it was something Ben would like. I'd already paid for it when I thought of Assleigh, as Sara referred to her, and that there was no telling if Ben would ever be at my place in a situation where I'd offer him a beer. I stuck the bottles in the pantry, thinking I could always bring them over to Tizzy's. With Theo's curiosity, he'd probably love to try it.

The doorbell sounded just as I was putting the cart back in the closet. Caleb had an eager look as he came up the stairs. The animation in his face gave his appearance a little more life than usual. I looked at yet another plaid shirt and navy-blue cotton pants and wondered if he wanted any wardrobe advice. It was amazing what clothes could do. I imagined him dressed in different outfits. It was hard to keep my thoughts from showing as I pictured him in a tuxedo, then a tracksuit, then a regular suit, and finally a pair of jeans and a pullover sweater. The last one would have been my choice.

The only breakfast things to clear off the table were some wrappers from the crackers. I spread the newspaper over the table in case he got carried away with the ink. I put out the supplies and invited him to sit. He didn't need any demonstration this time and went at it right away. He had apparently been thinking about it because he started creating his own things. Meanwhile I asked him about his wife's neighbors again.

'I told you I watched her doing yoga in the yard,' he said as he went wild with the art project. He'd lost interest in the hearts and flowers again and made a centipede with a creepy expression and a selection of spiders and bugs. 'What about if we say I want to catch her in my web,' he suggested. 'That isn't exactly what I would have thought of, but if that's what you want.' He nodded and I went back to my questions. 'So that's all you know about her?'

Caleb had fallen in love with a sort of fluorescent pea-green ink and was making what I assumed were outer-space creatures. 'Sometimes there was someone with her.'

I tried not to appear too interested as I asked for a description of the person, which was – to use a cliché – like pulling teeth, since he wasn't that observant. Once I heard that it was a he, I started to think Michael, but when Caleb added that his black hair was in a ponytail, I knew it couldn't be. Michael had dark longish hair, but it was definitely not black and it barely brushed the back of his neck. Unfortunately, that was all I could get out of him.

I left him to work on his final cards and went into the kitchen to put together a new pot of vegetable stew.

When I went back to the dining room, Caleb held up the card he'd made. 'Now we just need you to write something for the inside,' he said.

I looked at it and tried not to show my reaction. It was original. He'd made a heart with a piece blacked out and a bug running away with something red in its mouth. Another had little green outer-space creatures and a pile of pumpkins with a witch flying over. 'I thought I would make it seasonally appropriate,' he said, clearly proud of his work.

I'd tried to get him to make something a little more romantic, but he was enamored with his own creations. It was a challenge to come up with some content that went along with his art. While he continued to play with the art supplies, I wrote: *A piece of my heart is missing without you, You're out of this world to me, There's no trick with you, it's all treat.* And finally, *I'm bugged that I can't talk to you.*

I hoped she had a sense of humor, which was doubtful since he didn't seem to. But he could see the connection of what I wrote to the artwork. It was all like an equation to him. We made sure to add a line that it had been designed and executed for his Prime Number, as he called her, by him. He said he was going to leave one of them at her door with a bag of candy corn.

I thought of the quote I'd created for Maeve: that there was no good or bad art, just personal expression. His work was certainly that.

NINETEEN

There was something almost too quiet about Sunday night. Despite the way everything had become 24/7, it felt like the world took a last-minute deep breath before the new week began. But instead of doing the same myself, I was busy at my computer. I'd spent the whole time after Caleb left going through some more of Maeve's notes. I found a half-done piece she'd written and gave it a polish. I kept her title of *First Time the Star.*

I wondered how Michael would react when we went to the first gallery reception where there were a number of the Scotty paintings on prominent display. If he was uneasy, he hid it well and, if anything, he acted as if he was in the place he was always meant to be. He'd never been one of the solitary artist types. He positively beamed when Zander introduced him to the invited guests. He had the story perfected, saying that the image of the Scotty had been lingering in his imagination since he was a kid. Seeing how happy he was after all his frustration for so long, all of it seemed worth it.

I was pleased with what I'd typed in the computer, and kept on going. This time I created an entry I called *The House on Harper.* I remembered how Maeve had talked about her attic enclave, and I found bits and pieces she'd noted about the house, though I knew that I still needed to get another look at the outside to pick out some details to include.

I remember the day we moved into the house. It was like a dream come true. Michael would have been happy in a high rise with a view of the lake, but I want a place with a porch and a yard. I had wanted to live on Harper for as long as I could remember. I had walked past those houses with their interesting details, thinking someday one of them would be mine. And the sales of the Scotty paintings made it a reality. We'd been sharing a small apartment, and Michael had used the room above the coffee house as a studio. The house gave us lots of space and the sun porch on the side was perfect for Michael's studio. It would be what I considered part of the public space in the house. He liked the idea of company being able to wander through his studio to see his workspace and discover the painting he was working on.

For me, it was all about the third floor. I never thought of it as the attic. It was my own personal space. I wasn't like Michael, throwing everything open for the world to see. I kept it for invited guests where I could limit their access. Michael and I were different, and I liked to think we complemented each other.

I planned to fill out the piece with the history of the street and the way it was like its own little neighborhood within the bigger one, after I'd had another look at the houses, so I could put in some specific details about the different styles.

I even found a way to use something from Rina's rant and what I knew about Maeve's relationship with Michael's daughter. I called it *Baggage.*

I had to accept that Michael didn't come unencumbered. Things would have been different if I had known he was married. I never would have gotten so involved until I knew he was free. But I have to wonder if his ex would have been any less hostile if they'd been divorced when he and I got together. I knew she was upset that his success had come when she received no benefit. She blamed me, but he was the one who wanted out. The personality of an artist?

I wanted to get along with his daughter, Suzzanna, but discovered that it had to come from both sides. She maintained a separate relationship with her father, becoming his assistant and part of his entourage. Did she simply not like me, or did she blame me for her parents' breakup?

When I finally called it a night, I had a feeling of satisfaction that I'd found my stride with putting together the manuscript. No need for chamomile tea or crochet.

I spent Monday writing more entries. I used the poetic license that the publisher had talked about and filled out some snippets with my own words. It was pretty clear that things had changed. While Michael never tired of the gallery receptions and parties at the home of wealthy art collectors, Maeve did. I began to see entries in the journal that said things like: *Not another party. Why do they even call them that? They're no fun, for me anyway. I would call them endurance evenings. Michael doesn't seem to care if I stay home.*

And then it was Tuesday and time to get ready for the writing group. I always vowed to look over their work before the last minute, but it never turned out that way. Reading their material again never took long – it was writing the comments that took time. Having been on the other side of it, I knew how much the comments meant, even to Ed. Everyone was like Daryl in a way. They didn't really want to hear criticism, but not insincere sugary kudos either.

Ed's pages were easy. He'd made it clear he only wanted help with his grammar and punctuation. Even so I added, *Good Work. Keep it up.* I agonized with Daryl. I wanted to draw lines through half her copy and find a way to tell her it was crisper without all of it. But I didn't. Instead, I reminded myself that a lot of it was taste. Not every style of writing pleased me, but it might be fine with other people. I ended up saying: *Keep your eyes open for extra sentences. Always good to be straightforward. Definitely coming along. Keep going.* Tizzy was easy. She actually wanted me to edit her writing. No problem if I took out sentences or made suggestions of word changes.

And then there was Ben's. I'd left it to last because I had all kinds of emotions about it. He'd been doing so well at expressing himself and now he'd gone back to the cold, terse style he'd started with. He had zipped all his emotions back up. Finally, I wrote, *What happened to the cop who helped the homeless guy? I want him back.*

I wasn't even sure that Ben would come to the group session. The way he'd rushed off the last time – not even coming in, but just dropping off the food from his sister's and then saying he had to get home – had sounded ominous to me. Despite what Ben said about wanting his cake and eating it too, he didn't seem cut out for juggling women.

When seven rolled around, Tizzy, Ed and Daryl all arrived together and went back to the dining room. I could hear by Ed's tone that he was anxious to get started, and I was going to follow them when I heard the knock.

'Sorry,' Ben said, coming in the door. He had the impersonal cop tone, then it broke as he asked me if everything was OK. What was I supposed to say?

'Things are kind of up in the air. I wasn't sure you'd come,' I said, trying to emulate his detached tone as the two of us joined the others.

Tizzy sensed the discomfort of the moment and tried to cover it. 'One of Veronica's clients died and she's trying to piece together the person's memoir.' I flinched at what she said, even though it was hardly a secret anymore, and I had not told her not to tell anyone.

Nobody was interested in Ben anymore and everyone looked at me, waiting for me to say something. The only ones who didn't know about Maeve were Ed and Daryl, so I decided I might as well fill them in. Ed was interested because he'd heard about the incident. Daryl seemed more concerned with my comments on the previous weeks' pages, and kept trying to cover up the new tattoo of a rose on her finger.

I tried not to talk about my work during the group's time, and I think they mostly agreed, but after what Tizzy had blurted out, they all wanted details. I explained the difficulty in the situation of working from note fragments. Tizzy interjected that she and I had already met the first Mrs Angel, only it was really Mrs Wolinski, which led to a discussion on pretentious names. The one that bugged them the most was when someone put their initial first before a middle name. That would have made me V. Helen Blackstone. I suppose it was pretentious, but it did kind of stand out.

As long as they were all talking about Maeve, I was curious

about how they thought I should proceed. 'You know it was the husband,' Ed said. 'It's always the spouse. Maybe he wanted a divorce and it would cost too much and easier to just get her out of the way. You need to find out more about him. Maybe he was into kinky stuff that she didn't like.'

Everyone else groaned at Ed's comment, but he was right about needing to find out more about Michael Angel, as in, was there an immediate reason he might want to be free of Maeve? I put my hand up to stop the conversation and get down to their writing. I was surprised when Ed seemed disappointed. But he recovered quickly and wanted to be read first. His pages were the usual sexual acrobatics. And when anyone suggested he needed more romance and less heaving body parts, he glowered.

Tizzy and Daryl's work were read without incident.

I couldn't tell if Ben had any pages. Would he even have time since he was dealing with Assleigh? I had to stop thinking of her with that name or I'd mistakenly call her that to him. It would make me look like everything I didn't want to be – petty and jealous.

He pulled out some rolled-up papers from his jacket pocket and handed them to Tizzy to read, explaining it was about a cop making a domestic violence call.

He had to deal with a fight between two women over a man. One woman was graspy, but also seductive and beautiful and they had a history together. The other woman was kind and funny. The cop talked to the two women, trying to make peace and figure out who to arrest. The seductive one was insistent that he should not arrest her. She blamed the other woman, and said that the man belonged with her. The kind, funny one offered herself up, saying she hadn't meant to cause a problem between them. The man tells the cop to arrest the seductive one. And then it was time for comments.

'You ought to spice it up a little. What about making it a *ménage à trois*?' Ed said with a leer.

'It sounds to me like it was a variation on the King Solomon story about the two women fighting over a baby,' Tizzy offered.

'And the judge says he'll cut the baby in two and give them each half,' Daryl added. 'One of the women says to give the baby to the other woman rather than that. And then the judge determines that she loves the baby enough to be willing to give it up rather than allow it to be hurt, and he decides she should get it.'

Ed seemed perplexed until Tizzy explained it, and then he shrugged and said it wasn't quite the same.

It was close enough to the situation with Ben to make me embarrassed, and I was glad that only Tizzy knew about the return of Ben's wife. And maybe a little uneasy at the way he'd described the other woman. In my mind I'd imagined Ashleigh as a sharp-tongued shrew, not a hot babe. The other woman was kind and funny. OK, I knew that never in my wildest dreams would I be described as a hot babe, but *kind and funny?*

The group broke up after that and I followed them to the front door. Ben was in the rear and kept looking back at me. I had tried to keep a neutral expression, but I guess I didn't do a very good job. 'Do you need dinner?' he said with a hopeful look.

'I have my own,' I said. 'I made a big pot of vegetable stew.'

The others had already gone out my front door and he hung back. 'Can we at least talk?' he asked. 'I need to explain.'

I am not good at being tough or even staying angry, so I agreed. Even though the others were already on their way down the stairs, he went through the charade of leaving.

When he returned, he was holding a piece of chocolate angel food cake. 'You said you had dinner, but you didn't mention dessert.'

I didn't know what to do next and I was glad when he went right to explaining.

'You know how you always say write what you know,' he said with a small smile. 'It just didn't come off like I meant it. The woman who wins is the one who has substance and a heart. I played up the other one's looks to exaggerate.'

'You did a good job of talking your way out of that,' I said.

'That's one of the things you learn in cop school. Conflict negotiation.' He didn't make a move toward the couch. 'Well?' And I picked up that he was waiting to see if I was going to need more. I didn't want a flowery speech. I might write them for others, but they didn't really do much for me. I always thought that the people I wrote love letters for got points for the effort more than the words. A bunch of clichés floated through my mind. *It's the thought that counts, actions speak louder than words* and *pretty is as pretty does.* I smiled at him. 'I'm good.' I expected him to say he had to rush off as he'd done before, but he didn't make a move and glanced toward the couch. It was probably a mistake, but I invited him to sit and offered him a bottle of the pumpkin ale with a warning that it wasn't chilled.

TWENTY

Tizzy was going to be my wingman again, or should I say wing-person. It was getting so confusing with how people wanted to be referred to. Now there was 'they' and 'them' in addition to 'he' or 'she'. I don't think she really cared how I referred to her as long she got to come along. I was standing on the corner waiting for her. She had gotten Alex to let her go by telling him it was connected to the reception we'd gone to in his stead.

The sky was almost not cloudy, sort of like a half-smile. There was enough sunlight getting through to make shadows, but not bright enough to give the sky more than a faint apricot hue and certainly not enough to add any warmth. A breeze sent a shower of leaves cascading around me as it cut through my sweater, making me understand the value of a nylon jacket.

Tizzy came down the street with a spring in her step, obviously looking forward to our adventure. I was glad to have her along on another undercover mission. We were good at playing off each other's conversation, which we wanted someone to overhear. It was also good to have another pair of ears to make note of what went on, too.

I had told her this was the combo plan. I was looking for material to put in the book and also to figure out who killed Maeve.

'Ed's probably right,' Tizzy said when we'd started walking to the train. 'Theo did more research and it pointed out that most murders were committed by people who knew each other. Who could be closer than a spouse?'

'But what Theo really meant was that the murderer *knew* the murderee. There are other people who knew Maeve. After meeting Rina, I was ready to make a citizen's arrest. But I need to consider everyone in Maeve's orbit before I make a judgment. And, it's always good to have proof, too.'

'You have a point,' Tizzy said. We went up the stairs to the Metra tracks just as the train was pulling in.

I had given up on talking to Michael Angel again. He'd been rather hostile, and I was worried that he'd press me more about seeing what I'd written. No way was I going to give him a chance to demand I change anything. It had been Tizzy's suggestion we go to the gallery where we'd attended the reception. It was a public place, and it would seem natural to talk to them about Michael Angel and hopefully Maeve. I might even be able to check on his alibi for the time that Maeve was killed.

I had done my best to dress like a wealthy art collector, which meant my ninja outfit with the addition of a colorful silk scarf that looked almost like a Hermès design.

Tizzy was the perfect wing-whatever. She could start a conversation with anybody, and she picked up on my cues easily. And she was helpful at taking care of details, like finding out the directions to the gallery since Theo had driven us there when we went before. It turned out to be just a short walk down Randolph.

As soon as we walked in, we were greeted by a woman dressed in a black skirt and black sweater with some interesting silver jewelry, making me realize my clothing choice was perfect. Her eye glazed my scarf. It was arranged so the pattern wasn't quite discernible, but I think it passed her muster because she offered us both a warm smile.

'Do you have an appointment?' she asked, and I suddenly felt deflated. I should have figured that. I started to say no, but Tizzy gave my arm a nudge and took over. I almost choked when I heard her start talking with a Southern accent. She turned toward me just long enough to give me a wink and I remembered that she'd called the place before and must be trying to disguise her voice. Tizzy really took being my wingman seriously. She threw around her boss's name and his connection to the Hyde Park Art Center in a whirlwind of comments meant to imply that we were more than lookie-loos. It seemed to work. The woman brightened and said she'd be happy to waive the requirement in our case and introduced herself as Melanie Gilbert. She subtly asked for our IDs and asked us to sign the guest book.

'We like to escort our visitors so that we can offer background on the pieces,' she said. In other words, a sales pitch. It was probably also to make sure we didn't touch anything or have a snack as we looked – or try to take a souvenir.

'It would be a pleasure to have your expert comments,' Tizzy said, laying it on a little thick in her Southern belle voice.

There had been such a crowd at the reception and, since I had no idea the gallery would be connected to my client, I hadn't really paid that much attention to the artwork. The only thing that had registered was seeing the unpleasant woman I'd met at Maeve's who had turned out to be her stepdaughter.

'Let me tell you a little about us first,' our escort said. 'We like to say that art is in Zander Paul's genes. The gallery was started by his late father, who introduced him to the world of artists and collectors. The goal of the gallery is to bring the two worlds together. Zander is intent on carrying on the tradition of discovering fresh faces in the art world, along with offering works of known masters.'

I started to ask her questions about how the gallery worked. Did they own the paintings, and how did they pick what they were going to include? She seemed a little put off by my questions. 'There's no reason for you to worry about any of that. Just enjoy the viewing,' she said.

I was concerned that my questions might be brushed off, and had a ready reason for asking, with a slight stretching of the truth. 'I'm a writer,' I began. 'I'm pitching an idea for an article about contemporary art, and I'm trying to gather up as much background information first as I can.' My profession was a convenient shield for asking a lot of questions.

'Oh,' she said with sparked interest. 'Of course, we'd love it if you mentioned the gallery by name. Actually, it is a mixture between artwork that Zander Paul Galleries owns, and those by artists looking for a place to display their work who we have offered space to. We also take works from collectors who want to take advantage of the appreciation of works they own.'

It sounded like a lot of words to say they wanted to cash in on a painting that had gone up in value.

Personally, art was an emotional thing for me. I liked it or I didn't, irrespective of someone telling me how I should feel or how much it was worth.

'Some galleries feature just one artist or a couple of them. We have an eclectic group,' she said, leading us into a large area, painted a stark white. It looked a lot different without the crowd at the reception blocking the view. The artwork was spaced so that each piece stood by itself. She stopped at an abstract painting that looked like a red square in the middle of a white canvas and started on her pitch. She pointed out some grayish lines along the bottom of the red box and, as she named the artist, said that he had tried to capture the shadows on a pile of canvases in his studio. I squinted and tried to see what she was talking about. I supposed that the marking on the bottom of the red square could indicate a kind of shadow from a pile of canvases, but it escaped me why that was important. She did a little pitch on the artist, with most of the emphasis on how the value of his paintings had been escalating since another of his paintings had been seen in the background during an interview with Brad Pitt about possibly being the first non-British James Bond. 'Everyone knows what impeccable taste he has,' she said, looking at us. We both nodded and murmured something about it being impressive.

I looked ahead at all the artwork in the room, figuring she'd give us a pitch on each of the paintings and then move on to the sculpture in the middle. I really wanted to cut to the chase. Yes, it was a cliché, but it said it so perfectly. I'd looked into the derivation and it came from the film industry in the 1920s, and literally meant cutting to the exciting chase sequence which was the best part of early movies.

'I'm really interested in Michael Angel. Do you have any of his works?' I said before she could begin her pitch on the next work of art.

'Yes, we do. In fact his daughter just joined our staff. It's too bad she isn't working today because she could give you even more background on him,' Melanie said. I feigned disappointment while thinking how grateful I was that she wasn't there.

'We have a whole gallery dedicated to him. Let me show

you.' She led us into the next room and my eye went right to a canvas on the back wall. 'That's his newest. It's seasonally appropriate,' she said with a smile. The black dog was in the foreground, staring out with its soulful eyes that somehow also had a feeling of fun. A decorated altar was in the background with a vase of marigolds, a blue patterned cup, a loaf of bread and a skeleton in dancing mode. 'It's called *The Scotty and the Day of the Dead*,' Melanie said. I noticed she'd pulled out a piece of paper and looked at it surreptitiously. 'The holiday is celebrated on the first and second of November, honoring the departed with traditional marigold flowers, a favored drink and food, with a skeleton added for fun.' She stopped and looked at the paper again. 'It's supposed to be joyous rather than somber.'

To say that I loved it was an understatement. No matter what I thought of Michael Angel personally, I loved the painting. I glanced at the card with the price and almost choked. Maybe if I won the lottery.

Tizzy moved toward an adjacent wall that had several landscapes. I joined her, noting that each had a nude woman in it rather randomly placed. Melanie rushed to join us and began what sounded like a scripted pitch.

'These are done by Michael as well. They show the breadth of his talent.' She went on about the style of trees, the way he handled the light and the graceful nude figures. I nodded and pretended to be impressed, but maybe I just wasn't into nude women. I was glad to move on to another of the dog pictures. She followed me, going on about the deeper meaning of the Scotty and how the soulful eyes seemed to exude love. I was more interested in the painting itself. It was called *The Scotty and Friends*. The black-haired dog was in the center, flanked on one side by a stylized Jack Russell terrier. Michael had captured the short-haired dog's *bon vivant* type of personality. A black-and-white cat that resembled Rocky was on the other side. It seemed like the cat was smiling. Just looking at it made me smile. I didn't dare look at the price tag.

I asked Melanie how they discovered new artists. 'Zander goes to all the art fairs and small art shows, hoping to find the next big star.'

'And that's how he found Michael Angel,' I said as more of a statement than a question.

She stopped for a moment. 'I think that was more of an experiment,' she said rather cryptically.

She pointed to an adjacent wall and another of the Scotty paintings. 'That one is called *The Scotty and the Lake*.'

I loved that one, too. The foreground of this one had a tree branch lacy with leaves dangling over the Scotty dog. He had the same expression that drew me in. There was something moody and maybe a little sinister about the lake in the background.

'We have prints available on this one, for the budget minded,' she said. I didn't want to tell her that the best my budget would allow was the postcard I'd bought at the reception.

Tizzy nudged me and I got my mind off the paintings back to the reason we were there. 'I'm sure you've met Michael Angel,' I said to Melanie. 'What's he like?'

'Utterly charming,' she said. 'It's such a pleasure to have an artist who likes to meet our patrons. It's like he was born for the spotlight. And now he's nominated for that important honor and being featured in a documentary.'

'What about his family?' I asked.

'I told you his daughter works for us, and she's also been acting as his assistant lately.'

'Then he's not married?'

'It's not really our concern,' she said hesitantly.

'I suppose it isn't,' Tizzy said. 'Veronica is only asking for the article. She wants to know about the life of the artist. Is he like Picasso with two wives, six mistresses and countless lovers?' I had to keep myself from laughing at how direct her comment was. It was probably from more of Theo's research.

Melanie blushed and seemed uncomfortable. 'He has had two wives, but I don't know about the rest of it.' Then her voice dropped. 'His second wife just died in a horrible accident in their home.'

Tizzy and I nodded with reverence, and probably both realized at the same time that her comment had just ended any more chances of probing into his personal life.

She brought us back to the front and seemed anxious to be

done with us. But before she could escort us to the door, two people came in. I recognized Zander Paul and Sophia from the reception. I suppose she had a last name, but I'd only ever heard her referred to by her first name and her YouTube channel. There had been a lot going on then and I hadn't realized they had any connection to Maeve, and so I had only given them a cursory appraisal at the time.

Trying to appear casual, I checked them out. He looked the part of a gallery owner. A combination of business and arty. The suit and the open-collared dress shirt were the business part, and the nubby scarf in tones of brown that hung loose against the lapels was the arty part.

Sophia was distinctive rather than pretty. Her dark hair was so shiny, it looked shellacked, and she accentuated her generous lips with bright red lipstick. I was pretty sure the scarf she was wearing was a real Hermès.

Melanie explained that she'd been showing us around and that we were Michael Angel fans. The gallery owner, thinking we might be buyers, introduced himself and Sophia, and waited until we gave our names as well. To say he was solicitous was an understatement. I hoped I could use that in my favor.

It took a moment before I noticed the dog at Sophia's feet. 'He looks just like the dog in the painting,' I exclaimed. I remembered that at the reception she'd said something about the resemblance of her dog to Michael's paintings, and that was how they'd all come together, but I was curious about hearing her version again when it had relevance.

'Everybody says that,' she said with a smile. 'My sweetie Drexel wasn't that actual model, but I think somehow he crept into the imagination of the artist.' She pointed out the small counter set up in the corner. I recognized the display of posters and other merchandise as the spot where I'd gotten my postcard. 'Hard to believe that he'd never laid eyes on my darling when he painted that.' She grabbed a T-shirt with the image of the painting. She looked from me to Tizzy. 'You don't know who I am, do you?' she said. She turned to her escort. 'Tell them,' she commanded. Then she laughed. 'If I say it, it sounds self-serving, but if he does, it sounds better.'

'She's Sophia of the Second Chance Sophia YouTube

channel.' He gave it a moment to see if either of us responded, but Tizzy was following my lead and we both had blank looks.

'She, with her trusty companion Drexel, turns trash into treasures. She can fix anything with Sukey's Super Stick and a few other supplies.' Sophia fluttered her eyes as if she was embarrassed by his hyperbole and then stepped in. She had pulled out business cards and handed them to the two of us. 'This has the link, in case you're interested. I'd love for you both to subscribe.' She made it sound like getting a personal invitation was supposed to excite us. I glanced at the card and saw the painting was her logo. She saw me looking at it. 'Everybody loves that picture. It's like every one of my subscribers had gotten a T-shirt or a poster.'

While Tizzy and I were making friends with the dog and eyeing the merchandise, I noticed that Zander had pulled Melanie aside. No doubt she'd clued him in to how we weren't potential customers.

The solicitous manner was gone when he rejoined us. He linked his arm with Sophia. 'We just stopped in to drop something off,' he said. He nodded to our guide. 'Melanie can help you with whatever you need.' Melanie watched as the three of them went out the door.

It seemed like she suddenly remembered what I'd said about writing an article. 'They're off to a charity event in Highland Park,' she said. 'Part of the gallery business is socializing with potential collectors.' I was enjoying her use of words. The way she said collectors instead of buyers, and how she tried to keep the whole thing above what it was: turning art into cash. 'I believe Michael Angel is meeting them there. He never says no to an event. Some of our artists seem to feel out of place with that crowd, but not Michael. He seems to come alive when there's a lot of people.'

I wondered about the event he was supposed to have gone to when Maeve had her accident. But I couldn't think of a way to ask her without it seeming suspicious.

'She certainly saw a different side of him than I did,' I said to Tizzy when we left. 'All I got was anger. And what was that voice about?' I asked with a laugh. As I thought, she'd been worried the woman might recognize her voice from the phone call. 'Well, Scarlett, how about getting some lunch?'

'I'd love to, but I have to get back to work,' Tizzy said, batting her eyes in a mimicry of the *Gone with the Wind* character. 'Alex is understanding, but even he has his limits, and there is some work I have to get out today.'

We took the train back to Hyde Park and, when we got to my corner, I started to thank Tizzy. 'Why don't you come to my place after work? I don't have sherry, but I have cooking wine. We could talk over everything. You may have noticed something I missed.'

'Yes,' Tizzy said with a smile. 'That's the job of a wingman.'

TWENTY-ONE

I t was just as well that Tizzy had been in a hurry to get back to work. I went right to my computer and wrote down notes from our trip. They were just snippets that I would use to come up with an entry for the memoir. I decided it would be about the dog paintings themselves. I would just throw in a couple of lines about the landscapes and use what Melanie had said about it showing the breadth of his talent. I'd have to be careful not to go too over the top about the Scotty works and then seem indifferent to the others. I was sure that Maeve adored all his work. What was it that the headmistress of the Dupont Academy had said: 'Love is blind.'

When I'd gotten down everything I could remember, I wanted to let it jell a little before I wrote up the piece. I was considering going across the street to the coffee shop and having a bowl of soup. Wednesdays they had cream of mushroom and it was my favorite.

Before I could do anything, my landline rang. It was Caleb reporting that he'd left the second of the new cards that he'd made. He sounded sure his artwork and my words were going to get through to her. Even though it would mean the end of the gig, I hoped he was right.

Talking to Caleb made me curious about which house his wife lived in and I wanted to get some details of Maeve's house to add to the piece I'd written about it. The soup would be my reward.

Of course, the weather had changed in the short time I'd been home and a sharp wind was blowing in off the lake. Even the hint of sun from earlier was gone and the sky now had a gray, moody look which made the idea of something hot seem even more appealing.

The chill and clouds did nothing to dissuade the group of joggers who ran past me as I turned on 57th. The world could be ending and some students would probably still be jogging to the lakefront.

As soon as I turned on Harper, I went into observation mode. I noted how narrow the street was compared to mine, and how it curved, making it impossible to see all the way to 59th. Although the houses had been built at the same time and there was a uniform feeling in their size, each was individual. Now that Halloween was the next holiday, a lot of the houses had pumpkins and gourds displayed on their front porches. I stopped when I got to Maeve's house. I made note of the little balcony outside her workroom and the sunburst design in strips of leaded glass at the top of one of the living-room windows. Being there reminded me of the big kitchen and the layout of the first floor. I forced myself to remove the memory of Maeve on the stairs and tried to imagine how it would have looked to her when they first moved in.

For now, the house appeared quiet, and there was just a tiny shred of police tape left on the front-door handle from when they closed it off. I would have liked to look at the backyard, but I didn't dare.

I considered taking a picture with my phone, but I could only capture parts of it. I pulled out my notebook and pen and wrote down the details I'd noticed. Then I began throwing down words that came to mind. Brooding, holding secrets, scene of the crime. I stopped realizing none of those would be useful for what I was working on.

'Are you looking for someone?' a man's voice called out. It was the kind of voice that got my attention right away, with its deep, melodious sound. I found the source of it was standing on the front porch of the house I'd thought might be Caleb's.

'No,' I said quickly, uncomfortable that I'd been observed.

'So then what is it? Are you here because of what happened next door, or are you interested because of the history of the street?'

I was glad that he didn't add that I might be casing the house with the intention of robbing it later. I held up the notebook and introduced myself. 'I'm a writer for hire,' I said. 'I live over there.' I waved my arm in the direction of my building.

'And I was dashing down a description to use in something I'm working on.'

His expression relaxed and it was hard to miss that he was extremely good-looking. His dark eyes had a sparkle and the black turtleneck made him look somehow poetic. I caught a glimpse of some bracelets on his wrist. When I saw that his black hair was pulled into a ponytail, I realized he was Maeve's yoga partner, whom Caleb had seen.

'So that makes you almost a neighbor,' he said. 'We get a lot of people looking at the houses, curious about the history, and then what happened next door . . .' His voice trailed off and he studied my face to see if I knew.

'I heard,' I said, and both of our expressions turned somber.

'What exactly are you writing? Maybe I can offer some insight.' I wondered if it was truly an offer of help, or if he didn't believe me and was trying to corner me. I pulled out a business card and walked up the porch and handed it up to him.

'So you can see I'm legit,' I said. He looked over the card and seemed satisfied.

'There's been a slew of people hanging around. Podcasters, some woman with a YouTube show and now newspeople with their satellite vans.' He sounded a little weary. 'You were going to say what you were writing.'

I wasn't about to bring up Caleb, so I threw myself in with the crowd interested in Maeve's place and added that I'd been hired by her to write something.

His dark eyes lit with interest. 'So, you're the one she hired.'

Then he knew about the memoir. I wondered what else he knew – like maybe the ending she had dangled in front of me. If nothing else, he might tell me enough about Maeve's yoga practice that I could write something about it. 'I'm trying to put something together based on the notes she gave me. Would you be willing to answer a few questions?' I asked.

He glanced up and down the street and then back to me. 'It's kind of cold out here. I was just going to have a mug of hot cider.' He stepped toward the front door and held out his arm in a welcoming gesture to complete the invitation.

I realized it was going inside a stranger's house next door

to where a murder had recently happened, and I hesitated for a moment, but my gut told me he was OK. I went up the stairs and followed him inside.

He was telling the truth about the cider. I smelled the cinnamon and apple scent as soon as I got inside. 'I should introduce myself,' he said with a friendly smile. 'I'm Kent Goodman.' He pointed toward the living room off to the side of the entrance hall and invited me to sit while he got the cider.

There was a moment when I had a horrible thought that Kent was going to come back with the cider and an axe in hand. My gut had said he was OK, but just because he was good-looking with a great-sounding voice and a friendly manner didn't really exclude that he could be an axe murderer. There was this phrase in mystery writing, *too stupid to live*, when characters did unbelievably stupid things. I didn't want to be guilty of that in real life.

The living room looked lived-in. Books and magazines lay on a coffee table in front of a couch, which had one of the cushions moved, as if someone had been reclining on it. As soon as he set down the drinks, he rushed to replace the cushion and offered me the seat, while he kept at a respectful distance, sitting in a wing chair to the side.

'So, Kent, I gather you knew Maeve,' I said, leaving it at that and not bringing up that I knew they'd done yoga together.

'Since you live around here, you probably know that this two-block stretch is like a small town within the neighborhood. We do a lot of holiday celebrations together. We shut it off for Halloween, have carolers at Christmas and a carnival for the fourth of July. Most everybody takes part. Sometimes not the whole family, but at least one member.'

'What about next door?'

'Her husband did help make a scarecrow once, but it was mostly Maeve who got together with the neighbors. She and I were garden buddies. My wife travels a lot and never had much interest in the yard. My kids took after her and are off at school anyway.' He urged me to try the cider while it was hot. 'I can't believe she's gone.'

I considered if I should tell him I was the one who found her, but that would push me to the center of the conversation, and I was more interested in hearing what he had to say. I didn't know what story was circulating, whether it was murder or an accident, and I didn't want to get in the middle of speculating. I wanted to use whatever time I had with him to get information.

Because of my work, I'd become a good listener. Not just aware of the words, but the intonation, the space between the words, and if there was a subtext of meaning. Everything about the way Kent's voice dropped into a pit of despair as he said, *I can't believe she's gone*, made me believe there was more story behind it.

'She was so excited about the house when they moved in. She rushed over to introduce herself. Having a backyard was a big deal to her, and she was trying to figure what to do with theirs. I offered to show her ours and then to help her plan theirs, since she seemed overwhelmed.'

'What about her husband?' I asked.

'Yes, Michael Angel, the big-time artist.' It was impossible to miss the contempt in his voice. 'His only interest in a garden seemed to be painting it.' My ponytailed host glanced over at me. 'You must have been up in her workroom, and she probably had you do an art project,' he said.

'Yes,' I said. 'Then you were up there, too?'

'It was where she felt the most comfortable. The whole downstairs was arranged around Michael's studio and the flow of people who came to see him and his art.'

'You must have gotten to know her pretty well if you did a lot of gardening together,' I said. 'What did Maeve tell you about the memoir?'

'Not too much, other than she said she wanted to show the artist behind the dog. It seemed to be particularly important to her, now that he was nominated for that art prize.' A car rumbled down the street and he looked out the window. 'She really adored him and made all kinds of excuses for him. Artist temperament and such.' Kent looked down at the cider and I saw that his brow was furrowed, as if he'd thought of something upsetting. 'I don't know how well you know him, but he does the artistic thing very well. Moody and bursts of temper. And he was hardly discreet about other women.'

'It sounds like you spent a lot of time with Maeve,' I said.

'Like I said, we were gardening buddies. My wife doesn't know the difference between a marigold and peony. Michael's only interest in anything green was painting those landscapes. We helped each other plan out our gardens and execute them. We joked that we'd always have petunias,' he said, with a take on the line from *Casablanca* about always having Paris.

He led me to the kitchen that looked out on the yard. Part of it was lawn, but the back section and along the sides had a selection of plants that seemed at the end of their season. 'We both had vegetable gardens and flowers this year. I grew tomatoes and she planted lettuce and scallions. We shared our harvest,' he said. 'I helped fix some things around their place, too.' He seemed to be remembering something. 'I never did get to the basement door lock . . .' He glanced at me. 'But this isn't helping you with what you are writing. Maybe you should tell me what kind of information you're looking for.'

'What you're telling me is great,' I said. I'd started taking some notes, thinking I'd write about her garden.

'We talked a lot when we were digging up the backyards. She was the most giving person. Always thinking of others.' Kent took a sip of the cider, and I had the feeling he was using it to cover his emotions. 'Her husband abused her good nature and I think she had some plan in mind to take back control of her life.'

'Do you know what she was going to do?' I had a feeling it was connected to that mystery ending.

'She was rather mysterious, and kept saying something about what goes around, comes around, and that she was probably deserving of what was happening. I was certain it had to do with Michael. I gather with the award and the documentary he had become insufferably full of himself.' He held the mug in his hand. 'She didn't offer any details, but she definitely had something in mind.'

It seemed like too much of a non sequitur for me to suddenly bring up the yoga they did together, but it did seem they were more than garden buddies. I sensed that he was in love with her.

'It's all like a bad dream,' Kent said in a low tone. 'I'm sure in the end it will turn out to be ruled an accident.'

'I suppose the police talked to you,' I said, and he nodded.

'They asked me the expected questions. Did I know her, and did I see or hear anything?' He shook his head sadly.

'Well, did you see or hear anything?' I asked.

'I wouldn't want you to think I was a nosy neighbor, but I saw Michael leave with a woman that day. Later I was out raking some leaves and Michael came back alone for a short time and left again.' My host stood and said something about having to get to a philosophy class he had to teach and I got it, our interview was over. I had hoped to ask him if he knew anything about Caleb and his wife, but I couldn't figure out how to do it without it seeming weird.

By process of elimination, I now knew which house was Caleb's, and I checked it out on my way back down the street. It was a dark brown with a covered front porch that left the house in deep shadows, which hardly looked inviting.

My mind was on overload when I went home, and I forgot all about the plan for the soup. I wanted to write down some more notes, and did better writing them by hand than using the computer. The phone rang while I was scribbling fast and furiously on a yellow legal pad. I considered ignoring it, but when the caller ID said Suzzanna Angel, I went for it.

I said hello, girding for whatever rudeness she was going to spew, but instead she greeted me in a friendly tone.

'I understand that you are working on Maeve's memoir,' she said. 'I can imagine it's difficult without her to guide you. It's too bad that I wasn't at the gallery when you came with your friend. Since the story is really about my father, with Maeve mostly as a guide, I thought I might be able to help you.'

Her friendly tone actually made me more uneasy than if she'd been nasty. 'I'm managing pretty well on my own,' I said. So she knew about our visit. I had hoped to keep it quiet, but she must have looked at the guest book.

'I'm sure you are, but I know it all from the inside. Maeve had really been left behind. There were so many things lately – parties and receptions that she didn't go to, the documentary that's in the works. I could fill you in.'

I didn't like her, but she had a point. I was already envisioning creating more about the parties and the people who attended them. And I certainly wanted to know about the documentary. 'I'd appreciate that,' I said.

'You could show me the draft you have and we could go from there,' she said. Then I got it, she was trying to do what her father had tried to do. It was one thing to talk to her and write something up, but I certainly wasn't going to let her look anything over and then start wanting to change it.

'I'm sorry, I don't work that way,' I said. 'I'd be happy to listen to whatever you had to say. We could do it on the phone or in person. Your choice.'

She made an angry *tsk* sound. 'Well, I don't work that way,' she said in a snippy tone. 'I should be a collaborator on it. You'll just get everything wrong. Maeve was trying to hang on to Michael, but he'd outgrown her. Serves her right after what she did to my mother's marriage.' Her voice had risen in anger.

I didn't know what to say, other than to tell her the truth. 'As I said, I'd be happy to talk to you, but no promises about what I'd include.'

All the friendliness was gone and the person who'd answered the door that first time returned. 'My father said he'll sue you if you say anything defamatory about him. If you know what's good for you, you'll let me help you.'

I forced myself to be pleasant and repeated that I'd be happy to talk to her, but that was it. She hung up without a word. I guessed that was a no.

It took me a minute to recover from the call. Had she just threatened me? I included it all in the notes with *What are they afraid of?* underlined twice.

TWENTY-TWO

The afternoon was fading and Tizzy would be coming soon, but even so I sat down at the computer ready to use the notes to work on the manuscript. I found what I'd written about Maeve's house and wanted to add some personal touches to it, like how she felt about the place. I'd begun to take some liberties – actually, putting words in her mouth. I doubted there was anything Michael Angel would object to. The whole idea of them suing me was preposterous and sounded like an empty threat. But, just in case, I took some time to think about libel and slander since I always got them confused. I felt like Theo as I started doing research on defaming someone. Basically, libel was based on the written word and slander the spoken word. I would have to write something that damaged Michael's reputation and was untrue. It was easier for a private person to win a suit than a public person. I was confident that Michael qualified as a public person. But I wasn't going to say anything damaging anyway. When I'd finished with my reading, I started writing.

The house on Harper meant different things to Michael and me. He could parade people through his studio. Their chance to see where the master did his painting. For me, it was about the yard and a chance to have a garden that would change with the seasons. And my own space on the third floor. I liked that it was private and for invited guests only. It was an art teacher's dream. My guests and I would do a project while they visited. They were always hesitant, but I'd push them to try, and in the end, they were pleased with their creation.

When I stopped, I looked through the stacks of papers that Maeve had given me. I was curious if there was anything about

Kent. There was no mention of him by name or even referred to as a neighbor. But I did find the line, *We'll always have petunias.* I wondered if she'd meant that as a prompt and that, when we got to it, she would have told me all about him and their gardening time and their relationship. I would never know now.

I heard my phone chime, announcing the arrival of a text. I fought the urge to be like a Pavlovian dog and jump to look at the small screen, but I told myself it might be important, and the fact that I waited a little bit meant it was a conscious decision to check it, not an automatic one.

It was from Caleb saying he needed to talk asap. I called him right back.

'I don't know what I'm going to do,' he said after I'd barely managed to say hello.

'About what?' I asked, trying to get him to focus.

'It's my wife. I think she's found somebody else.' He sounded distraught and unfocused, and I figured the first thing to do was get to what exactly had happened. He had told me very little about the situation with her. I didn't even know her name. He called her my Prime Number.

'Are you divorced?' I asked. There was a silence on his end of the phone and I wondered if I'd overstepped with the question, but then he finally answered.

'Sort of,' he said. It seemed like a vague answer from anyone, but even more so from a mathematician, since numbers weren't ambiguous. I thought of another way to find out about the situation between them.

'What about the house? Is it hers?' I meant, as in, she got it in the divorce.

'It's a rental,' he said in a noncommittal tone. The next question could have been who paid the rent, but I sensed it would go nowhere, so I moved on.

'What makes you think that?' I asked.

'When I went to drop off the card I made yesterday, I saw a man inside.'

'That doesn't mean anything. It could have been a plumber,' I said. Then I paused with a thought of a question of my own. 'How did you even see she had company?'

There was a grumbling sound from his end. 'I thought it would be better to slip the card under the kitchen door. There's a deck by the back door and I looked in the window.'

I wondered if I should bring up how that might seem a little creepy and, if she saw him, make things worse between them, even though I was convinced he was harmless. 'What were they doing?' I asked, almost afraid of the answer.

'Just standing there,' he said. 'And it wasn't a plumber. Unless they started wearing bracelets.'

'You really noticed some details,' I said.

'Only because he seemed to be handing her something,' the mathematician said. I tried to find out some particulars about the bracelets, but he vaguely remembered seeing beads. Interesting that both Michael Angel and Kent wore bracelets made of beads.

'It was probably just a neighbor who wanted to borrow something, or maybe a piece of mail got delivered to him by mistake and he brought it over. It sounds pretty innocent to me.' I hoped I was convincing, though I had no idea if it was true.

He took a moment to consider what I'd said. 'You could be right,' he said finally, sounding a little brighter. 'What would she want with a man who wore jewelry?' He let out an unhappy sigh. 'If she would just talk to me. It would be so much better.'

'Did you leave the card?'

'I forgot,' he said, and I had the feeling he'd hit his forehead with his hand in a move of frustration.

'You said your daughter lives with her, maybe you can give it to her to give to her mother.'

'No, no,' he said with sudden passion. 'I won't do anything to put her in the middle of things.' I was touched by his wanting to be a protective father, and surprised by his emotional response.

'You can try leaving it again. But it's probably best if you put it in the mailbox or leave it on the front porch as you've done before.' It wasn't my job to give relationship advice. All I did was help my clients communicate, but it wasn't the first time I'd gotten sucked into doing more. I didn't feel like much of an example at the moment, considering my situation with Ben, but I went ahead anyway.

'It's hard for me to tell you what to do since I don't know all the circumstances, but I think that your continued thoughtful gestures will help. Maybe next time we should send her a note with a blanket apology,' I suggested.

'Do you really think that would work? I'm not very good with the mushy stuff, but I really love her. I just want to be able to go back home and spend time with my wife and daughter. You'd have to come up with something great.'

I didn't want to tell him, but I was already composing a note in my mind that would apologize for everything wrong in the world first, like climate change, and then make it more personal. It would be tricky without knowing exactly what it was, but I was sure I'd figure out something. 'But in the meantime, be sure to leave the cards you made,' I said.

'You're right. I'm sure I overreacted. Thank you, I feel better,' he said. 'I'll make sure to leave a card on the front porch.'

I let out a big breath when I hung up. Caleb seemed to have calmed down, though I had to wonder who her company had been. I'd begun to realize that there was no way not to get involved with my clients' lives when I was doing such personal work for them.

I took a break and went back to flipping through the stack of papers Maeve had given me. It was like a treasure hunt, and I always seemed to find something new. A paragraph popped out at me.

Imagine that, a documentary about Michael. I had the filmmaker up to my workroom for a meet and greet. I thought Jennifer wanted to get something about my point of view, but all she talked about was Michael and how much time they were spending together so she could 'capture the man behind the art.'

I flipped ahead and found another batch of notes I hadn't noticed before.

I know it's Michael's nature to charm women and now, with his success, they are drawn to him. It's just who he is. I can deal with it as long as it's a temporary crowd, but not if it's just one. I know what I will do if it ever comes to that. I wonder how she'll like him then.

TWENTY-THREE

'Long time, no see,' Tizzy said with a laugh as she reached the top landing. 'It's not a cliché, but more of an idiom. And is actually a translation of a Chinese greeting?'

'Then I guess it's OK to use,' I said with a smile. I brought her into the living room, but she followed me back to the kitchen as I went to get the cooking wine and look for some snacks.

'I was talking to Theo before I left and he said we should check out Sophia's YouTube feed.'

I was anxious to tell her about my afternoon, but decided that it was best to concentrate on one thing at a time. We'd just focus on Sophia and her YouTube show for now, and then later I'd bring up my visit with Kent, the call from Suzzanna, and even Caleb's worry about his wife's visitor.

I found some mini quiches in the freezer and popped them in the microwave while I poured the drinks. I arranged the food and drinks on a tray. She grabbed some napkins and we brought everything back to the living room. I tried with no success to get YouTube on my TV, so the only other option was my computer or phone, neither of which seemed ideal.

'Let me call Theo,' Tizzy said. I tried not to eavesdrop on their conversation, but with cell phones it was hard not to. The sense I got about them was that they were both on the same side, allies, friends. It was reassuring to me that relationships like that existed. Maybe someday it would be true for me.

She clicked off and turned to me. 'Theo feels kind of left out. He was actually going to call and ask to join us. He's offering his laptop, a pizza and, of course, his help.' She looked at me with a question in her eye.

'It all sounds good to me,' I said, and she called him back, giving him the go-ahead.

'Lucky for us, he was sure we'd say yes and he's already ordered the pizza. He'll be here in a few minutes.'

Theo had never been to my place before; as soon as he came in, he started looking around. The horn-rimmed glasses were so prominent, it was hard to see his features, but he seemed to have a friendly expression. 'I love these old buildings,' he said, glancing toward the frosted French door that led to my office. 'It seems so sad when people try to modernize them and take away all the charm.'

'You don't have to worry about that here. I can't afford to do it. I have to make do.' I pointed at all the things plugged into the surge protector. 'When they built this building, they didn't have a clue about all the computers and such we'd have to plug in.' I looked down the hall to the dining room. 'Believe it or not there are still pipes in the ceiling left from gas lamps.'

'Really?' he said in an excited voice.

'You'd better show him,' Tizzy said.

'There's really nothing to see.' I took him back to the dining room and pointed at the ceiling fan I'd had installed. 'The gas pipes are behind it. There must have been a chandelier. Of course, the gas has long been shut off to them.'

He seemed disappointed that there wasn't more to see, so I showed him the metal disc on the floor under where the person at the head of the table would have sat. Before I could explain what it was for, he chimed in. 'It was to call the servant,' he said, then let out a dry laugh. 'The thought of having a live-in servant seems so strange now, but it must have been common. I bet you have a small bedroom off the kitchen meant for the help.'

'You're right,' I said, and offered to show it to him. He left the pizza on the table and put his messenger bag on a chair and followed me. I used the room as a catch-all. He peeked in the small bathroom.

'I'm sorry for being so nosy, but I'm fascinated by things from the past. I love helping Tizzy research information for her book.' He offered me a warm smile. 'Thanks for letting me come over and join you two. Ever since Tizzy told me about your adventure today, I've been doing research on YouTube shows and on Sophia. It's really fascinating how anybody can do one.'

'We can talk while we eat the pizza,' Tizzy said. We were

back in the dining room and I offered them both seats while I got plates and utensils. 'Anyone can do one, but not everyone gets followers. It's about the person or people. They need to attract interest and have a subject matter. But it helps if you have some money as well. There seem to be ways to pay to get attention that leads to getting followers.'

Tizzy started to serve up the pizza and I asked Theo what he'd like to drink. He asked for a glass of my cooking wine. 'It's legendary,' he said with a smile. 'Tizzy thinks it's wonderful how you have given the wine personality.'

'It's pretty basic stuff,' I said. 'I hope you're not a connoisseur.'

'It wouldn't matter if I was. I read that there were some blind tastings among wine lovers and they couldn't tell fancy wine from cheap stuff by the aroma or taste. It makes you think all that swirling and sniffing is just a pretention.'

'It's certainly lost on me. One sip and it goes right to my head, no matter what it costs.' I was glad that Theo let my comment pass and didn't start doing research on why alcohol affected me as it did. He was more intent on the pizza.

Tizzy handed him a plate with a slice. 'I got your favorite, Margherita pizza,' he said to his wife. 'People think it's a new creation, but it goes back at least to 1889 when it was presented to the Queen of Italy. The basil, tomatoes and mozzarella were reminiscent of the colors of the Italian flag.' He looked at me. 'Don't worry, no meat.' I was impressed by his consideration and thanked him. Tizzy was a lucky woman, and even more so because she appreciated what she had.

When we were done with the pizza, we moved back into the living room and Theo set up the laptop on the coffee table and positioned it so we could all see the screen.

He signed onto my WiFi and started typing something in. 'I want to show you her very first show after she changed it from being just about her and the dog.'

The beginning was similar to a regular TV show. There was a montage of Sophia and her Scottish terrier in different places, and it ended with them sitting on chairs across from each other. I'd watched the occasional instructional video on YouTube, but this was the first actual show I'd seen and I was curious. As the program began, Sophia addressed the camera. 'Welcome to our new home.' She and the dog walked around a big space that appeared to be a loft. I guessed it was one of those industrial buildings that had been turned into living spaces. As she did the tour, she pointed out that it was empty except for the two chairs. She started going on about how they didn't have any furniture and she'd spent all the money on rent. She seemed like a natural for the screen. As I'd noticed before, she was interesting-looking rather than pretty, and it came out even more as I watched her on the computer. It was crazy, but she and the dog did appear to have a special rapport. She kept going on about being without furniture and that there had to be a way to find stuff on the cheap.

Supposedly so they could think about it, she and the dog went for a walk. It all seemed very random and choppily filmed to make it feel real, but I was suspecting it had started with a script. Not with exact dialogue, but a story.

It cut to them walking down an alley and passing a discarded couch. It had an interesting shape and she called it a divan, though that wasn't exactly correct. A divan was supposed to be a long, low sofa with no back or arms. What can I say? I'm a word person. This one had a back, but no armrests. The faded pink covering had some cuts in it and the stuffing was coming out. Sophia sized it up and decided it had good bones.

'It looks pretty ratty to me,' Tizzy said. She made a face. 'I wonder if it smells.'

If it did, Sophia didn't seem to care. Drexel danced around her feet as she grabbed an end of the furniture and began to pull it. Out of nowhere, two men were helping her and then it was brought into her loft. Her neighbor came in and wrinkled his nose at the condition of the couch as they had a conversation back and forth.

'He becomes a regular,' Theo said. When Tizzy and I looked at him, puzzled how he knew, he admitted to watching a number of them. 'So I could curate a collection to show you,' he explained.

There were several shots of the couch in various stages of being re-covered. It was implied that Sophia was doing it, but I wondered. In the end, it was covered in a red suede-like material and was stunning. She added some throw pillows to complete it. The neighbor returned, awestruck by what she'd done, and said, 'That's amazing. You took something nobody wanted and turned it into something everybody would want. I'm going to call you Second Chance Sophia.'

'That's where they got the name for her channel,' Theo said, acting as our guide. 'There are more of her doing the same with furniture, but we'll skip ahead.' He fiddled with the laptop and another of her programs came on.

An ad for something played and then the actual show started. In this one she had a broken vase and a cup with a saucer that was broken in two. Something about the cup got my attention, but before I could think it through she had started to prattle with Drexel sitting close by, watching. She held up a bottle of Sukey's Super Stick. 'It bonds anything together, permanently,' she said in a cheery voice.

'I wanted to show how she'd progressed. Now she has enough followers that she receives some of YouTube's ad revenue and she has the glue company paying her to show off their product.'

Tizzy and I weren't nearly as excited about it as Theo was. 'Wait until you see what I show you next,' he said. There was more hitting of keys before something showed on the screen. As before, it began with an ad. Sophia was in the loft, which was now furnished with a lot of stylish pieces she seemed to have saved from somewhere. Drexel was sitting on a chair watching her as she bubbled over with enthusiasm. 'Drexel, look what we got,' she gushed. The camera moved and the painting of *The Scotty in the Sleeping Garden* was propped up on a chair. 'Don't you just love it,' she said to the camera. 'It was painted by Michael Angel.' She turned to Drexel. 'It looks just like you. Did you sneak out and model for it?' The dog gave out a yip as if to say no. She gave the dog an affectionate pat. 'Everybody loves you. Really we should call my channel Drexel and his friend.' She spoke to the camera again and asked her viewers to let her know if they loved the painting.

Theo ended it there and found another of the videos. This time, Sophia was surrounded by a display of 'merch', as she called it. There were posters, T-shirts, mugs, tote bags and postcards, all featuring the painting. She was very excited about it all, claiming there had been such an outpouring of love for the painting, she'd had to do something so her viewers could share it.

Tizzy shook her head. 'Wow, she makes it seem like she's doing them a favor.'

Theo pressed on and found another show. This one had her at the art gallery. Zander was there, along with Michael Angel and Maeve. She took the entourage into a gallery filled with the Scotty paintings. I hadn't seen these before and was fascinated by them. The Scotty had a background of the beach and what looked like a carnival. Before I could see all of them, Sophia had positioned the camera on the group. She introduced Zander as her boyfriend and did a pitch on his gallery. She gave a glowing introduction to Michael and, almost as an aside, introduced Maeve. She looked at Michael. 'Now, you're a famous artist, thanks to us.' She pointed at Drexel and herself, slipping her arm through the artist's. He appeared a little uncomfortable, but tried to smile as he said thank you. 'I introduced your wonderful paintings to my almost a million followers. And now we've become friends besides.'

Theo stopped it and started to explain the story behind the story that he'd figured out. 'I thought at first that it was all about her wanting to be a star. This whole YouTube thing offers that opportunity to anyone. But as I watched the videos, I changed my mind. Though Sophia seems to try and make it seem like she's just having fun and it all just sort of happened on its own, I think she's very shrewd. The idea of being a star might have appealed to her, but I think she had another goal. It's all about monetizing. First, with getting enough followers to get ad revenue, then being paid to display products and then the merch.' He smiled. 'That's the short version of *merchandise* that those of us in the know use.' There was a twinkle in his eye, making it clear he was making a joke about himself. Then he got serious and went on retracing the steps of her buying an obscure painting and turning the painting and the artist into a big deal. 'She's probably made a fortune off all those posters and T-shirts. And Michael Angel hasn't fared too badly either.'

Theo would have gladly gone on and on about YouTube channels and the money you could make, but Tizzy stopped him. 'The point is to help Veronica get information to use in the book she's writing.'

'You just needed to be patient,' he said, 'I was getting to that.' He started on the keyboard again and then pointed at the screen. 'Is this good enough?' He showed us a thumbnail that had the title *In Memoriam*. We nodded and he clicked on it.

He sped through the usual beginning and stopped when the video actually began. Sophia and Drexel were sitting in her now well-furnished loft. As always, the painting of *The Scotty in the Sleeping Garden* was prominently displayed behind them. They both looked sad and were wearing black armbands, though it was hard to tell on Drexel's black fur. 'Thanks to this wonderful painting, Drexel and I became friends with the artist and his wife. Maeve liked to stay in the background, but she was truly the person behind the artist, and our friend. She was a gifted art teacher loved by her students.' Sophia was more subdued than usual and her eyes were tearing up. 'I can't believe that she's gone – the result of a terrible accident.' Drexel jumped in her lap to comfort her as she swallowed back her emotions. 'To honor her memory, Drexel and I are making a donation to the Dupont Academy. Maeve's favorite thing was to inspire the artist in everyone.'

'That's true,' I said. 'She had me making pictures on my second visit.' I grabbed a pen and some paper and made a note of which show it was and then scribbled down something about the donation. 'Thank you, Theo, that is something I can use at the end of the book. She said something about a surprise ending, but I'm sure that wasn't it,' I said with a heavy sigh.

Theo's eyes sparked with interest. 'She told you there was a surprise ending?'

'I'm not sure that was exactly her words, but it doesn't matter, because she's not here to tell me what she meant.'

Theo's mind seemed to be clicking. 'I wonder if I can figure it out.'

'Theo, I know you love to do research and draw conclusions, but I think this is out of your reach,' Tizzy said.

He seemed disgruntled, but also might have realized Tizzy

was right and he changed the subject. 'She called it an accident. Does that mean it's official?'

'The last I heard it was being left as inconclusive until they get results back from the tox screen to see what – if any – drugs were in her system.'

'If it was foul play, any ideas of who?' Theo asked.

'Maeve seemed to be a really nice person. She was loved at the school. I just talked to one of her neighbors who I think had a crush on her. But . . .' I took a breath and collected my thoughts. 'From what Tizzy and I found out, Michael's ex-wife was very angry at Maeve and blamed her for being left before the gravy train pulled in.' Tizzy and I traded glances and laughed at variation on the cliché.

'You know where that came from?' Theo asked. 'It's from the 1920s, during the financial boom, and was railroad slang for a run that had good pay and little work.' He seemed amused by my surprise. 'I know about your thing about clichés. It made me curious about their derivation.'

'I told you, Theo is curious about everything,' Tizzy said as she gave his arm a squeeze.

'Back to the suspects,' I said. 'I just got a call from his stepdaughter, Suzzanna. She did a number on me about wanting to help with the manuscript, but her real motive was to see what I have. She seemed to be representing her father and, reading between the lines, they seem worried there is something damaging about him in the material she gave me. She ended the call with what seemed like a threat.'

'You didn't tell me,' Tizzy said.

'It just happened this afternoon, between the time we went to the gallery and when you came over.'

'What are you going to do about it, the threat?' Tizzy asked.

'It was really the threat of suing me, and I don't think there is much chance of that, so I'm ignoring it.'

Theo had been typing into the laptop as we were talking. 'I agree with Veronica,' he said. 'What it really comes down to is if whatever they're worried about being disclosed is true. My guess is that it is, and they're just trying to scare you into glossing over anything negative about him.' Theo looked back at the screen. 'Do you know where that phrase *reading between the lines* came from?' he asked.

'No,' I said, embarrassed that with all my fussing I'd used a cliché and not even realized it. It was nice of Theo to call it a phrase rather than what it was.

'I never would have guessed it,' he said, looking at his wife and me. It comes from cryptography, when a code was used that had the real message on every second line. So you had to read between the other lines of text to get it.' Tizzy and I agreed what he'd found out was fascinating.

'And then there's Michael himself,' I said. 'Everyone seems to agree that being the spouse puts him in first position. And I heard something from the neighbor that contradicted his alibi that he was gone the whole time at an event they were using to get some material for a documentary being made on him.' When I mentioned the documentary, it reminded me of what I'd found in Maeve's notes about Jennifer Soames. 'There's someone else who might be involved.' I told them that Maeve had written about Jennifer spending a lot of time with Michael. 'And then later, Maeve wrote something that made it seem she knew he was a womanizer, but then wrote something to the effect that if she found out that he'd settled on one woman, she was going to do something that would cause him trouble. When I read it, it seemed to me to be a threat. I have to wonder if Maeve was referring to Jennifer.'

'If they were spending a lot of time together, I bet you're right,' Tizzy said.

'And you can be sure that Michael knows whatever she was threatening,' Theo said.

'Maybe he did something criminal,' Tizzy said. 'And he'd gotten away with it for all this time.'

'I don't know,' I said, shaking my head. 'Maeve was very nice in all my dealings with her, but she was really desperate to keep the whole project a secret. Maybe because she was worried.'

'Are you going to mention this to the police?' Theo asked.

'Hardly,' I said, rolling my eyes. 'I don't want to bring any attention to myself since it might end up making me a person of interest.'

'I don't like that term,' Theo said. 'It seems too imprecise. It's like that thing where people say they're engaged to be engaged. You're almost a suspect and the cops have their eyes on you. It's not even defined by the US Department of Justice.' 'I think this particular homicide detective says it to annoy me,' I said. 'He knows I wrote a mystery and it's the soft kind, more about people and the puzzle than gore. Derek Streeter doesn't even carry a gun most of the time. Everybody keeps their clothes on and eats a lot. Derek succeeds when the cops overlook important clues. Maybe if I wrote something like Ben . . .' I said, looking to Tizzy before explaining to Theo that he was a cop.

'I know all about Ben,' he said. 'And Daryl with the job that convinced her to get tattoos and Ed with the pages so full of heaving and throbbing that no one except Ben can read them out loud.' Tizzy obviously shared even more than I realized.

Theo nodded. 'Yes, I understand why this detective wouldn't be a fan and might resent you offering him any information. So, what's the plan. Investigate on your own?'

It was a good question, and I wasn't sure of the answer.

TWENTY-FOUR

I had enjoyed having Tizzy and Theo's company. I did a quick cleanup and went back to looking through Maeve's notes, curious if there was anything about Sophia. It would have been nice if it was all on my computer and I could have just done a search, but I was stuck actually speed-reading the pages, looking for some mention. I found a couple of snippets in the pages and mixed them in with what Theo had showed us on YouTube.

> *Who would have thought that Michael and I would have gotten involved with a YouTube star? I didn't even know who Sophia was. I only found out after she bought the Scotty painting. It was easy to see why she acquired it. Her Drexel could have been the model. It was fun being included in one of her videos. It was nice that she appreciated my value as an art teacher. You could say we appreciated each other. I was amazed at her knack for finding things and turning them into treasures.*

I left it at that, thinking I'd look at one of the later videos again so I could get exact details of the treasures Sophia had created. And maybe find the video Maeve had been in to pick up some details. Finally, I called it a night, and fell asleep without the need of chamomile or crochet.

In the morning I made a deal with myself. If I spent the morning writing, I'd treat myself to a bowl of soup at the coffee shop in the afternoon. Thursday was cream of potato soup, another of my favorites. I repeated what I'd done so many times, which was to comb through more of the pages, looking for something I'd missed. It was easy to miss things because there were often just random paragraphs or thoughts and not in a particular order. This time I found something from their early days. She seemed to have some concerns about money that she had given to Michael. It was a little vague, but it sounded like he'd done some creative bookkeeping when he managed the coffee house and she had given him the money to make up for it. Wasn't 'creative bookkeeping' another way of saying embezzling? I wondered if there was more.

The deal worked and the morning slipped by without me noticing as I racked up some more pieces to include in the book.

'Sorry you can't join me, no cats allowed,' I said to Rocky as I put my jacket on. The black-and-white cat looked up at me from the couch and he had a pleading look that I'd seen when he was up for adoption. Then it had said, *Please take me with you.* This time it seemed like he was saying, *Do you really have to go?*

The wind swirled through the tree out front, sending a shower of semi-parched leaves around me as I stepped onto the sidewalk. I didn't bother closing my jacket since I was literally just walking across the street.

It always felt inviting in the small coffee shop and, since it was the slow time after lunch, I took a big booth in the window where I could look out at the street. There were always people coming and going and the inevitable group of joggers on their way to the lakefront.

The soup arrived, steaming hot with a basket of bread and butter. Since it was homemade, it was always a little different, though always delicious. I was savoring a creamy spoonful when I felt a blast of air as the door opened and someone came in. Before it could fully register, someone was in my face talking in a low, terse voice.

'What did Maeve tell you about me?' Michael Angel demanded. He didn't give me space to say anything before he continued. 'You should know that Maeve was crazy.' He was leaning on the table so we were eye to eye. 'What have you found out from all your snooping?'

'It wasn't snooping,' I said. 'I went to the art gallery that features your work.'

'You weren't exactly honest about who you were,' he said, almost spitting the words.

'That's not true,' I said. 'I gave them my name and even gave Melanie my card. I said I was writing something. I just wasn't specific.'

'Whatever you were doing, I don't like it. You went to my neighbor's, too.'

'It's a public street and he started the conversation.' I didn't like having to defend myself, and instead tried to turn the questioning on him. 'How do you know about my conversation with Kent?'

'I saw you go in there, and I asked him. He said you were looking for information about Maeve.'

'And he told me she liked to garden,' I said, trying to keep things calm.

He had moved closer to me and I could see anger building up inside of him. 'You better take my daughter up on her offer.' His eyes flared and his voice was almost a growl. 'One way or another, that book won't come out without my approval.' He tried to lean even closer with a menacing stare. 'I could ruin you, or worse.'

I felt another blast of air as the door opened again. I tried to look around him to see who'd come in, but he reacted by putting his hands on my arms. 'I'm talking to you.' I was surprised and annoyed at being grabbed and was going to push him away, but someone else did it for me. Michael stood upright in surprise and found himself staring at Ben.

'What's the problem?' Ben said.

'Just a misunderstanding,' Michael said as he backed his way to the door. The whole time he was glaring at me, and he did that thing with his fingers where he pointed at his eyes and then at me. The meaning was clear, he would be watching me.

'Thanks,' I said to Ben, and then I saw that he wasn't alone. A petite woman with over-tweezed eyebrows was standing next to him.

'You must be As—' I stuttered on the syllable and almost called her Ben's sister's nickname for her, 'Ashleigh,' I said, relieved that I managed to get her name right.

'And you are?' Her voice was harsh and demanding.

'I'm Sara's upstairs neighbor,' I said, trying to hide that I was checking her out. She was pretty in a sharp sort of way and, though she was wearing a light coat, I saw the short, clingy dress just as Sara had described. She stared back at me and if looks could have killed, I would have been dead. She obviously had figured I was more than I'd said. All this and I was still recovering from the interchange with Michael. Why was he acting so threatened? What did he think I knew? Did it have to do with what I'd figured out in my latest go-through of the pages? The thoughts swirled through my mind as I tried to deal with the current circumstance. Ashleigh made a point to wave her left hand at me so I could see the gold band with a diamond on her ring finger.

'Who was the guy? Your boyfriend?' she said.

'Yeah, who was he?' Ben repeated.

'The upset spouse of a client,' I said.

Ashleigh was still staring at me, and a look of recognition came over her face. 'You're the writing teacher?' She turned to Ben. 'You made her sound like a gray-haired librarian type, like Donna Reed in that movie they show every Christmas.' I knew she was referring to a scene in *It's a Wonderful Life*, and the actress who had been made up to look like a dried-up fidgety woman. Why had Ben said that? Obviously, so she wouldn't think of me as competition.

'If everything is OK,' Ben said, snagging her arm, 'we have to go.' He went to the door with her in tow and looked back just before they went outside and mouthed something which I gathered was an apology.

I looked down at the almost full bowl of the creamy soup, which was now cold. It didn't matter because I'd lost my appetite anyway. I asked to get it packed to go.

The whole episode of Michael's appearance, the veiled threat and then having Ben and Ashleigh show up had given me a super adrenalin rush. When I got upstairs, I put the soup away and flopped on the couch to recover. The adrenalin receded, but it left me with sort of a brain fog. I tried to think of doing normal things to get myself back together, like to check Rocky's dry food and clean his litter box, but I couldn't seem to boost myself off the couch. I needed to calm myself and instinctively pulled out the plastic bag with the crochet square

I'd just started. I was glad it was a really basic one, just a single and then a double crochet in a toast-colored worsted yarn. Even with the simplicity of the pattern, when I looked back at the rows I'd done, I saw that I'd made a mistake and screwed up the order of stitches which threw the whole pattern off. I gave the yarn a yank and started ripping, as my mind went back to what had just happened. Without meaning to, I ripped the whole thing apart and was left with a pile of yarn. As I went to start over, I had an uneasy feeling as I considered Michael's sudden appearance. He must have been holding a lot of anger and then seen me through the window.

I wondered how idle his threat was. He'd said he'd ruin me and that the book wouldn't come out, no matter what he had to do. How had it gone from what seemed like a nice memoir to this? Maeve was dead and he had sort of implied I might be too if I persisted. Maeve had said there might be a problem if Michael found out about the memoir, but I never thought it would be something so serious. I wondered if I should try to back out of the whole thing. Maybe I could borrow some money to give back what I'd been paid.

But there was a part of me that didn't want to be scared off. And no way was I going to deal with Suzzanna's 'help'. I began to feel a new resolve to finish the manuscript and to find out what he was hiding and make it public. And if I found Maeve's killer, so much the better.

I'd chained the first row and begun working on the pattern of stitches. My mind switched to Ben. Not really Ben – it was more about seeing Assleigh in person. It was OK to call her that name since it was only in my head anyway. Why had they gone to see Sara? She was the one who came up with the name for Ben's wife, clearly expressing her feelings about her. I imagined various scenarios, but the predominant one was that Ben had brought her over to tell his sister they were trying to make a go of it and attempt to make peace between them. Maybe Ashleigh'd talked him into it. Or maybe he was a willing participant. There had to be something about her that attracted her to him in the first place, since obviously he'd married her.

Looking to distract myself from the Ben situation, I went

into my office and grabbed the packet Maeve had given me. I'd noticed that every time I looked through the papers, I found something new. I started with the first page and began to read through her notes again, hoping there'd be a clue to what Michael was so worried about.

The afternoon faded into darkness without me noticing. I reheated the soup and ate it while I continued to read. The beginning pages had stops and starts as she had attempted to write entries. I had to force my shoulders to unhunch and skipped ahead back to the journal pages that I had glossed over before. I got that she felt guilty when she realized he was married, but she was so infatuated with him that she convinced herself that Rina was in competition with him, while she wasn't. Rina had been holding him back, and she would help him soar.

I heard my cell announce the arrival of a text. I figured it was probably from Sara with some sort of update, but when I looked it was from Ben. He was standing outside my door and didn't want to knock and scare me and asked if he could come in.

He was holding a bunch of sad-looking flowers and there was no reserved cop look this time. The best way I could describe his expression was 'hangdog'. 'They were the only ones left at the market,' he said, handing them to me. 'You have to give me credit for intent.' He blew out his breath and rubbed his forehead. 'I'm sorry,' he said.

I waved for him to come in and he went into the living room and sat on the couch.

'You could have just texted me the apology,' I said.

'No. I'm not that kind of guy. I believe in person is the best.'

I had to give him credit for that. Most people would have taken the easy way out and just sent me a message telling me about the change in his situation. But now it was my turn to step up and deal with him. I didn't want to be the one who was dumped, so I decided not to wait for him to say his piece. Despite my efforts to distract myself, I had kept going back to seeing him with Ashleigh. It was pretty clear what was going on and OK, it was a cliché, but true. Three was a crowd.

It would make me feel better to speak first as if it was my decision.

He had that look on his face as if he was trying to put the words together, but I put up my hand. 'No worries, I understand,' I began. 'I get it. You want to give it a second chance and come up with a happy ending this time. Isn't that the fantasy of everyone who gets dumped? What was it? Did you bring her over to show Sara you were back together and hope you could make it so you all would get along?' I kept going, never giving him a chance to answer what I looked at as rhetorical questions.

'Whatever we started together was nice, but you really need to put all of your attention on her. I'm perfectly fine with you staying in the writers' group. I promise it won't be awkward.' I stopped to take a breath.

'Are you done?' he asked, and I shrugged.

'That was it,' I said with a sad smile. 'Just go and find your happy ending.'

'You seem to have it all figured out.' He glanced down at the wilted flowers. 'I bet some water might help these. And I hate to be a bother, but I just drove out to Weston to take Ashleigh home and back here to talk to you. I could really use a cup of coffee.'

I picked up the flowers, feeling sorry for them. They looked like I felt. Maybe if I cut off the bottom of the stems and put some sugar in the water they would revive. As for the coffee, I could do with a cup as well, and he did deserve something for his effort. It was pretty brave of him to face me. And now that I'd spoken my piece, I felt a sense of relief. Lastly, if I meant what I'd said about the writers' group, I needed to show him that I could be around him without it being uncomfortable.

He stayed in the living room while I took the flowers into the kitchen. I put the coffee on, then snipped the ends of the stems before putting them in a vase with lukewarm water and three teaspoons of sugar. I wasn't sure what to do with them after that. Normally when I got flowers, I put them on the dining-room table, but I wanted to show him I'd cared for his gift, so brought them into the living room. In the short time, they already had started to perk up.

He looked up from his phone as I set them on the coffee table. He was probably sending a message to Ass— No, I was going to have to drop that even in my mind . . . Ashleigh with some reason why he wasn't home. 'So you didn't give up on them,' he said. 'A good trait.'

He seemed to have more to say, but I wasn't ready to hear it, and went back down the hall to get the coffee. We both took it black, so I returned carrying just the two mugs.

'Now can I speak?' he said when I'd set them down on the table, maybe a little too hard. I had done my whole farewell speech and sounded so mature and unemotional, but honestly, I was upset at the circumstance. Maybe more than upset, more like angry.

'Sure, go ahead,' I said, sitting in the wing chair. There would be no more sharing the couch. We were back to teacher and student.

He took a sip of the coffee and set down the mug before turning toward me. I'd never noticed before, but he really had soulful eyes when he didn't have the cop face going. 'To start with, how about you're wrong – about everything.' He let the words hang in the air before taking a deep breath and continuing. 'Ashleigh went to Sara's on her own, on the train and unannounced. She had a present for Mikey – completely out of his age range – and tried to act like family. She knew that I was coming over later and gave Sara the impression that I knew she was coming over earlier so they could spend some time together. Her real motive was to get Sara to like her and want us to be a couple.'

He leaned toward me. 'As if there was any chance of it happening. You do know my sister doesn't like her. If she said anything to you about her, I'm sure Sara used the special name she calls her. She doesn't think I know, but I do.'

I tried to give a noncommittal shrug as he continued. 'Ashleigh is doing everything she can to force the issue. She could do things one-sided when it came to walking out, but getting back together takes two to tango.' He cracked a smile, knowing I'd react to the cliché. I bit my lip and held it in. How fidgety old-maidish would it sound if I went into an explanation that the phrase originated in a 1952 song and gained popularity as an expression, before I offered alternative ways of saying it.

His face lit into a chuckle. 'You're thinking of other words, aren't you?'

'Maybe,' I said, uncomfortable that I was so predictable. 'Was there something else you wanted to say?'

'Just that I'm staying out of the dance, but trying to keep things peaceful so that she'll sign the papers.' He went on about how annoyed Sara had been. 'I had to use all the resolution tools I learned at the academy to keep things calm between them.' He kept his eyes on me. 'Are we good now?'

'Is that something you learned at the academy too?' I didn't know what to do with the matter-of-fact way he'd asked if things were now OK between us. I was stunned that I had been so wrong. And relieved.

'No,' he said with a mirthless laugh. 'They left it up to us to figure out how to deal with our personal relationships.' There was a moment of dead air, and in some rom-com movie we would have fallen into each other's arms, but neither of us made a move. He took another drag on the coffee and looked at me. 'Now that we've taken care of that, are you going to tell me who that guy was?'

It took me a moment to figure out who he was talking about, and then the episode in the coffee shop replayed in my mind. 'Remember the woman who may or may not have fallen down the stair on her own. That was her husband.'

'As a police officer, one of my jobs is to size up a confrontation and, while I couldn't see his face, his body language looked threatening. What was that about?'

It seemed like we were both glad to talk about something other than personal stuff, even though it seemed that even after all that he'd said, I was still in the third-wheel position. I figured that his mind had been kind of occupied with Ashleigh, so I didn't know how much he remembered about the situation. I repeated the whole story of how Michael Angel had been trying to stop the project I was working on, or at the very least get approval of the manuscript. I added that he seemed to think there was some damning information about him in it. 'He's under the impression that his wife gave me a more complete draft than she did. It's really just notes and prompts, along with some journal entries. She intended for us to work on it together. Every time I look through the papers again, I find something new. Whatever he's so worried about has to be in there somewhere.'

'You probably know what my advice would be as a law enforcement professional,' he said, cracking a smile.

'You would tell me to leave it alone,' I said.

'Right,' he said with a nod. 'Just fulfill the contract and create a pleasant memoir of the woman and her artist husband. Let him know that's what you're doing. You don't know what lengths he'll go to keep whatever it is a secret. She's dead and most likely it was homicide. Let the cops do their job and pin it on him.'

'I don't know if I can do that. I feel like I have a commitment to Maeve to finish what she started.' I looked in my coffee cup and then drained the remains. 'Remember she thought that I might be able to figure the ending myself. Talk about catnip for someone who wrote a mystery.'

'Any ideas of what it is?' he asked. 'You do realize that could be why she got killed.'

TWENTY-FIVE

'And the reason you were in Maeve Winslow's kitchen when the paramedics arrived again?' Detective Jankowski asked, staring at me from across the table in the coffee-shop booth.

He'd made another surprise visit the next morning. I'd figured out that cops didn't make appointments when they wanted to interrogate you. He'd rung my bell, and when he glanced up at me leaning over the railing from the third floor, he'd suggested I come down and we go across the street to the coffee shop.

I knew it was the stairs, but also going to a neutral place made it feel more friendly. Less like an interrogation and more like him just checking the facts again. It might have worked the first time, but I knew his game by now. My guess was he was coming up empty with evidence for any other suspects, and so had circled back to me. Honestly, I could see why. Claiming to find a body had been used by killers attempting to cover up their crimes, and it probably worked sometimes. The only good news was that despite waiting for the tox screen, he hadn't put the investigation on hold.

'The same reason I told you before,' I said. He was familiar with the coffee shop as it was a favorite among cops, and had ironically chosen the same booth in the window I'd been sitting in when Michael Angel had confronted me. 'Maeve had hired me to do some writing for her and we were supposed to discuss it,' I said. 'She was expecting me, so when the front door blew open in the wind, I went inside, figuring she had left it unlocked for me.' I shrugged and put up my hands to try to tell him that was it.

'And . . .' he waved his hand for me to go on, but I did the same shrug move again.

'There is no *and*,' I said. Technically there was. I had been vague about where I'd looked for Maeve before going to the kitchen where I'd found her. I hadn't mentioned that since we'd had our last meeting in her workroom, I'd gone up there expecting to find her. I'd barely taken more than a few moments to look around before I went down the back stairs expecting to catch up with her. I'd left all that out before and didn't want to add it in now.

'And no one knew about what you were supposed to be working on with her?' he asked.

'No,' I said, reminding him that my work with Maeve was supposed to be a secret.

'Then you never discussed it with Suzzanna Angel?' he said, holding my gaze.

I started to shake my head and then it came back to me that I had said something about a memoir the first time I'd gone to the house when she had answered the door. That's when she had scoffed at the idea. The only thing I could do was tell Jankowski the truth.

'I did mention it vaguely to her,' I said. There was a glint in his eye and the slightest of nods.

'So maybe your visit was a little different than you have suggested. It was about giving back the check. Ms Winslow had doubts about your competence, since most of what you do is create descriptions of ice-cream flavors and write love notes. She had decided that someone who made up a mystery would make up lies about conflict and negative information to make her memoir more exciting.' He looked at me, trying to read my reaction to what he'd said. 'I understand how hard it must have been to have her insult your ability and demand the money back when you needed it so badly.'

I didn't have to ask who'd told him this new version of what happened. Was this a hint of the *or else* that Michael Angel had talked about? He and Suzzanna must have gotten together and concocted this story. Did she actually lie and claim that Maeve had discussed the memoir and my qualifications with her? They were trying to trash me and say that I'd write lies. Now I was really angry, but I couldn't really show it. I had to stay calm as I dealt with Jankowski.

I had been vague about the writing project until now, but since Michael seemed to be feeding him inflammatory information, I decided to lay it out for the detective.

'Here is exactly what happened,' I began. 'Maeve had pitched writing a memoir, sort of a *me and the famous artist*, and gotten a publishing deal. But when she tried to write it, well, she couldn't. Time was running out, so she hired me to fix up what she'd started and go from there. She had meant to keep it a secret from her husband until it was done. She said it was supposed to be a surprise. I thought a happy one, but the way he's been acting, trying to stop the project, demanding to see what I have, and now spreading a story that it's going to contain lies, makes me wonder about the happy part. There is probably stuff he'd rather not come out.'

'Can I have a look at those notes?' he asked.

'If you have a warrant,' I said. He tried to hide it, but I saw a flicker of disappointment in his expression.

'Well, then maybe you can tell me if you've found anything I should know about in them?'

'Why? Because you think her death wasn't an accident?' I said.

'I'm not saying that, but if I did, do you have any idea who might want her out of the way.'

'You're asking if I have a list of suspects,' I said.

'No. I'm just curious as to what you've uncovered so far in the memoir.'

'A lot about art and Scotty dogs,' I said, in an effort to keep it light. He just looked at me deadpanned.

'We collected some fingerprints,' he said, eyeing me for my reaction.

'And you want mine to see if they match?' The waitress showed up and dropped off a plate of breakfast for him and a cup of coffee for me. 'I have never said I wasn't up in her workroom. It was her place to meet with people.' I didn't add that it was also probably where she died.

He began to work on the food. I knew I should probably leave it be, but I couldn't help myself. 'There are people who might have wanted her out of the way.' He looked up with a piece of steak stuck to the end of his fork.

'Is this you or that character Derek Streeter talking?' he asked. I was surprised when he mentioned my fictional detective by name. I knew that he knew I'd written one mystery, but not who the detective was.

'You read it?' I asked. He moved the steak to his mouth and, as he chewed it, he nodded his head in a dismissive sort of way. When he swallowed the steak, he tried to explain.

'You've been a suspect before and I looked at it as trying to get inside your head.' He cut another piece of meat and piled some eggs onto the meat on his fork. 'And it was something to do when I couldn't sleep. They say laughter is a good antidote to stress.'

'But it wasn't supposed to be funny,' I said. He let go of the unemotional cop look for a second and smiled.

'I know.' He ate the forkful and slathered a piece of toast in butter and jam.

I might have gotten a little defensive. 'You're not my audience,' I said.

'Whatever,' he said, wanting to move on. 'You might as well tell me about those suspects of yours.' His tone was off-handed, but I noticed he'd put down the toast and picked up his pen and flipped open the notebook.

'This is from the notes and what I've observed. There's Michael Angel's ex-wife. Maeve seems to have taken up with him while he was still married to Rina. She has a lot of anger. When they were married, he was a struggling artist. Now he's bringing in high prices for his canvases and she's still working at an art supply store. Guess who she blames?'

He asked if I happened to know the name of the art store and he scribbled it down. 'Anyone else?'

'There's Suzzanna Angel. She could have blamed Maeve for the end of her parents' marriage. I've heard that happens. And when I met her, she seemed very hostile to Maeve.' I wondered if I should mention her last phone call to me, but decided to leave it be.

So far, I wasn't getting much of a reaction from him, which either meant he was hiding it, or I was really offering lackluster suspects.

'I'm sure you considered Michael Angel,' I said. 'I don't have to tell you that spouses are usually the first suspects.'

He glared at me derisively. 'You're right, you don't have to tell me.'

'Then of course, you checked his alibi?' I let it hang in the air.

'He would only need an alibi if it was murder, and I'm not saying it was or wasn't. But he did account for his time.' I considered telling him what Kent had said about Michael leaving and then coming back a while later. I didn't remember where he said he'd gone, but I had already figured that he could have gone wherever then come back and dealt with Maeve and then returned, making it seem like he'd been there the whole time. Then I had a better idea.

'How did you check it exactly?' I said.

He pursed his lips in an impatient expression. 'I certainly don't have to explain to you, but he went to a fancy charity brunch. A documentary filmmaker was there with him. I gather they didn't want the filming to be intrusive to the event, and so she operated the handheld camera.' He gave me a tired look. 'I've done this before.' I wanted to ask him how he knew Michael had been at the event the whole time. I might not be able to ask that, but he'd just given me the information I wanted to know. It was an old trick, making it seem like you already knew something, and I was surprised he'd fallen for it. I hadn't known the exact nature of Michael's alibi until Jankowski had told me.

Then he did something that surprised me. He volunteered some information. 'The medical examiner is waiting for some results before he makes a judgment about the cause and manner of her death. We were waiting for those results, too. We need to put the manpower where it's needed at the moment. But Michael Angel called raising holy hell. He was insistent that I investigate you again. Now I realize it's something personal he has against you.' His plate was empty and he waved for the check.

I went back across the street, thinking over the conversation. I had given more information than I'd gotten and I regretted it. As I went past the second floor, the door opened and Sara looked out.

'Can you come in?' she asked, seeming a little agitated. She did that a lot when she needed someone to keep an eye on Mikey while she showered or did something uninterrupted.

'Need some me time?' I said with an understanding smile. I could only imagine how hard it was to try to do anything when you had a toddler walking around with his hands out, just reaching to get into stuff.

'It's not that.' She grabbed my arm and pulled me inside just before Mikey ran out into the hall. 'You saw her, didn't you?' She shook her head with annoyance. 'Did you see those pinched-looking eyebrows? Doesn't she look like Cruella de Vil? Or maybe Satan's girlfriend.'

She seemed very worked up and I just nodded in agreement. She wasn't even paying attention to Mikey, and ignored it when he started bringing in her sneakers and trying to put them on her feet. His way of telling her he wanted to go out.

'I couldn't believe it when she showed up here, unannounced and not escorted by my brother. I thought I was going to throw up at the way she was so over-the-top friendly. She always looked at Mikey as being a nuisance, and suddenly she shows up with a present for him. Highly inappropriate since it says for seven years and above. I'm just so upset. What if Ben falls for whatever she's putting out there and gets back with her?'

'I'm sure Ben will do the right thing,' I said. 'It's hard when someone is so brazen as she appears to be. Just showing up here like that. It's not as if they're living together.'

'She made it sound like they were. She was about to tell me something else about their relationship, but then Ben showed up and interrupted her,' Sara said. 'I'd hate every holiday if I had to spend them with her again. I don't know what my brother was thinking about when he married her in the first place.'

I imagined that Ashleigh had been about to mention that she and Ben were still married. I was glad that Ben had kept her from spilling the truth. It would only have upset Sara even more, if that was possible. I wanted to do something to help my friend feel better and offered to keep Mikey company if she wanted to grab a shower. She hugged me like I was a life-preserver in the middle of the ocean. 'Assleigh would never do that.'

She usually asked me what I was working on, but she was too agitated, and after my meeting with the detective I was glad to put it out of my mind for a few minutes. Between writing the memoir and being concerned about who might have wanted Maeve dead, my mind was twisted in a knot. Dealing with a toddler was a refreshing change. I didn't even mind when he kept driving his toy truck up my leg to my knee and letting it slide back down while he laughed.

The escape from all things to do with Maeve ended when I went back upstairs. I thought over the conversation with Jankowski again. He'd brought up the documentary filmmaker as part of Michael's alibi. I went back through the notes and found the snippet about Maeve meeting Jennifer Soames. All it really said was that filmmaker had talked about spending a lot of time with Michael and her effort to find out about the man behind the art. It was just a generalized statement and I needed something more specific to put into the memoir. Since it had become abundantly clear that Michael would do whatever to try to thwart the manuscript, I couldn't very well be upfront about why I wanted to meet with Jennifer. It was better to deal with her the same way I had with Michael's first wife. In other words, undercover. That's where Tizzy came in. I'd gotten used to having help and hoped I could get it again.

'Do you feel like being my wingman again?' I said to Tizzy. I'd gone for a walk to clear my mind and ended up on the campus and her office as I'd done before. She got up from her seat and took me out in the hall, pointing to Alex's open door.

'Do I ever,' she said when she felt free to speak. 'You have made my life so exciting.' She squeezed me in a hug. 'Though Theo will probably be jealous. He really really liked being included the other night. By the way, he asked me to ask you if he can join the writing group.' She was on a roll and all I could do was let her continue. 'He's a poet and he wants to write a novel. After teaching students about English Lit, he wants to create some.'

'And you're OK with him joining?' I asked.

'Maybe not having him as another wingman. It's wingman, not wingmen. But I'm OK with him joining the writing group. You saw how he is, very specific. He'll probably corner Ed and tell him his sex moves don't add up.' She punctuated it with a laugh.

'What kind of poetry does he write?' I asked. We'd never had a poet in the group and I wasn't sure how to critique it.

'Light verse, amusing with words that rhyme.' She pulled out a piece of paper. He leaves them in little notes for me. She started to read.

> *Roly poly morning*
> *Came to me with no warning.*
> *Better than the buzzer on a clock.*
> *Even if it was a shock.*
> *Willing for it any time,*
> *Be it in your room or mine*
> *I'm always ready for a repeat*
> *Under the covers with you in the a.m.,*
> *is always a treat.*

Her voice had started to warble. 'I guess that's kind of personal. I probably should have had Ben read it,' she said with a giggle. 'You get the idea, not about the subject, but he doesn't write about heavy stuff. They're fun. And as for his novel. He wants to write something for kids about a superhero who is either Dr Smarty Pants, Dr Know It All or Cedric Von Brainiac.' She took a breath. 'But tell me about being your wingman. I'll get out my trench coat and fedora again.'

I told her about my visit from Jankowski. 'I got him to think about other suspects.' I looked at Tizzy. 'I think he's pretty much off me as one of them, even though Michael Angel is doing whatever he can to cause me trouble. It made me think about his alibi and a contradiction in it.' I told her what Kent had said about him coming back home. 'The one who gave him the alibi was Jennifer Soames, the woman who is making the documentary about him. I want to see if I can get something from her for the memoir and see what she says about his alibi. I thought we could set something up to meet without her knowing who I am, since there's a good chance Michael Angel warned her about talking to me.'

'I'm in,' Tizzy said. 'We could really talk to Theo first. He was curious about her after the reception, and I think he did some research on who she is.' Her phone began to ring in the office and she switched into working mode. 'Better not mention the poem. I'm not sure he meant for it to be shared.'

I had checked Tizzy's availability and asked if she was agreeable to me using her name and saying we were from the university. 'Well, we are, or I am,' she said, giving me the go-ahead. When I went home, I tracked down Jennifer's phone number and set up a time to meet her the following week, claiming we were interested in doing a short documentary.

As I gathered up Maeve's notes, a page slipped out. I saw that it was from her journal. There was a bit about some things she needed at the grocery store and that parent night was coming up at the school, and then at the bottom of the page there was a single line.

He's meeting with her again. This is real. I'm the odd one out.

TWENTY-SIX

I t was an uncomfortably quiet weekend. Ben sent me a text saying that he had to work overtime on both days. Sara let me know that Quentin didn't have to work that weekend and they were off to spend time with his family. Even Tizzy and Theo weren't around. They drove up to Madison to see their daughter at the University of Wisconsin. I had no choice but to continue to comb through all the pages again, looking for tidbits I could make into something about Maeve. I found something sweet from their anniversary. She had just written some sentences and I created an entry and called it *Sweet Moment*.

> *It was our third anniversary. Michael woke me up with a pot of my favorite spiced tea drink that he had made from scratch. When I thanked him for the chai tea, he teased me and said I'd really just said tea tea, since chai meant tea in Hindi. He thanked me for marrying him and putting up with all his moods. He said he felt bad about our wedding. We'd gotten married at city hall and had no reception. Michael didn't care, but he worried that I would have liked something with a white dress and a party afterwards. As we sat together drinking the fragrant concoction, I told him that it wasn't the wedding that mattered, but what had come after it. We'd talked about how far we'd come since then. It was a perfect moment.*

I'd used a little poetic license and put the words about chai meaning tea in Michael's mouth, using something that Maeve had said when she had made some for me. But I didn't have to enhance the way she described the day. She very clearly did love Michael, from the time he'd been an unknown painter managing the coffee house until now. Whatever anger she seemed to have was connected to her worry about losing him to someone else.

I wrote some more entries, but they were all over the place in terms of time. I was going to have to figure out a structure and then fit them all in.

I was actually relieved when it got to Tuesday and I knew the writers' group was going to meet. I looked forward to noise and having people in my place after all the recent days of my own company. I did my usual clearing of the dining-room table, this time adding an extra chair for Theo. I wasn't clear about where he was in the novel, but I thought he'd be a good addition to the group.

Theo was certainly anxious to be part of the group. He and Tizzy arrived before seven and were already around the table when the others arrived. I started to introduce him, but he stopped me. 'I'm Theo, Tizzy's husband, and I think I know who all of you are,' he said with a friendly smile. He stopped on Ed and took in the track pants and the commuter mug. 'You're the one who writes the stuff none of the women can read out loud. I'm sure I can do the honors whatever you write, no matter how suggestive.' He turned to Daryl. 'I know you're sensitive and I promise to be kind.' He looked at her wrist and hand. 'Nice tats.' She appeared confused, and both uncomfortable and reassured at the same time. 'You're Ben, the cop,' he said as Ben slid into a chair. The friendly smile faded a bit as Theo glanced over at me and I wondered what else Tizzy had told him.

I was right. Theo was a good fit. His comments were all diplomatic, but accurate. Ben looked a little peeved when Theo said that his work seemed lacking in emotion. After the debacle about the short story, Ben had brought in the beginning of a story with an uptight character. It was clear that Tizzy had told her husband about the progression that Ben had made and now seemed to have been lost. Theo hadn't brought anything to show them, but he promised to bring the beginning of his novel and in the meantime just offered the possible names of the main character. Nobody said anything and it was up to me to ask him who he thought his readers would be.

'Kids,' he said enthusiastically. He was already thinking about it being a series.

I suggested he choose Cedric Von Brainiac then and they all agreed.

When the group broke up, Theo started to hang around the table, but Tizzy pulled him away, promising that I was coming for sherry the next day.

Ben threw me an uncertain glance as he was about to go through the door. I was hungry and I couldn't see what was wrong with accepting a plate of food, so I gave him a nod.

When he returned with the plate of dinner, he seemed distracted. I asked him about working all weekend. He merely nodded and said he didn't want to talk about it. I was left wondering if he'd really been working or if he'd been tied up with Ashleigh instead. He didn't stay long, saying he had another long day with overtime coming up. Only when he was at the door did he ask if there'd been any developments about Maeve. He seemed tired and it was late so I didn't bother telling him about Jankowski's visit.

I had come to look forward to joining Theo and Tizzy in the early evening. It was the time of night that I found the loneliest, imagining families gathering around the table for dinner. It was probably more of a fable leftover from when my family was whole than a current reality, since it seemed like these days people grabbed some take-out food and ate in front of the TV.

Theo answered the door, glad to see me. He was anxious to tell me how much he liked being part of the writers' group and couldn't wait to bring in his first pages for them to see.

'Tizzy will be down in a minute,' he said, taking me into the front room which was already set up for our get-together. I caught the scent of his martini and wanted to move closer for a bigger whiff. I commented again on how I loved the aroma of gin.

'It's the juniper berries that it's made from,' he said. 'That's the predominant scent. But it varies depending on what botanicals are mixed in. The name gin is a derivative of the French word for juniper berries, *genièvre*.' He smiled at me. 'That's just the kind of thing Cedric Von Brainiac would say.'

'Really? What makes gin smell the way it does is appropriate for a kids' book?'

'You're so right,' he said. 'That's why I need to be in a group. I get carried away and forget the obvious.' He bypassed Tizzy's waiting glass of sherry and pointed at the empty glass next to it. 'I wasn't sure what you were drinking,' he said. I considered asking for a splash of sherry with a lot of soda, but even that might give me a buzz and I wanted to be completely alert.

'I'll stick with club soda,' I said. I didn't go into why I was drinking something non-alcoholic, again afraid he'd get caught up in doing research about why alcohol affected me the way it did. Instead, I brought up what Tizzy had said about him doing research on Jennifer Soames.

'You know me, I hear about anything or anyone and I want to find out more. I'm like a kid asking endless questions. My computer is like a magic carpet taking me to the answers.'

I was afraid he was getting back to the idea for his Cedric Von Brainiac book and tried to keep him focused on Jennifer. 'Where did your magic carpet take you?' I asked.

He seemed pleased that I'd used his descriptive phrase. 'First, I made a few detours and got caught up in the need for content now. With all the Internet and pay channels, there's a big need for programs to fill all that time. And I found that niche stuff, which never would have found a home before, now does. Eventually I got to checking out Jennifer. I found her Wikipedia page, which she probably wrote herself. It described her as someone who is an expert at it all, producing, directing, editing, and even acting as narrator if need be. She went to Columbia College and started out as an intern for a broadcast channel's news department. There was something about her being award-winning, but when I followed the trail to what it really was, it was an honorable mention for a student project. That's what I call putting a spin on something,' he said, pleased with his own figuring. 'Of course, she has a website. I was curious if she is someone who makes films for the love of it, or the commerce.' His expression drooped slightly. 'I was hoping it would be clear that she did it for the love of it. I guess I'm a romantic, but I like to think that creative people all follow their passion.'

'So, what about her?' I asked.

'Probably both, judging by her credits. She claims to get deeply involved with whatever she works on,' he said, then he shrugged. 'But who knows if that's real, or the way she wants to be perceived.'

Tizzy came in with a bottle of club soda and some lemon slices and filled my glass as she asked what we were talking about. Theo filled her in, repeating what he'd found out about Jennifer Soames.

'Veronica thinks she might be a little too deeply involved with Michael Angel,' Tizzy said as she took her seat.

We all picked up our glasses and toasted the end of another day before getting back to talking about Jennifer Soames.

Theo had his laptop on the table and began typing in something and then he looked up. 'I think Veronica might be right. I remember at the reception that I thought she was Michael Angel's wife. I just looked up "body language" and I can see why I thought that. The way they were standing and the way she looked at him and laughed at something he said and then touched his arm, made it seem they had an intimate connection.'

Theo looked at Tizzy and me. 'Why the sudden interest in her? Do you ladies have some plan in mind?'

'Veronica thinks she might know something about what happened to Michael Angel's wife,' Tizzy said.

'And she might have something I can use in the memoir,' I added.

'I'm helping Veronica with the meeting. We decided it was best not to tell her what we really want, so we're telling her we're interviewing her because we're interested in doing a documentary.' She looked at her husband and saw his expression slipping. 'We would have included you, but three people might be too many.'

'At least let me help you come up with a cover story,' he said, sounding disappointed that he couldn't be part of our masquerade. He went back on his computer. 'The local PBS station has a lot of short features about different spots in Chicago. What if you said the university wanted to make something about the campus and then let the PBS station air it?'

He really wanted to be a part of it, so Tizzy and I agreed to use his cover story. It also sounded plausible.

Theo showed me her website and found a blog that mentioned what she was currently working on. It was all about Michael Angel, and how she was working on two projects about him. One piece was for a network news show that was a profile of him and focused on his nomination for the prize. Concurrently, she was working on a documentary about the man behind the dog, as she called it.

I brought up what I read in Maeve's journal. 'She seems to have seen Jennifer as a threat.'

'After seeing her at the reception, I think we can understand why,' Theo said. 'I think the woman who turned out to be his daughter does, too. They were both stuck to him—'

'Like glue,' Tizzy said, finishing the thought with a shake of her head at her husband. 'If you're going to hang out with us and be in the group, you'd better remember that Veronica has an aversion to clichés.'

'I wouldn't call it an aversion exactly,' I said, thinking about how it made me sound. 'I sometimes use them myself. They get the point across quickly. I just think that in writing, it's better to be original.'

'OK by me,' Theo said. 'I love a challenge. Let's see how else I could say that. The two women hung onto him like appendages.' He gave it a moment, then dismissed it. 'How about stuck to him like they were made of Velcro.'

'Better,' I said. 'But you could probably just say they stuck with him.'

'I love hanging out with you ladies,' Theo said, and passed his glass close enough so I could take another hit of the wonderful fragrance.

I liked the way Tizzy made sure that he felt included. They were a team.

'We're not doing anything illegal,' Tizzy said with a nervous titter as the two of us stood in her office. Her boss Alex had left for an all-day seminar and Jennifer was supposed to arrive there any minute.

The plan was to let her see us in the office and then hustle her out of there. We were going to do a variation on the good cop, bad cop, only in the sense that we would play off each other. One of us would think she was right for the job and the other would have doubts.

'Showtime,' Tizzy said as we heard approaching footsteps. A moment later the filmmaker came into the office.

'Jennifer Soames,' she said, introducing herself as she looked at the two of us, probably trying to figure out who was in charge. She was about my age, but much more confident and direct than I could ever hope to be. She had a duster-length sweater over pants, with a burgundy scarf wrapped in a loose, keyhole style.

Since I'd presented Tizzy as being the one in charge when I set up the meeting, she took over, introducing herself and then me. 'This is Véronique Schwartzstein,' Tizzy said, giving me a wink. I had to choke back a laugh by appearing to have a coughing spell. I had said I didn't want Jennifer to know who I really was, but Tizzy and I hadn't discussed an alias for me. On her own, Tizzy had made my first name sound French and then translated my last name into German. Since I wasn't the one in charge, Jennifer didn't seem that interested in me anyway, and gave me just a cordial nod before turning her attention back on Tizzy.

'Why don't you tell me what you have in mind,' Jennifer said, glancing around the dull-looking office.

'Yes, we should show her the location,' Tizzy said. 'Why don't you explain, Véronique.'

I swallowed back another smile at the unfamiliar name. 'I don't know if you're familiar with the campus,' I said. 'But there's a pond next to one of the science buildings. My associate thinks it would be a good subject for a short film about a highlight of the campus.' I kept a serious expression, implying that I wasn't necessarily in favor of it.

'Oh, Véronique,' Tizzy said with a frustrated wave of her arms that sent her kimono jacket into a swirl. 'There absolutely is a story there. The change of the seasons. How much it means to the neighborhood kids. I bet there have been proposals on that bridge. Maybe we could do a reenactment.' She waved to Jennifer. 'Let me show you and then you can be the judge.' Tizzy threw me a dismissive shake of her head before leading the way out the door. We flanked her as the three of us walked across the campus.

'Why don't you tell us a little about yourself? Like what are you currently working on?' I said.

'I'm in the midst of a documentary about an artist. His name is Michael Angel.' She glanced at us to see if we recognized the name.

'I know who he is,' I said and looked to Tizzy. 'Those paintings with the dog. She's doing a film about a person. But we're interested in something about a place.'

Tizzy picked up on my cue. 'But it must be harder to capture a personality than to do a background on a place.' She turned to Jennifer. 'Isn't that so?'

'It is different working with a person,' the filmmaker said. 'And you're right, it is more complex.'

'You must have gotten to know him quite well,' I said. 'And probably the people around him.'

She nodded in agreement. 'Speaking about the people around him. Didn't I hear that his wife died? Some kind of accident,' Tizzy said. 'I think I heard that he wasn't home. He was at a party.' Tizzy shook her head in disapproval, as if he was somehow at fault for not being there.

It worked and she became defensive. 'He wasn't off having fun,' Jennifer said. 'The social gatherings he goes to are really about mixing with wealthy collectors. We filmed a bit of it for the documentary.'

'So, then he was there with you the whole time,' I said. She gave me an odd look.

'It wasn't a date,' she said, trying to make it sound like a joke. 'I just grabbed a few shots and got a few people's opinion on his art while he socialized.'

She seemed a little overwhelmed with our questions and I worried about pushing her too far too soon and pretended to be talking to Tizzy. 'Let's give her a chance to look at Botany Pond first and then we can talk some more.'

Tizzy picked up on what I meant and changed the subject to that of our supposed short film. We'd stopped on the curved bridge over the small body of water. Being that it was September, the area around the small pond next to the ivy-covered building was in fall beauty. Ducks were still swimming and lily pads floated on the water. The grass was still green and the ginko tree still had most of its leaves. Tizzy explained that the bridge had been the gift of a long-ago graduating class and another class had given a stone bench. Jennifer took out her phone and took photos.

'I was talking to my contact at Channel Eleven, and she liked the idea of a film about something at the university.' Tizzy looked out over the water. 'This could be just the beginning. I think she said something like: if you get them made, we'll put them on.'

'That is once we decide on everything,' I said. 'Like who we want to work with.'

I glanced at Jennifer and she had definitely picked up on the idea that there could be more work. My comment was meant to imply that we were talking to others and she seemed to have understood that.

'Why don't we continue this over some coffee?' Tizzy said, slipping me a nod. Jennifer agreed, seeming anxious to please us.

I suggested the coffee kiosk that Tizzy and I frequented.

'That sounds excellent,' the filmmaker said. 'It'll give me more of a chance to see the cinematic virtues of the area.' I kept a serious expression as I listened to the verbiage, making it seem that I still wasn't sold on her.

We grabbed a bench in the courtyard and Tizzy went to get the coffee drinks.

'How close to finished are you with the Michael Angel project?' I asked. 'I'm curious how long something like that takes.'

She explained that it was stop and start because it was spread over a span of time. 'We'll finish when the award he's up for is announced.'

'Do you work from a script?'

'Not exactly. I come up with an idea of what I want to

include, but a lot is done in the editing.' She started to say
that we would have a choice about the film about the pond.
'If you want to cover the four seasons, it'll take longer.'
'What about when something happens that changes everything, like Michael Angel's wife dying? How are you dealing
with that?' I asked.
She seemed a little perturbed but was trying to hide it. 'The
film I'm making is really about him, so we'll probably just
make a mention of what happened at the end.'
'You must have gotten to know her. I would think you'd
get personally invested in the people you're making a film
about.' I left it hanging, hoping she'd go on.
'I interviewed her only once. It was up in her workroom.
That's where she meets people. I mean *met* people. We had
tea and did an art project. We talked about Michael and his
art. That was it. She was busy being an art teacher and, as far
as I could tell, had tired of being the one standing off to the
side while he was the center of attention. Being the wife of
someone famous has its challenges,' Jennifer said with a shrug.
'What about him? He must be having a hard time dealing
with your film now that his wife died.'
'You don't have to worry. I can pivot when things change,'
Jennifer said. Tizzy returned with the coffee drinks and handed
them out.
'Since you are on the inside,' Tizzy said to Jennifer, 'you
must have gotten more details about what happened to Michael
Angel's wife. I heard it was an accident.'
Jennifer's body language changed as she figured something
was going on besides her viewing Botany Pond. She straightened and eyed the two of us. 'Who's your contact at Channel
Eleven. I've done a lot of work with them and know everybody
there.'
Tizzy and I both froze, but only for a moment. 'I can't name
names,' Tizzy said, appearing offended. 'Nothing personal,
but I can't have you speaking to them until we have our deal
set.' She got up and gestured for me to do the same. 'We have
your information,' my friend said. 'We'll be in touch.'

TWENTY-SEVEN

Tizzy and I started to retrace our steps across the campus to her office, but she got a text from Alex wondering where she was. He'd left the seminar early. I'd hoped that we would have a chance to talk over our meeting with Jennifer, thinking that she might have picked up something I missed, but when we got to the circle in the center of the campus, we separated, agreeing to meet for sherry again.

I felt adrift after the abrupt ending to everything and, as I walked back along 57th, decided to stop at the coffee shop. It was mushroom soup day again.

Since I tended to go there during off-time, it was usually quiet, so I was surprised when I walked in and the place was super busy. I took a booth in the window that was the only open spot.

The server knew me by sight and greeted me when she dropped off a menu.

'Busy,' I said, glancing at all the full tables.

'The other room, too,' she said, gesturing toward the overflow space that had been a separate storefront. I pushed the menu back, telling her I didn't need it, and ordered the soup.

While I waited, I took out my ever-present notebook and pen. The meeting with Jennifer had been successful in at least one way and I began to write down some notes. She'd given me an idea for the memoir when she mentioned being in Maeve's workroom. I would write something about how Maeve entertained by having her guests do art projects and drink tea. I would make it into a scene using some of the conversation I'd had with Maeve, and I could even mention a specific art project. I thought of how I would describe the décor and the kind of tea she served.

Thinking about her serving tea stirred something in my memory, but before I could capture the thought, a ping on my phone announcing the arrival of a text grabbed my attention.

I made myself wait to check it out, still insisting I wasn't going be like a Pavlovian dog. The soup arrived and I even took a generous taste before I glanced at the screen. I'd been expecting it to be from Tizzy, but I was surprised to see it was from Ben. He'd written SORRY in capital letters with an explanation that everything had been in chaos lately and asked if we could get together on the weekend and he'd explain all. I gather he meant about all his overtime work and how abrupt he'd been the other night. I was embarrassed by how happy I was at the text and relieved that the way he'd been acting wasn't meant to cut off anything personal between us. Not wanting to seem too anxious, I ate some more soup before I texted back a yes. He sent back a happy emoji and asked what I was up to. I typed in eating soup at the coffee shop and hit send.

There were no more pings after that and I gave my full attention to the delicious creamy soup, feeling myself smile.

I barely noticed people coming and going or the servers rushing by until the one who'd waited on me came by with a cup of hot cider and set it on my table.

'I didn't order that,' I said, and she smiled.

'You must have an admirer. Someone ordered it and asked for it to be brought to you. Enjoy!' she said, walking away as another customer waved her over.

I looked at the amber drink and thought of Ben. He was really trying to smooth things over with the romantic gesture of sending me a drink. I let it all sink in for a moment and then texted him with merely the words, *Thank you.*

My phone pinged a moment later. *Thanks for what?*

I guessed that the two words weren't enough after what he'd done, so I spelled it out that I was wowed by the arrival of the cup of hot cider that he'd had delivered to me. I sat back wondering if I'd said enough. The sound of my phone ringing made me jump and I grabbed it to answer it.

'What, you want more praise?' I said, smiling.

'Don't drink it,' Ben said in a warning voice. 'I didn't send it.' I started to dismiss his concern, but he reminded me of my encounter with Michael Angel.

I could hear his cop radio going off telling him to answer

a call, but he wouldn't hang up until I had promised not to drink it, and to keep it so it could be checked. He didn't have to tell me to question the server about who had sent it.

I didn't want to let on that there was anything wrong with the drink and asked for a to-go cup for it before trying to get more details about who was behind it.

'Sorry, hon,' the server said. 'I don't recall. It seems like everybody came in at once and I was running around getting orders and delivery food. Someone handed me the cup and told me to take it to you – the woman sitting in the window booth by herself.'

I poured the cider into a to-go cup and carried the cup home as if it might be full of plutonium. I didn't know what to do with it when I got to my place, and finally left it sitting on the coffee table where I thought it could do no harm.

There were more texts from Ben checking to find out if I'd gotten any answers. Then he called again and suggested that I call Jankowski. There was a lot of noise in the background and I guessed he was on a call.

'No way,' I said. 'It would sound crazy and I don't want to stir things up with him.'

He sounded harried and said he had to go. I heard someone in the background yell, 'Freeze with your hands up.'

I brought the to-go cup with me when I went to Tizzy's. As soon as she heard the story, Tizzy reminded Theo of the kit he'd ordered that could tell if there were drugs in a drink. He'd gotten it when we were conjecturing that Maeve's tea might have been tampered with.

'I knew this would come in handy,' he said as he retrieved the package and read over the instructions. He dipped a spoon in the drink and let a few drops drip on a testing medallion. 'And now we wait,' he said as the three of us hung over expectantly. Then two lines appeared and Theo checked the directions. 'That means there are drugs in it,' he said, sounding excited at first and then concerned as he looked over at me.

'I bet it was Jennifer,' Tizzy said. 'The timing is just too convenient.'

'You could be right. The name change probably didn't fool her; she must have known who I was. I wonder if that means she killed Maeve or she's covering for Michael Angel,' I said.

'You should call the detective and tell him all about it,' Tizzy said. 'If she tried to drug you, she must have done it to Maeve.'

Theo seemed thoughtful. 'But didn't you say that the police didn't find any evidence of anything at the scene? That's why they're waiting for the tox screen.'

'I'll have to think about what I can do,' I said.

'At least take this with you,' Theo said, dropping the test kit in my purse. I thanked them both and got up to go.

Rocky was waiting for me when I got home and, hoping to calm myself after the whole issue with my drink, I did some routine things like feeding him and checking the mail before considering my own dinner. Not that I was really hungry. While some of the leftover stew was heating, Caleb called.

'We have to think of something else. She's still not responding,' he said, sounding despondent.

I reminded him of our idea of the note with the blanket apology, but he wasn't cheered by the thought and said it wouldn't work. I had no idea what else we could do, besides packing him in a box and getting him delivered to her house. I didn't share that idea with him in case he thought it was a good plan.

'I'll think of something,' I said before hanging up. I tried to eat the warmed-over vegetable stew, but I was too tense from everything. I tried chamomile tea and crocheting, but neither helped. Finally, I looked through my notes, thinking maybe I could put the wired feeling to good use and work on the memoir.

It was crazy, but writing did what the chamomile and crochet couldn't do. I was in the flow, making up a whole scenario of Maeve in the attic room. I was seeing it all in my mind's eye and then something popped up in my memory and I put my hands over my eyes in dismay. How could I have forgotten? There was no way that I could tell Jankowski. Was there any way I could make things right?

As I went to stack up the pile of Maeve's papers, the photograph I'd seen before fell out. I started to just give it a cursory look, but this time I checked the back of it. I was stunned by what I read and then the pieces started to fit and I thought I knew what it was that Maeve was going to tell me.

Not surprisingly, I slept poorly and awoke filled with nervous energy. I had no idea what to do with what I knew. I needed a release to even be able to think straight. I pulled on some sweat pants and a sweater and headed outside, hoping to walk off some of the tension. Without even considering where to walk, I headed to Harper.

I didn't have a plan and I felt like a guitar string that had been tightened too far. Maybe that was why when I saw the woman on the front porch of the house next to Maeve's and figured she was Caleb's wife, I lost it. It made it even worse when I saw the white envelope on the ground next to her foot.

I stormed up the stairs, glaring at her. 'What is wrong with you? Why won't you talk to him? Let him apologize and, even if you don't accept it, he'll be able to let go.' I probably seemed a little unhinged and I realized I hadn't bothered to comb my hair, which must have added to the crazy look.

She took a step back and put out her hand to fend me off in case I moved any closer. 'Who are you?'

I had a moment of panic and I wondered how to answer. I was supposed to be invisible, stay in the background, letting the notes speak for my client. But she was just too hard-hearted and I was going to have to come out of the shadow.

'I'm a friend of Caleb's. He really, really wants to work things out.'

She put her hand down and eyed me with interest. I'd never really thought about what she looked like when we were composing all those notes, but seeing her in person, she appeared like the perfect match for him. She had nice features, but did nothing to enhance them. Her clothes were so unremarkable that they didn't register even as I looked at them – other than noting she was wearing pants and some kind of top with a hoodie over it.

She gave me a sharp look. 'Not another one. Caleb is easy picking for any predatory female.'

'You think I'm his girlfriend?' I said, incredulous. I pointed at the envelope on the ground. 'Your husband hired me to help him write love notes to you. He never told me what caused the rift between you, but he's desperate for you to talk to him so he can do whatever it takes to work things out.'

'I knew he didn't write those notes. I figured he copied them out of a book or something.' She peered at me again. 'He actually hired you to write them?' She jiggled her head as if that would help it make sense. 'He's the most passive person you can imagine.' She glanced down at the note and box of candy corn. 'Did you pick out the things he sent along?'

'That was all him. And the artwork on that is from him as well.'

She leaned down and somewhat reluctantly picked up the envelope. She took a moment before carefully opening it and looking at it intently. I felt an obligation to add my narration. 'It's none of my business and actually more profitable for me if you don't talk to him, but he's a good guy and no matter what he did, he seems to regret it.'

'I'm not surprised he never told you,' she said as her expression hardened. 'He had an affair with a teaching assistant and there's a child. An affair is one thing, but a baby is another thing entirely. It doesn't go away.' I noticed her shoulders drop and her expression softened. 'But if I'm honest, I know it wasn't his fault. She went after him, seduced him with the idea of having his child.'

I was astonished at what she'd said. The thought of him being pursued seemed kind of crazy. He hardly oozed sex appeal. My thoughts must have shown in my face.

'You have to understand, he's like the rock star of mathematicians,' she went on, shaking her head as if thinking aloud. 'He solved an unsolvable problem and is rated as one of the greatest living mathematicians.'

'Really?' I said stunned. 'What happened with the woman?'

'She thought he would marry her, divorcing me first. He was befuddled by the whole thing, except that he wants the baby to have his name and share parenting with her.'

Now I understood why Caleb wouldn't tell me what happened. 'Wow, that's really messy,' I said. 'But could you at least talk to him?'

She looked down at the note and traced the heart he'd made

on the front. 'He really made this for me?' I could tell she was softening. 'It certainly is something that he went to all the trouble of hiring you and actually doing artwork . . .'

We were still standing at the base of her stairs and I glanced toward the lavender house with the fish-scale siding. I noticed a group of people going up the stairs and inside the house.

'What's going on over there?' I asked. She looked up from the card and followed my gaze.

'It's that odious man next door. He came over here to complain that my cat was wandering in his yard. He's always having people over. I think he has them hang out in his studio and watch him paint. It doesn't seem to matter that his wife died recently.' She gave the house a disapproving glare as more people went up the stairs.

I watched the arrival with an entirely different thought. It could be a cover for me. Did I dare try to slip in and make things right? The whole episode with my tainted drink and then my writing the piece about Maeve entertaining in her workroom had sparked my memory. In all the confusion that came after, I'd forgotten completely about breaking the cup and trying to cover my clumsiness with moving it and switching it with an unused one from the counter. I remembered there had been liquid in the broken cup that I'd left in my haste to remove the evidence. 'Evidence' was the key word here. That cup and the paper around it were evidence of who else had been in the workroom with Maeve. I couldn't tell Jankowski about it on the chance that he'd consider that I had tampered with evidence. Maybe it was a foolish idea, but somehow I thought if I put the cup back, I could get Jankowski to revisit the workroom without knowing I was involved. There was no time to figure that part out now. The immediate need was to put things back where they belonged.

I made a fast exit from Caleb's wife, though by now I knew her real name was Rebeka. She went back inside, hopefully to call Caleb, and I slipped down the driveway of Maeve's house. I could see the crowd in his studio as I went toward the back of the house. Seeing the leftovers of the vegetable garden in the backyard made me think of Kent and of something he'd said about the basement door lock had needed to be fixed. Did I dare try to slip up to the workroom? My heart was thudding as I plastered myself against the building to keep out of sight until I reached the few steps down to the basement door. Convincing myself that I hadn't lost my mind and was just trying to make things right, I tried the basement door and discovered the lock was still broken.

Taking a deep breath, I went inside. The inside was a jumble of boxes and laundry things. I found the crude staircase and, when I opened the door at the top, saw that I was in the kitchen. Was I really going to do this? I gave a last look back at the basement stairs. There was still a chance to retreat. But I propelled myself forward. The sound of voices coming from the front of the house would hopefully cover any noise that I made.

The back stairs were dark, and I touched the wall to keep my balance as I traveled up them. The next staircase was less worrisome and better lit. My breath came out in a gush when I reached the attic. I probably should have gone right to moving the cup back, but I wanted to check out the storage room first to see if there was anything to prove my conjecture about what Maeve was going to tell me. This time I lifted the ghostly looking sheets to see what was underneath and my mouth fell open.

But now speed was of the essence. I went back to the main room and retrieved the cup and paper around it. There was still a hint of the spicy smell of the chai drink. My hand was shaking as I took out the test kit that Theo had given me. I took some droplets of the liquid and dropped them on the medallion. Two lines showed up, meaning there were drugs in the tea. As the paper around it unfolded, I realized there was even more evidence than I'd thought.

Now to get out unseen. Before I could make a move to go, I heard someone coming up the stairs. There was no escape and I considered hiding under the sheets in the storage room, but then I wasn't alone anymore.

'What you doing here?' a voice demanded as someone strode into the room. I tried to shield the cup from view, but it was too late. 'Where'd that come from?' And a hand made a grab for it.

I had been so focused on it being Michael or Jennifer, I hadn't considered who else had made a visit to the workroom. 'So it was you,' I said. The adrenalin was making my mind click and suddenly I understood the motive. 'It was about money, wasn't it?'

'Shut up,' Sophia said. 'There's no reason for anything to change. And with you out of the way, nothing will.' She seemed in panic mode and grabbed something off the table as she glared at me. 'You're an intruder and I'm just trying to protect myself.' Her voice was low as if she was reasoning with herself. That's when I noticed that she'd picked up an artist's utility knife. The razor blade stuck out of the end as she stepped closer and waved it near my face before she moved it down toward my neck. I didn't want to think about what damage a swipe at my carotid artery would do. I was horrified to realize I was cornered with no way to get past her.

There was a momentary standoff as she seemed to be preparing herself for the attack. What she'd done to Maeve was more passive; she'd probably waited until Maeve had passed out from the drugs before she suffocated her. Slashing me would take a different sort of mindset. I took advantage of the pause to search the room for some kind of help. Just as Sophia seemed ready to use the knife on me, there was a clatter of footsteps on the stairs. Instinctively, she turned her head toward the sound and in that moment I made my move and grabbed the back of one of the wheeled chairs. I pulled it close to me, planning to use it as a shield to keep her a distance. She turned back and, in a panicked move, lunged toward me. I blocked her with the chair and steered it in a dance that kept her at bay. In a last move, I gave it a push, hoping to hit her in the knees. She tried to step out of the way, but wasn't fast enough and it rammed into her leg, throwing her off balance. She tried to right herself as she made another lunge toward me, but her foot caught on one of the wheels. Her short skirt fluttered upward as she fell backwards and landed with a thud into the seat.

'What's going on?' a shrill voice demanded, as a woman walked up the last step and stared at the two of us. There was no mistaking the too-thin eyebrows and the too-short dress.

'Ass— I mean Ashleigh?' I said in surprise.

'You better get over there with her,' Sophia said, waving the knife at us as she tried to stand. But instead of getting out of the chair, she squealed in pain. Her eyes widened. 'What the . . .'

It took me a moment to figure out what was going on, and then I remembered how my attempt at fixing the cup handle had turned out. 'So, sorry,' I said in mock concern. 'I forgot that I spilled Sukey's Super Stick in the chair. As I recall, the catchphrase claims it never dries out and bonds anything together, permanently. I guess that means skin, too.'

Undaunted, Sophia tried to wheel the chair closer to me with her hand outstretched as she tried to slash me. I moved away and she tried to roll the chair after me.

There were more footsteps and a barking dog, as Jankowski reached the top step with Drexel nipping at his pant leg. Michael and Suzzanna came up just behind him. 'Arrest her,' Michael said, pointing at me. 'I told you there was an intruder.'

Jankowski looked over the scene and shook his head. Drexel, seeing his mistress, ran to her and jumped in her lap.

The detective's eyes settled on me. 'Why don't you start by explaining what you're doing here,' he said.

'Don't listen to her,' Sophia said. She looked at the artist's knife in her hand. 'That's right, she's an intruder.' She glared at Ashleigh. 'That must be her sidekick.'

Jankowski momentarily turned his attention to Sophia. 'Don't worry. You'll get your chance to tell your version,' he said.

He turned back to me. 'The floor is yours, Ms Blackstone.'

'She killed Maeve Winslow,' I said, looking directly at Sophia. 'She drugged her tea and then suffocated her with . . .' I looked around the room and saw a plastic trash bag. 'Probably something like that. And then she pushed her down the stairs, so it would look like she fell. You know she didn't die from the fall,' I said. 'There was almost no blood from the gash on her head, meaning she was dead before she fell.'

His expression didn't give a hint of his thoughts. 'Conjecture is fine, but where's the evidence?' he said.

'That's what I came here for,' I said, pointing to the cup with the paper around it. I hesitated, wondering how to explain. Finally, I simply told the truth about moving the cup and the paper to cover that I'd broken the handle. 'I didn't realize it was evidence,' I said. 'My plan was to put it back and somehow get you back here to look at it.' He looked in the bottom of the cup and saw there was some liquid. I offered him the kit I had and he begrudgingly used it and saw the results.

'That's OK for now, but we'll have to redo the test in the lab for it to mean anything official,' he said.

'If you want to see who was here with Maeve, just look at the paper,' I said.

He used a pencil to open it wider and glanced over it. 'It's just a bunch of doodles,' he said.

'Yeah, made with fingerprints.'

From the corner of my eye, I saw Sophia flinch and try to hide her hands. A spark of interest flared in Jankowski's face, despite his best effort to keep a neutral countenance. 'And I suppose you know her motive,' he said. A uniformed officer came up the stairs just then.

I waved for Jankowski to follow me, and he told the officer to keep everyone in place. Michael pushed around the detective and tried to stop us. 'There's nothing in there,' he said as he made a move to shepherd us back into the main room.

'I beg to differ,' I said. Jankowski looked from the artist to me.

'Why would you listen to her?' Michael said, blocking the way. 'Besides, you don't have a warrant.' He sounded desperate by now.

'This is clearly a crime scene,' the detective said. 'I need to make sure there aren't any victims in there.'

Jankowski stepped around him and went into the storage room. I began to peel off the sheets. There were Scotty pictures all over the room, with one in progress on an easel. I pointed to the signature on one of the paintings. 'It's just initials,' I said. 'It looks like an M and an A or it could be an M with a W leaning against it.'

Jankowski looked at the initials and then shrugged. 'I don't get it. What are you trying to say?'

'Maeve is the one who did the paintings.' I still had the photograph in my pocket and pulled it out and showed him the picture of the short-haired kid next to the Scottish terrier. 'When I first saw this, I thought it was Michael Angel with the dog, but when I looked at the back, in tiny writing it said: *Seven-year-old Maeve with her best friend Monty.*'

Jankowski still didn't seem to be getting it, and I had to explain that Michael always told the story that the dog had been his inspiration.

'He stole her story. She was the artist, but he took the credit,' I said when Jankowski still seemed confused.

When I looked back, Michael had his hands over his face and was shaking his head in despair.

'Assuming that's true, how does she come in?' We'd rejoined the others and Jankowski's gaze had settled on Sophia.

I again explained what I'd been hired to do and the notes that Maeve had given me. 'Maeve said in one of them that everything would have been different if she hadn't gone for sandwiches that day at the art fair. The day that everything changed. I misunderstood at first. I thought she meant if she hadn't gone for sandwiches, she would have been there to witness the moment that changed everything, but she meant something else entirely. If she had been there, everything really would have been different. Then she would have been there when Sophia and Zander admired the painting of *The Scotty in the Sleeping Garden* and wanted to buy it. Zander was no fool and knew that the copyright stayed with the artist even when a painting sold. They'd already come up with a plan to market merchandise connected to her YouTube show, using the painting that so resembled her dog co-star. Since Michael was the only one in the booth, he went along with their assumption that he was the artist. He was so glad to have the sale and at more than the asking price, that he gladly wrote something down giving them the copyright.' I paused and looked at the detective. 'But it wasn't his to give away because Maeve was the artist.

'And they kept the ruse going. I gather that Maeve was OK with it, which meant so much to Michael. He wanted to be a star artist, and he was better at playing the part than she was.

Maeve had hinted there was going to be a big disclosure at the end of the book. She was going to tell me about it when we got there, but she said I might figure it out on my own. Sophia must have realized what Maeve was going to do. She was going to disclose that Michael wasn't the real artist, just when the national prize-winner was announced, causing him the utmost embarrassment. I don't know how much Sophia made from selling all that merchandise that she didn't have the right to sell but, aside from whatever legal action there was, Sophia would have to pay back whatever she'd made to the real copyright owner, Maeve.'

Sophia interrupted with a wail. 'It's all his fault,' she said pointing at Michael. 'How was I supposed to know that he lied? Maeve was going to ruin everything. Make it so he'd never get that prize even if he won. She said I had no right to sell all that merchandise. I tried to get her to leave things as they were, but she was too angry. I acted like I understood and agreed to meet her up here so we could talk it over.' Sophia cut herself off then, realizing she had already said too much.

'And I suppose you know why the victim wanted to ruin her husband,' Jankowski said to me.

'That was in the notes, too. She'd been able to deal with his short-term relationships, but when he got involved with one woman, she snapped.'

I saw that Jennifer had joined the crowd and she glowered as her gaze stopped on me.

'I suspect it had to do with her own guilty feelings of meeting him when he was married to someone else. Despite her charm and those dimples, she was a woman on a mission.' I looked at the group of them in the attic. 'Isn't it amazing how easily everybody dismissed Maeve as just being an art teacher and not an artist. But even now, women artists still don't get their due.'

The detective appeared tired, and I was sure he would have loved a cup of coffee. He had written down a bunch of notes and he turned his attention on Ashleigh. 'How does she fit in?' he asked, looking at me.

Before I could speak, Ashleigh took over. 'I'm here because

of her,' she said, pointing at me. 'I was following her to
see what she was up to so I could tell Ben.' She glared at me.
'Ben and I are still married and I need her to bud out.' She
glanced around the group and held up her hands, showing off
the silver nail polish with pearl pieces attached. 'Trailing her
was easy. I was going to be a cop if I hadn't gone into nails.
I'm hard as nails,' she said, striking a tough pose. I wanted
to tell her that the cliché wasn't referring to the nails on your
hand, but it didn't seem the time. 'She has to understand that
we are back together. We're going to do the whole thing this
time – a house, a dog, kids. He's too soft to tell her. It was
up to me to let her know that he's gone from that writing thing
she roped him into.' She stepped closer to me, looking me in
the eye. 'I mean, really, did you think he'd stick with you
when he could have this.' She did that move of waving her
hand in front of her face, meant to highlight her attributes.
'Just look at her nails.' She grabbed my hand and held it up
for them all to see. 'No polish, not even buffed.' Her eyes
went skyward, as if my nail condition was that horrendous,
before her glance moved around to the rest of them, apparently
expecting them to nod in agreement.

'I see this is something personal. You'll have to work that
out on your own time,' the detective said with a weary shake
of his head. He waved at Sophia. 'You'll be coming with me.'
He seemed annoyed when she didn't get out of the chair and
waved to the uniformed officer to help.

'Sorry,' I said, holding back a smile for what I was about
to say. It wasn't really a cliché anyway, but rather an idiom,
and in this case just a true statement. 'She's glued to her seat.'

TWENTY-EIGHT

I went home and collapsed on the couch. Jankowski had assured me that he'd want to talk to me some more. And there was still the issue that I'd gone into the house uninvited and it could be viewed that I'd tampered with evidence. I was pretty sure that – all things considered – there wouldn't be any charges against me, though. Most likely, I'd get a warning to stop playing detective and mind my own business.

By the time I'd left Maeve's house, the newspeople were already on the sidewalk doing a remote report. I'd gone out the way I came in, by way of the basement. Kent had let me go through his backyard and driveway so that I escaped getting caught up in it. Ashleigh chose to let the newspeople grab her as she reached the sidewalk. I can only imagine what she had to say to them.

My landline rang and I considered letting it go, but I saw it was Caleb. 'She called,' he said in an excited voice. 'I knew my artwork would turn things around. She agreed to talk to me and I think she's going to forgive me.' He sounded happier and more enthused than I'd ever heard. He seemed clueless about what had just gone on next door to their house. But then he'd always seemed wrapped up in his own world. I guessed his wife was too.

'Thank you for your help, but I wanted to let you know I won't be needing it anymore. You can save whatever artwork is left for some other clients you get.'

I choked back a laugh at the thought as I hung up. Next there was a text from Tizzy. Word of what had happened – at least sort of – had made it to the campus and she wanted details. We made a deal to meet for sherry but they'd come to me.

I appreciated the company and the pizza they brought. 'Tell us everything,' Theo said. 'I'm so glad I could be a part of it.' I'd told him about using the kit he'd given me and offering it to Jankowski.

'You should have seen Jennifer's face when she realized Michael was a fraud. She'll really have to pivot with the documentary now.'

'Was it Sophia who spiked your drink?' Theo asked.

'It's the only thing she didn't do. I'm pretty sure it was Suzzanna, thinking she was helping her father by trying to scare me off. I don't think she knew that her father wasn't the real artist.'

'Any idea how Sophia figured out that Michael wasn't the artist?' Tizzy asked.

'She started to ramble before Jankowski took her away. Something about visiting Maeve at the Dupont Academy and seeing some sketches of the Scotty dog in her desk. When Sophia had asked her directly, Maeve had admitted she'd done them.'

There was no way to explain Ashleigh's appearance without explaining the whole situation with Ben. 'I had no idea it was that big a mess. Wow, they're still married,' Tizzy said. She put her arm around my shoulder and gave me a reassuring squeeze. 'I'm sorry he won't be in the group anymore, but at least Theo will be there now to read Ed's work.'

Her husband nodded with a smile, saying he was up for the challenge. 'What's going to happen with the memoir?' Theo said.

'I've already talked to the publisher. She wants the book, and just as Maeve intended it. It'll be about the paintings and their relationship, leaving it so it implies that he's the artist until the big reveal at the end.'

'What about the award?' Theo asked, shaking his head.

'I believe the award is connected to the art and who created it, not Michael the person. I expect there will be an announcement that he has been disqualified, with an explanation.'

'What about the paintings of the dog?' I chuckled at Tizzy's question.

'They'll probably go up in value because of all the notoriety, and because the supply is now limited to what she already painted. I found something in the notes about her writing a will and leaving her worldly goods to the school she loved so much. The paintings should be part of that,' I said.

We discussed what would happen with Sophia and Zander. 'I'm sure when they get her fingerprints and compare them with the paper wrapped around the cup that had the fingerprint art project, she'll get charged with murder. I wonder if they allow prisoners to have YouTube channels?'

We agreed that Zander would probably not be charged, as it seemed Sophia had worked alone. All he'd done was to gamble on buying some obscure paintings that his gallery made a bundle on after his girlfriend made the artist a star. I was sure Drexel would go to him.

I was grateful for Tizzy and Theo's company. It was good to have someone to talk everything over with. When they left, the whole impact of the day hit me, and I knew I was too spent to even write down some notes about everything. I was spent *and* wired. There was so much to process about the memoir and about Ben. After what Ashleigh had said, it made sense why he had stayed away with the claim of work. His text saying he would explain on the weekend probably had to do with somehow trying to keep our relationship going while he and Ashleigh started their new life together. Even if it did make me more interesting, I knew I wasn't cut out to be 'the other woman'. And if it was true that people had types they were attracted to, I was all wrong for him anyway. I looked down at my slightly ragged nails and shook my head, remembering her silver claws.

I felt myself hit bottom. I was disappointed and sad as it hit me that Ben and I were truly over, but then it was like there was a spring waiting that gave me a bounce back up and I knew I would be OK. Nobody could say I wasn't resilient. I put on the kettle and took out the chamomile tea. Settling on the couch with the flowery scented drink, I took out a ball of shell pink yarn and a hook. I started to make a foundation chain, thinking of what stitch pattern I'd do. I thought about Sara. She wasn't going to take the news about Ashleigh well.

'I am so glad to have you,' I said to the black-and-white cat who was cuddled next to me. I began to feel a sense of peace after the day I'd had as the tea and stitching began to work their magic. I felt as if my whole body had let out a big sigh. The ping on my phone startled me and I flinched. I thought about ignoring it, but I was too curious to ever be good at that.

It was from Ben asking if we could talk. He was outside my door.

I didn't know if I had it in me to deal with his situation right now. I was going to put off talking to him, but maybe it was better to let him say his piece and be done with it for good.

He was leaning against the door frame and straightened when I opened the door. There were no flowers this time. He looked drained and I invited him in.

'Sounds like you had quite an afternoon,' he said. 'So, you nabbed the bad guy, or should I say girl.' He had a weak smile.

He wanted to hear all about it. But I figured it was just a stall before he got to the why he'd come over. I gave him all the details. He loved that Sophia had gotten glued to the chair. And then it got very quiet as there was nothing else to keep him from talking about the real reason he was there.

I offered him one of the pumpkin ales I'd gotten by mistake. He might as well have one for the road. He didn't move from the couch while I went to get it. He took the bottle and I slipped into the wing chair.

'Well, I guess this is it,' I said.

'What do you mean?' he asked.

'You weren't there, but Ashleigh made it pretty clear to the world that you're back together and that you were done with me and my unpolished nails. She said you're going for the whole thing this time around – a house, cousins for Mikey and a dog.'

'She said that?' he said, stroking his forehead. 'I'm sorry. I really am. She's a force of nature.' He'd dropped his hands and took a deep breath. 'She told me that she had gone there, but I didn't realize she went that far. That was just her grandstanding. The same as when she came to Sara's. She hoped it would help with her negotiations. She has some other guy already. It was all about money and me giving her more. I finally caved and gave her what she was demanding.' He let out his breath. 'And she finally signed the papers.'

'What?' I said, incredulous. 'This is going to take me a

moment to process.' I was stunned. 'It was all about squeezing you for money? You could have told me what was going on.' This time I put my hand on my forehead as I tried to make sense of it all.

'I'm sorry, and I probably should have, but I guess I preferred the fantasy that the two of you were fighting over me,' he said with a smile.

'Don't you wish,' I said. The tension was gone and the mood was changing. 'So, what now?'

'I don't suppose we could just ignore what happened,' he said, looking at me intently.

I shook my head. 'I'm afraid Ashleigh is a little too memorable for that.'

'How about we start by you joining me on the couch.' He patted the spot next to him in welcome.

'Are you sure no one else is going pop up out of nowhere? There aren't any old girlfriends or another ex-wife?'

'You imagine I'm a lot more popular than I am,' he said.

'There's something else,' I said, still in the chair. 'Now that I've seen your type, I'm not so sure we're right for each other.'

He eyed me closely, trying to see how serious I was. Mostly, I was joking, but I suppose there was a touch of truth in it. 'Maybe I should look up that ex-husband of yours,' he said, 'and check out your type.'

'OK, agreed, neither of us will be judged by our past,' I said. He patted the spot next to him again and this time I moved around the coffee table and settled next to him.

'Now that I'm a free man again, how do you feel about being my plus one at my partner's birthday party on Saturday night?' he asked.

'I'll have to check my calendar. It's kind of last minute,' I teased.

'Well?' he said, looking at my phone.

'OK, I don't have to check. I'm free.'

'That's what I was hoping,' he said, putting his arm around my shoulder. 'So then we're good?'

'And then we're back to where we left off,' I said.

'Or . . .' he said, giving my shoulder an affectionate squeeze, 'We could kick things up to the next level.'

'You mean tell your sister?' I teased.

'I was thinking more of something that just involved the two of us,' he said with a twinkle in his eye. 'What do you think?'

'I'll take it under consideration,' I said.

'Well,' he said after a moment. 'Have you considered?'

'Yes, and yes,' I said with a smile.

ACKNOWLEDGMENTS

It is always a pleasure working with my editor Carl Smith. He makes the editing process fun with all his comments and asides. Piers Tilbury has come up with another eye-catching cover. Natasha Bell is always great dealing with the final workings of the books. Behind the scenes, Penny Isaac did an excellent job of copy editing.

Jessica Faust continues to help me navigate the publishing world.

The Hyde Park Classics Facebook group has been a great help keeping me in touch with Veronica's neighborhood. Through the group, I met Abbi Bardi who is almost a real live Tizzy. Penny Fisher Sanborn and Pam Fisher Armanino are my backup for memories connected to Veronica's building. Jakey opened up a whole new world of YouTube videos for me. And thanks to Burl and Max for being there.